In the
Wick of Time

In the Wick of Time

A MAGIC CANDLE SHOP MYSTERY

Valona Jones

CROOKED
LANE

NEW YORK

Copyright © 2023 by Margaret Toussaint

Published in the United States by Crooked Lane Books, an imprint of The Quick Brown Fox & Company LLC.

Crooked Lane Books and its logo are trademarks of The Quick Brown Fox & Company LLC.

Library of Congress Catalog-in-Publication data available upon request.

ISBN (hardcover): 978-1-63910-507-6
ISBN (ebook): 978-1-63910-508-3

Cover illustration by Mary Ann Lasher

Printed in the United States.

www.crookedlanebooks.com

Crooked Lane Books
34 West 27th St., 10th Floor
New York, NY 10001

First Edition: October 2023

10 9 8 7 6 5 4 3 2 1

This book is dedicated to
Suzanne and Michelle.

Chapter One

Sage dumped a full measuring cup of sand into the small paper bag, and I added a votive candle. My twin had twisted my arm to help her prepare the luminaries for the All Good Things Nursery and Landscaping booth at the waterfront. Though the luminary celebration and the holiday boat parade were days away, we were getting sixty of these prepped ahead of time because today the nursery had a full staff. Well, almost full.

"Your manager still out?" I asked, placing another completed bag in the wooden crate. With my stiff back today, I was grateful for the stools Sage provided. They were a welcome respite after I'd already stood all day in The Book and Candle Shop.

Sage stopped working, tucked a strand of dark hair back in her ponytail, and looked at me, her green eyes clouded with concern. "Yes. It's the strangest thing. Loren Lee is never sick, and he's called out of work more times than not in recent weeks. I'm worried about him. This illness is more than a vomiting bug, Tabs, and he isn't taking this seriously."

My name is Tabby Winslow. My fraternal twin and I co-own The Book and Candle Shop, near Savannah's Johnson Square. We don't look alike, but we share plenty of other genetic traits, including a secret one. Sage moonlights at the nursery because plants are her hobby. Regardless, she and I are united in our efforts to make the family business thrive. Our very future is tied to our shop; so is our longevity.

"What's his aura look like?" I asked.

"Murky and thin. If I didn't know better . . ." She scooped another measure of sand, then rested the cup on the worktable as her voice trailed off.

"What?" I asked.

Sage glanced toward the distant employees and customers before confidentially saying, "I saw him yesterday when he dropped in to check on the nursery. He looked like death."

I froze mid-breath. Until now, Loren Lee Suffield had been in excellent health. For most illnesses, my family members could boost a person's health with energy transfers, and I'm sure Sage would've shared energy with her boss to make him feel better. But . . . there was one disease we couldn't help. I spoke what she couldn't say. "Is it cancer?"

"I don't know. He doesn't believe in doctors. He's been self-medicating with folk remedies for decades. I offered to drive him to a doc-in-the-box yesterday, but he refused. I became quite pushy about it, and everyone here heard our argument. That's why the owner surprised me by calling me in to work an extra afternoon shift today. I thought I'd get the sack for giving him a hard time, but the owner, Ms. Chatham, wanted extra coverage for the holiday rush."

"Why isn't he seeking medical attention if it's that bad? It's one thing to address minor ailments yourself—that's good common sense—but when illnesses persist it's time for a health professional. Is he hardheaded?"

She snorted, then covered her mouth at the rude sound. "Some of my best times here have been going toe-to-toe over the outdoor display area. He reuses the same holiday displays year after year. That's why I'm so glad he listened to me about selling potted trees and palms as Christmas trees. With people wanting to leave a smaller footprint on the earth, those living trees opened a new revenue stream for the nursery. We've been selling them with and without lights, but Loren Lee is missing the whole sales frenzy. It frustrates me that he won't admit how sick he is."

I sympathized with her. If my boyfriend let his health slide like Loren Lee, I'd insist he seek medical attention. My twin needed help. Ideas rolled through my head like ocean breakers, foaming, spilling, and receding. Short of kidnapping the man and taking him to the emergency room, our options were limited.

Sage started filling bags again, and we processed several more luminaries before something else occurred to me. I sent her a message on our telepathic twin-speak line. *Is this disease Loren Lee has akin to a Dorian Gray phenomenon? The better the nursery does, the worse his health gets?*

Don't you think I'd know if this place stole his energy? I've surreptitiously studied all the employees here. None are energetics like us.

Energetics didn't begin to encompass our entire "extra" skill sets. Sage and I were the latest generation in a family endowed with special abilities related to a person's natural electrical field. In other words, we push and pull energy from our bodies and auras to suit our needs. However, our late mother kept secrets from us so we weren't burdened by all the danger from our talents. I hated the phrases "for your own good" and "out of an abundance of caution." Consequently, we were stuck figuring out the energetic world on the fly.

Mary Nicole Frazier breezed into the potting area looking like she owned the world. "How's it going back here, Sage?" Not a hair of her sleek chin-length bob looked out of place, not a speck of dirt showed on her shiny nails, not a scuff marred her designer sneakers or her high-dollar clothes. I'd been here half an hour, and I had sand all over me. Self-consciously, I curled my less than perfect fingernails into my palms so she wouldn't see them.

Sage had hated Mary Nicole on sight, and Ms. Perfect Appearance would never make my favorite person list either. The smug way she looked down her nose at everyone irritated me. I'd had enough of that when classmates called us freaks. Her attitude rubbed me wrong, but she shouldn't act better than us.

To make matters worse, Sage and Mary Nicole both applied for the vacant assistant manager position here, the last assistant having impulsively yachted to the Bahamas with a customer last month with only a few hours' notice. I didn't know how we'd manage our family business if Sage worked here full-time, but we'd figure it out if she landed the job. I would never stand between my sister and her happiness. Thank goodness Auntie O had moved home and helped us in the shop.

Energy shifted in my sister. Uh-oh. If Mary Nicole had a grain of sense, she'd know what that frosty smile on Sage's face meant.

"Everything is great," Sage said. "Only a few more luminaries to go. Loren Lee and Ms. Chatham will be so happy our staff is keeping up with the holiday extras along with running the nursery."

"Yes, Ms. Chatham has no complaints about the nursery. I spoke on the phone with her a few minutes ago." Mary Nicole's face pinched. "I'm sorry. I should have led with the bad news, but I don't know how to tell you. I'll just come right out with it. Loren Lee died."

My jaw dropped. The blood drained from Sage's face. I felt her pain blasting through our twin-link. Instinctively, I showered her with good energy.

"He's dead?" Sage hugged herself. "He's been very sick, but dead? Omigosh. I'm stunned. This is terrible news. What happened?"

Sage's voice got louder and higher pitched with each word she spoke. The other employees hurried into the workroom and drew close in twos and threes. I heard them whispering to each other that Loren Lee had passed.

"Ms. Chatham went over to his place an hour ago to check on him and found him unresponsive. She called an ambulance, and EMTs pronounced him dead at the scene."

Silent tears rained down my sister's face. I couldn't sit here and let her suffer this alone. I slid off my stool and wrapped my arm around her shoulder, the energy transfer accelerating from multiple points of contact. Despite her being three inches taller, she leaned into me and welcomed the comfort I offered.

The entire staff were waiting for Sage to say something. I glowered at them, protecting Sage with a not-so-subtle extra curtain of energy because I didn't trust these people. None of them knew how rarely Sage showed any vulnerability.

After a long moment, Sage squeezed her eyes shut, then dashed her tears away with the heels of her hands, visibly pulling herself together. "Loren Lee just turned forty a few months ago. What a waste that his life is over. I can't imagine this place without him. He made a difference around here, and I swear the man had eyes in the back of his head. He kept his finger on the pulse of this nursery all the time."

"He was something, that's for sure," Mary Nicole said dryly.

Her snide tone made my twin reel. I worked to steady us both, keeping the energy transfer going and keeping my mouth shut. One did not step between quarreling lionesses.

"You won't miss him?" Sage said.

"He acted nitpicky and curt most of the time," Mary Nicole said. "He yelled at us if we did the slightest little thing wrong."

Several employees nodded in agreement with her.

I expected fire to jet out of Sage's nose any minute now from this show of disrespect. Didn't Mary Nicole have a shred of common decency?

"That's what bosses do," my twin said. "They set the standard. This place is the best nursery in Savannah because of Loren Lee Suffield's exacting standards."

"What's going to happen to the nursery?" a girl with a name tag marked Tina asked. "Will it close?"

Mary Nicole cleared her throat and waited until all eyes were on her. It took everything I had not to send a rogue energy current her way. In that moment, I disliked her as much as Sage did—more, because she'd hurt my sister.

"Ms. Chatham told me to assure everyone that nothing would change," Mary Nicole said. "The nursery stays open, and everyone's job is safe. She is already looking for an assistant manager. Now she'll expand her search for a manager too. She'll come in and do payroll. In the meantime, she appointed me as the interim assistant manager."

To her credit, Sage didn't swear aloud, but she used our twin-speak silent communication to share her thoughts on the matter with me. Until she began making sentences, I let the raw language run in one side of my thoughts and out the other. *This is completely messed up. Mary Nicole will run this place into the ground in a few weeks. I won't work for her.*

You're quitting without even talking to your boss?

I don't know what I'm going to do. I can't believe Loren Lee is dead. Why didn't he let me take him to be treated yesterday?

I don't know.

I can't believe the way she's going on and on about him, painting him as a tyrant. He did his job. She sits on her stool behind the register. She's never in the aisles tending plants. From what I know of Loren Lee, he would've already given her the first and second warning about sloppy work habits. How'd she score the assistant boss spot when she's one of the laziest workers here?

Again, can't help you. These are your people. I only know what you've told me.

"Sage, are you all right?" Mary Nicole said.

She's talking to you, I said in my twin's head. *Say something.*

"What? Sorry, I'm so upset by the news. I can't get past the fact Loren Lee is dead. Seems like any minute now he'll walk through this room and tell us all to get back to work in that gruff manner of his."

Mary Nicole nodded, then a malicious glint appeared in her eyes. "Speaking of which, be sure y'all clean up the mess you made."

Energy snapped and sparked in my twin. *Don't do anything*, I said. *Too many witnesses, and this puffed-up gal can't help herself. She isn't criticizing you as much as she's letting everyone know she's in charge.*

People fled the workroom, leaving Sage and me alone.

"Close call," I said softly. "You nearly wielded your energy in front of others and for no good reason other than she irritated you. We know better."

"You're right, but I don't like it," Sage said in a matching low voice. "Mary Nicole sneaks around here taking credit for other people's work. How come the boss lady can't see through her lies? It's as if Ms. Chatham wants to hear what that liar has to say. I don't stand a chance at a promotion, and I really want it. Mary Nicole will force me out of here."

I patted Sage's shoulder. "You're the reason for the nursery's extra surge of business this month. You know that, and everyone who works here knows that. If Ms. Chatham picks Mary Nicole for the promotion, she'll suffer the consequences of her choice. You make a difference here. I see your energy all over the place. The plants respond to you, not Mary Nicole."

"Thanks, but now I have a new problem. Trying to maintain my cool around a bossy, attention-grabbing woman. Perhaps I never stood a chance at the job opening anyway. I'm only part-time, and I've never picked up the phone to call Ms. Chatham about anything. I'm not a suck-up like my competition."

Due to Sage's longevity here, I knew some history of this place. The owner inherited the nursery from her late husband, and until today, she'd relied on Loren Lee to run the place. She kept her distance and let him have free rein. "Ms. Chatham is lucky to have you, Sage. If she can't see that, she doesn't deserve you. There are other nurseries in Savannah. No matter what happens with the assistant manager and the manager opening, you will land on your feet. Of that I have no doubt."

Energy roiled around Sage, flashing and sparking like a fireworks display. "I don't want to leave this place. I fit in here. I make a difference here. I want to be here."

"We'll see. I have a *feeling* things will work out the best for you."

Sage laughed, picked up a broom, and swept the spilled sand. "You sound like Mom."

I picked up the empty votive cartons and tossed them in the recycling bin. "Lately, I've had the sense I'm more like Mom than I ever knew. Trust me, that's not a comforting realization."

"I loved Mom, but her secretiveness exasperated me. Auntie O has her own agenda too. Did you know she hid my birth control pills?"

"Oh dear. Project Baby again?"

"She won't be satisfied until we're both preggers. Why is she in such a hurry? And why can't she accept that it is our choice? She makes me feel like a broodmare. At least you have a strong partner in Quig. He's rock solid."

Her comment concerned me. "Did something happen with you and Brindle? I thought you two were fine."

Sage stowed the broom and began moving crates to the loading dock. "We're good together when our schedules mesh. Brindle's been pulling back on our relationship lately, and I start to feel vulnerable when he's so distant."

I grabbed a crate and followed her. "Yikes. Turmoil at work and in your love life. That's a heavy load to shoulder at one time. Especially on top of losing a mentor you admired."

"Don't I know it. I need answers, so I'm heading to his place as soon as I leave here. Tell Auntie O I won't be home for supper."

"Tell her yourself. Quig and I are eating at our place tonight. I'm supposed to grab a bottle of wine on the way home."

"Wine is a good idea. I'll give you a lift and grab a bottle to take to Brindle's."

* * *

The evening passed uneventfully, but I couldn't shake the nagging sense of wrongness. Sage sent me her standard message of "busy" when I pinged her, so she might not be the source of the feeling. But still. I *knew* a lightning strike approached, and I couldn't do a darn thing about it.

Chapter Two

I covered the shop on Saturday, and with Gerard, our full-time clerk, off on the weekends, my helpers rotated between Auntie O and her roommate Frankie Mango. Today Frankie joined me as Auntie O had a hair salon appointment.

He wore starched trousers, deck shoes, and a white polo shirt. A heavy gold chain adorned his neck, rings gleamed on his hands, and a clunky watch graced his wrist. He looked like someone's idea of a character in *The Sopranos*. His clean-shaven olive skin and shock of graying black hair added to the mobster impression.

Frankie and I have good energy together, but we also give each other space. I didn't know how much Auntie O had told him about me, but I knew he manipulated energy much like my family members. He'd followed Auntie O home to Savannah when she'd decided retirement in Orlando, Florida, didn't suit her. They'd purchased the building between the one Sage and I owned and Quig's place, which, now that I'd permanently moved in with Quig, served as "our" place. Anyway, Frankie and Auntie O lived above a Bristol Street shop in our block, same as the rest of us did. This specific location nurtured our family, and we had no plans to leave it, ever.

In the Wick of Time

While Frankie opened the register and restocked low inventory, I ran a duster over the books, the whimsical tabletop sculptures, soaps, lotions, candles, aromatherapy room spritzers, wind chimes, and the newly restored Brenda's Bees product display. Swags of evergreens with ribbons and seashells accented each product grouping, adding a lush cedar aroma to our shop. Both Harley and Luna, our shop cats, supervised from atop the highest shelf in the room. I cleaned the front door and the glass countertops with window cleaner and plumped cushions in our reading nook. A few minutes of plucking bad fronds from ferns and herbs, and we were ready for customers.

Then I made candles and soaps in the adjacent stillroom with our cats supervising from the sunny windowsill. The origin of stillrooms dates to medieval times when each establishment or grand castle had a distillery room in the back. That room functioned as part science lab, part medicinal, part workroom, and part kitchen. In our stillroom the restful robin's egg blue wall color reflected my good intentions, necessary for the creation of any aromatherapy blend. I hummed along with wicks and wax combinations until a few hours later when I noticed Frankie watching me from the doorway.

"Smells divine back here," he said, sniffing copiously. "Something between a day at the beach and a coconut smoothie. Did you create a new scent?"

I beamed at Frankie's compliment. "Thanks. This is a trial run of a new blend. Glad you like the aroma. It's a little south of our 'Beach' candles. All our best sellers are the ones Auntie O and Mom perfected, but every now and again I try something new. Nothing ever got the same traction as Auntie O's blended scents."

"It's only natural you want to put your stamp on the shop, Tabby. Trust me, this blend will have wings."

"I hope so. Sage and I keep doing the math, and our income level doesn't quite meet the bar Mom and Auntie O set. We're not doing bad per se, but we are so close to the profit-loss line that a bad month might sink us. I asked Auntie O several times what they did differently, but she keeps saying we'll figure it out. It's frustrating not to have the answer."

"Do the skew numbers match up for the most part?"

Stock keeping unit (SKU) numbers were inventory codes for individual products. Since our consignors changed from time to time, those wouldn't line up exactly. However, our overall stillroom income and our total consignment income should be comparable through time.

"As far as I know." I wiped down the stainless steel counters until they gleamed. "Sage keeps the books now."

"Maybe the buying power of your earned income is less due to inflation."

"Or Mom and Auntie O supplemented their income with off-the-books work. That makes more sense to me. Enough about our income stream. We don't often get time alone together. Tell me about your family, Frankie."

He made an umpire's gesture of *you're out*. "All gone."

"Not even an aunt or uncle left?"

"Nope. I'm an only child of an only child. Dad didn't stay in the picture. Grandparents gone on both sides of the family tree, so meeting Oralee made my year. She's my family now, along with you girls."

I leaned against the island. "Were you born in Florida?"

"I'm not truly from anywhere. My mom moved often, so she taught me at home before it became popular."

Though he didn't answer my question, his reply made me pause for a moment. "I would've liked homeschooling. Kids are mean."

"The world is mean. Be glad you had that real-world seasoning in grade school. I got pancaked by mean adults in my late teens, and it nearly flattened me."

"How awful. May I ask what happened?"

"A big misunderstanding taught me a valuable lesson: the bullet that doesn't kill you makes you stronger."

I stared at him, understanding crystallizing in icy shards in my veins. "Omigosh . . . You got shot?"

He frowned as if remembering the pain. "Twice. Made the stunning realization of that line of work being hazardous to my health and decided on a career change. Bottom line, people like us make other people nervous. Our stronger energy currents evoke a flight-or-flight response in nonsensitives. When they don't see any danger and they can't dial back the alertness, they get testy and lash out at whoever is nearby."

"I learned that lesson as well. Luckily, tourists are less discerning."

"Indeed." He turned and headed to the store as the door chimed again.

"You got guidebooks in here?" a man asked.

"We sure do," Frankie said from the sales floor, turning to face our customer. "Let me show you our selection. Where you from?"

As their voices drifted away, I realized Frankie had revealed a slice of his history. He'd been in a dangerous job and taken two bullets. Even so, what kind of job would result in a teenager getting shot? That he still walked around seemed a miracle. He didn't even limp.

He cared for my aunt, and she cared for him. They were lucky to have each other. I felt happy for Frankie and even happier for my aunt. She'd been married in her twenties, but that didn't last long. So what if Frankie had a past? He'd grown into a responsible person.

Turning my attention back to work, I drew in a big whiff of my just-poured candles. I needed a name for this new scent. *Savannah Sunshine* popped into my head. I mouthed the name a few times to test drive it, and then I lettered it on our custom labels.

I crated the votives six to a mini-carton and shrink-wrapped each set in a plastic sleeve. The labels went on the six Savannah Sunshine pillar candles and two sets of votives. Adding them to our inventory system came next, which I promptly did.

As I carried them to the showroom, I saw my two least favorite cops in the world getting out of their unmarked vehicle. Detectives Chase Nowry and Sharmila Belfor had haunted our shop after the Blithe McAdam murder, but I'd gotten used to not seeing them around. Their visit meant trouble.

Unbidden, the thought came to my mind: "Who died now?"

Tempted to run for cover, I stood my ground behind the sales counter. My cat Harley came in and circled between my legs until I picked him up. Frankie Mango joined me, as if the counter would shield us both. If only that were true. Whatever came this way wouldn't be good. Neither of these cops routinely shopped here.

Nowry's military-short gray hair and lean frame outlined in an old school power suit gave credence to his take-no-prisoners attitude. All were guilty in his view, guilty until proven innocent. Belfor's soft curves displayed in more modern clothing told a different tale, though her steely eyes spoke cop-loud of her law-and-order profession. Of the two, I trusted Belfor to listen better, to be less likely to slap the cuffs on me.

Neither Frankie nor I called out a greeting to the detectives as they made a beeline for us. When Frankie stayed mute, I said, "How can I help you today, Detectives?"

"Looking for Sage Winslow," Nowry said. "Is she here?"

"This is her day off from the shop. Perhaps I can answer your question."

Nowry nodded toward my sunny stillroom. "You make the candles in there?"

His dour tone brought back unpleasant thoughts of an interrogation. My knees trembled, so I locked them to control the shakes. Memories of being held in a tiny police interview room loomed large in my head.

I clung to my cat Harley, silently challenging the cop into a staring contest. Oops. I should say something. "Yes. I made a batch this morning."

"You have plants in there too, right?"

Potted ferns and herbs were all over this room and the stillroom. How could he miss seeing the profusion of greenery? Still, it paid to cooperate. "We do. What's this about, Detective?"

"Loren Lee Suffield is dead."

"I heard of his passing."

"His death wasn't from natural causes. We're interviewing his associates in our investigation."

I didn't care for the man's sneer, nor his insinuation that Sage and our shop might be involved in the nursery manager's death. "So your first thought is to start investigating here? Are we ground zero for every homicide investigation now?"

He swatted my questions away as if they were annoying houseflies. "What do you know about Mr. Suffield?"

"I've seen him a few times. He is, I mean, he used to manage All Good Things Nursery and Landscaping, where my sister works part-time. He worked there many years."

"Did he come in here? Purchase things from this shop?"

"I don't know. I'm not here every day."

"We need to speak with your sister." He paused to flip through his notebook. "According to the acting interim assistant manager at the nursery, a Mary Nicole Frazier, Sage Winslow argued with the manager on his last day at work."

Mary Nicole's sneakiness ensured Sage never had a chance at the promotion. I hastened to explain. "Sage tried to help him, but he didn't want help. She told me he looked very ill for weeks prior to his death."

"Did he have a doctor?" Detective Belfor interjected, her sharp gaze boring into me.

"I believe the answer is no. I heard he tried self-medicating."

Nowry cleared his throat. "Be that as it may, we are looking for concrete facts about Mr. Suffield. Anything else you want to add to your story?"

My cat stirred, and I petted him until he settled. "It's no story. I'm answering your questions. I barely know—shoot, I mean, I barely knew him. Sage worked for him, that was my only connection to him."

"Which is why we need to talk to your sister. She isn't at the nursery or at home. Do you have any idea where she is?"

"She could be anywhere."

"Are you being evasive on purpose?"

"I'm trying to explain. She has a car. Thus, she could be at the beach, shopping, visiting a friend. I don't know where she is."

Sharmila Belfor pressed her business card in my hand. "Please pass this card along to your sister. We want to talk with her regarding Mr. Suffield's death."

"One more thing," Detective Nowry said. "You gals ever grind up plants in there to make extracts?"

"We have. What of it?"

"What plants get this treatment?"

"Herbs and spices."

"Nothing that's a poison?"

"Everything is a poison, Detective. It depends on the concentration and the dose."

He leaned over the counter. "So you also have the knowledge to make poisons."

Harley hissed at the detective. I set the cat on the floor, and he scampered away. "Even water can be a poison, sir," I stated matter-of-factly. "Mothballs, solvents, antifreeze, just to name a few common household products that are poison. No distilling is involved."

"Do you have poisons back there?"

I didn't like this conversational topic. "I have the tools of my trade."

"I want to see them."

We'd been down this road before with the cops. I never made the same mistake twice. "Not without a warrant you don't."

"Don't be that way."

I nearly snorted at his remark, but I displayed remarkable calm. I glanced at Frankie and he gave a minimalistic nod. His calming energy defused the tension in the shop. What would Nowry say if I came back with a don't-be-that-way regarding his style of interrogation? I held my peace, barring my arms across my chest and waiting. I could wait all day if needed, especially with Frankie's worry-free energy infusing me.

"You're making things difficult, Ms. Winslow."

The man had no idea how difficult I could make things, not that I would share that information with him. "I am protecting my family's intellectual property, Detective. We make our living with proprietary blends of candles, soaps, and related products. We aren't criminals."

He tapped his notebook in the palm of his hand. The repetitive sound annoyed me. His heavy gaze felt like it weighed our merits, and we failed. Clearly Nowry thought we were the murdering sort. Oh, what I wouldn't give to channel my inner Sage and blast him with a fire hose of energy and wash him out of our shop.

But that would be counterproductive.

Detective Sharmila Belfor picked up one of my new Savannah Sunshine candles and sniffed. "These are amazing. I see why you call them sunshine."

Pride swelled in my chest. "Made them this morning."

"I'll take two," she said, reaching for her wallet.

"We're not here to shop," Nowry groused.

"Speak for yourself. I need a hostess gift for tonight, and this is something my friend will love."

A few minutes later they were gone. Frankie and I looked at each other. "They don't cut you any slack," he said.

I put away the tissue paper and sanitized the counter. "No, they don't. Detective Nowry is old school and vindictive. Belfor is okay. It must be hard for her to work around such negativity. Thanks for the good vibes."

"Any time." Frankie got a faraway look in his eyes. "Tell them as little as possible. Cops find ways to twist your words against you."

"Sounds like you speak from experience."

"Oh, yeah."

Chapter Three

Sage stopped over that evening while Quig showered. She sported a sunburn and a fresh crop of freckles across her face, arms, and legs. "Looks like you had fun today," I said as we sat together on the couch.

Her chin lifted defiantly. "I went fishing with a friend."

Though it was December, our mild weather meant boating passed as a year-round recreation. "Didn't know Brindle had a boat."

"He doesn't. A guy from the nursery offered to take some of us out on his boat today, so I accepted. No one else showed up, not that it mattered. Larry Rau and I had a good time on the water."

How odd. Far as I knew, Sage had never been fishing before. Now she'd spent the whole day with a guy she knew from work. Fishing. "Thought you might be spending today with your boyfriend."

"My ex-boyfriend. When I went to his place last night, I saw him entertaining his receptionist, Alyss something or another. I swear everything on that woman has been lifted, tightened, and augmented. She's as fake as they come."

"Maybe they were working late."

"Absolutely not. I had a front row seat through the windows. They were dancing close. Very close. Like he does with me. I thought his body language meant something special. Now I know he snowed me. He used all the same touchy-feely moves with her. I started shaking all over."

Oh. Poor Sage. I surrounded her with good energy and scooted closer to wrap an arm around her shoulder. "I'm sorry. That must've been awful to see. Especially since you trusted your mutual exclusivity agreement."

"I knew something felt off. Brindle likes women a lot, more than he likes being tied down. He promised me we were exclusive, but he played me all along, saying what I wanted to hear and dating someone else during the week. But his promise tripped him up. Since we were exclusive, I didn't call and announce my arrival. I just showed up and got an eyeful."

"He's an ass."

Her eyes brimmed with tears. "My head knows that, and all the way home I told myself he doesn't matter. But my heart aches. I care for him."

"He doesn't deserve you."

"I thought about walking away without confronting him, but I wanted him to see that I witnessed his actions, that I saw him romancing her. He cheated in the worst kind of way."

Sage dashed the tears from her face. "Once I had the lay of the land, I used my key and marched inside. They were so engrossed in each other, neither one heard me enter until I threw my key at him and started yelling. His neighbors got an earful because I called him every name in the book. And her . . . I wanted to do terrible things to Alyss for touching him, but to what end? That cheater. I walked out. Took my wine home with me. He called five times last night and at least twenty this morning."

"I'm sorry I didn't know you were going through this until now. If you'd even hinted at what happened last night I would've come over. I gather you didn't take any of Brindle's calls."

"Not a one. Dumped his messages without listening to them. He knew my history and that I'd been burned before by a cheating boyfriend. I don't give cheaters a second chance. But I didn't put my tail between my legs and slink away. I changed my away message today to say I'd gone fishing with friends. Brindle loves fishing. That message may be petty, but I didn't care at the time, and I still don't care. He's ancient history."

"He didn't deserve you," I repeated.

Her lower lip trembled. "I wanted him, so I ignored his reputation as a player. Turns out he earned that reputation, though he swore we were a monogamous couple." Sage took a moment to gather herself. "He never lied to me before, until this. Liars never change. That will teach me to engage in magical thinking."

"I'm sorry your relationship exploded." I took a deep breath. "Turns out your breakup with him couldn't have come at a worse time. I have some bad news to share."

"You're scaring me."

"You should be scared. Detectives Nowry and Belfor came by the shop today looking for you. They asked pointed questions about poisons. Turns out your boss didn't die of natural causes. Someone helped him along with poison."

"For real?" Her eyes searched my face until I nodded. She gasped and sagged into the sofa cushions. "I'm stunned. Poisoned. Beyond stunned. I mean, who does that? Loren Lee devoted his life to the nursery. Someone killed him? That's terrible."

I hugged her. "It is bad. Very bad. The cops asked me about our work with plants, which led me to believe someone might've used a local plant to kill him. Nowry asked to snoop in our stillroom."

Sage pushed away from me, rose, and paced the living room, her quick strides making short work of each length of the room. "You said no, right?"

"Of course. He isn't getting in there without a warrant."

"Holy cow. This is bad news. Knowing how dogged those cops are, I'll need a lawyer soon. No way in hell would I trust Brindle with my freedom now. Ask Quig to hook me up with your guy."

"I don't need to ask Quig to be the middleman. I'll ask Herbert R. Ellis if he'll represent you."

"Thanks . . ." Her voice trailed off as she gazed out the dark window at the city lights. "Did they say which plant? It could be pyracantha, oleander, or sago palm, all of which are deadly, and there are more poisonous plants that I'm blanking on right now."

"They didn't say. You've never dried and ground up any of those, have you?"

"Never," Sage responded. "I've only ground herbs for our essential oils."

"Same here. When you're in the shop tomorrow, check the stillroom to make sure someone didn't set us up again by planting something suspicious back there. I would've checked earlier but I didn't think about it until now."

"Will do."

"I'm sorry this happened. It's bad enough having an abrupt breakup, but to be in the murder hot seat again, that's a one-two punch like getting hit with tornadoes during a hurricane."

"No need to be sorry. I should have known better than to trust Brindle."

"Is Larry going to take his place?"

"Not sure why Larry asked me to go fishing, other than we're work friends. I enjoyed getting out on the water and the peacefulness of fishing. That unexpected gift of Zen gave me a sense of relief."

"Larry already sounds like a better fit for you. He weathered your stormy mood without running headlong into another's arms afterward, and he enjoyed your company. It's fun to have that flash of attraction, but there's plenty to be said for companionship. Maybe Larry will become an outside-of-work friend. It's good to have friends who aren't lovers."

"I hear you, but now that I see how you and Quig are faring, I want both. I won't settle for another Brindle. I want the real deal."

"Your choice, Sis. You want to hang out with us tonight? We're watching *Star Trek* reruns."

"No, thanks. I won't intrude, but promise me this. If I am accused of murder, you'll conduct your own investigation. I don't trust Nowry and Belfor to hit on the right answer."

"Promise."

Chapter Four

The piece on Loren Lee Suffield's murder ran above the fold of the Sunday paper. It included the news of his poisoning and a summary of his time in Savannah. He lived alone, and his life revolved around the nursery. No hobbies, clubs, or activities were mentioned there or in his bare-bones obituary. Stark photos showed Detectives Nowry and Belfor grimly conferring outside the man's humble home on the way to Richmond Hill.

Quig focused on waffle-making as I read the newspaper and sipped my coffee at the table. I wore a robe, and he'd pulled on a pair of shorts. Quite the picture of domesticity, especially for a man who valued intellect, precision, and working out. The black-framed glasses he wore never hid the intensity of his dark brown eyes. He had a few height inches on me as well as a few birthdays, but he'd been crazy about me for years. Took me a while to admit I cared about him too. We'd moved in together a few months ago after more than twenty years of friendship.

"Wow. You read this?" I waved the newspaper his way.

Not that he saw my gesture. His gaze never wavered from the waffle maker, watching for the exact instant when the ready light blinked off. "If you're asking about the poisoned nursery manager article, yes, I saw it."

"Did you perform his autopsy?"

"Our newest medical examiner came up in the rotation. Dr. Chang ran detailed tests and found poison in Mr. Suffield's body. Initially, I had concerns about him wasting taxpayer money by ordering so many tests, but once the testing revealed poison, he became the golden boy. Everyone is singing Chang's praises. Nearly gave him a heart attack when the reporters came by on Friday to get his story. I found him hiding in the break room."

"No doubt as to the means of death?"

"The tests are very accurate."

Hmm. Good evasion of the question, but I had to try again. "When the cops came by the shop yesterday, they implied the poison came from a natural substance. Can you be more specific about the poison, so I know if Sage and I are in trouble?"

"No can do. It's a common practice to withhold critical information in a murder case. There are people who claim credit for killing homicide victims, and these people spin all kinds of stories of how they did it. By withholding information from the public, we screen out these imposters quickly."

How strange. "I can't imagine anyone lying about that. They must value notoriety over freedom."

"Something like that. In any event, I'd rather you let the cops do the investigating this time."

My heart panged at the fierce energy flaring in his aura. I had known this day might come, the day when Quig inserted himself between me and my twin. He had to know I would never abandon my sister, no matter how much I cared for him. If he wanted me in his life, he'd have to accept Sage as well.

Best to go along as I meant to be. "I have no interest in every murder case that comes along, only the ones that impact my family. Nowry and Belfor came after my shop clerk in the McAdam murder. This time, Sage thinks they're coming after her, and I believe she's right. I can't sit idly by and do nothing. I need to be proactive on Loren Lee's murder, so they don't catch us flat-footed."

The waffle light went out. Quig removed the perfect waffle, poured the next one, and then turned to me, his eyes heating behind his glasses. "I'll make sure you're safe."

I appreciated his pledge more than words could say, but I'd been looking out for myself for quite some time. "So will I. Knowledge is a good place to start. I wish Sage had been in the shop with me yesterday when the cops visited. If so, she'd have the preliminary questions out of the way. When I told her about their visit, she spazzed out, certain they'll arrest her on sight. I tried to calm her down, but she is very upset. I'm concerned about her emotional state right now. She's having a hard time with Loren Lee's death."

"Sage should talk to Nowry and Belfor soon. Encourage her to clear the air. Until she does, she remains a person of interest."

Just like Quig to go straight to the bottom line. "You know my sister. She doesn't take direction well."

"Help her help herself. She needs to own this."

"All right." I sent Sage a text message and waited for a reply. Nothing came back. I tried our twin-link. Same result. Radio silence. "She isn't happy with my message."

"She'll come around. Until then she's worrying for nothing."

I shrugged. "It's Sage. She's wired for hot or cold and nothing in between."

"Not to disparage your parents, but it is odd that the child they named Sage is less wise than her sister they named after a building material."

"As to that, thanks for calling me smart. I try to make informed decisions and do the right thing. Sage didn't get her name because of her hoped-for intellect. The tradition in our family is for the firstborn daughter to have the name of an herb. Sage being Sage shot out the womb first. Thus I have the honor of being named after a mixture of sand, lime, shells, and water."

"I love your name. It suits ya."

He meant that as a compliment, but the strong rip current of this conversation made me feel adrift and insecure. Concern for my only sibling did that to me.

*   *   *

Auntie O summoned me to the stillroom late Sunday afternoon after she closed the shop. "We gotta fix this, gals," Auntie O began when I arrived. Sage prowled the edges of the room, stopping now and then to pluck dead fronds off the window ferns.

A petite dynamo, our aunt brimmed with unflagging energy. Today she'd dressed in Christmas colors all the way down to her red and green striped socks. "The cops tried to find Sage here again today, and she hid in our secret supply closet. They expect her at the station tomorrow. That is not good."

"You didn't do anything wrong," I said to her. "Why not talk to them today and clear the air?"

Sage shook her head rapidly, her dark ponytail lashing her neck and shoulders. "They'll lock me in jail, same as they did to Gerard last time. I know it. I dread it. I can't do it."

Luckily my discussion with Quig had prepared me for this very conversation. Instead of trying to deal with the manifestations of her distress, I kept the conversation on an even keel. "No need to leap straight to DEFCON One. We don't know the actual threat level to your future or what defenses to employ. Let's assume they have a few routine questions for you." I gave an open-handed gesture. "I'll go with you, if you like."

"I won't drag you under too. Tina from the nursery called me after the cops visited All Good Things today. Mary Nicole filled their ears about my shouting match with Loren Lee the morning before he died." Sage stopped pacing and rubbed her temples. "Those were our last words to each other. Me yelling at him. I wish I'd told him how much I respected him."

"All it will take to turn that suspicion around is sharing the topic of your argument. Once you reveal you wanted him to get medical treatment and he refused, the cops should leave you alone. Avoidance implies guilt."

"Or prudence." Sage gathered her cat in her arms, snuggling her close. "You get me a new lawyer yet?"

Automatically, I looked for my cat to cuddle, but I didn't see Harley. "I left a message on Herbert Ellis's phone. Here's the deal with him. Unless it's an emergency, he doesn't return calls on the weekend."

"Smart man," Auntie O said. "Takes after his dad."

Her wry tone piqued my curiosity. "You knew Mr. Ellis?"

"Not in a personal way, but I knew of him. Seymour Ellis fixed on a gal early in life, like your Quig, and never wavered. A crying shame, if you ask me. I had a crush on Seymour as a teen, but he never glanced my way."

I grinned at her. "Savannah is the biggest small town I know."

"Don't I know it," Auntie O said. "Sometimes the dance of life loops repeatedly until we get it right."

"If that's the case, humanity is in deep trouble," I said. "Bad choices are made with increasing frequency these days. Bottom line, no one is safe."

Sage scowled at me. "Since when did you start spouting philosophy?"

"I've been questioning life for a while, but Quig is a master at it. He really gets into discussing the subjectivity of secular humanism."

"You lost both of us with those ten dollar words," Auntie O said dryly. "Let's return to Sage's safety. Does anyone feel she should spend tonight elsewhere?"

"If the cops are that interested in her," I said, "they'll grab her the minute she steps outside. She's better off hunkering down here."

"You could help me escape," Sage said.

Going invisible came at a high price. If I gathered energy from shadows, my energy burn barely mattered. Using white light energy to hide myself caused me to crash immediately afterward for hours at a time. "I could, and I will if that's what you want. The real question here is to what end? Hiding out annoys the police and increases their suspicions. If they pick you up tonight, you won't be able to reach Mr. Ellis to help you until tomorrow."

"Rats," Sage said. "I hate it when you're right. I'll stay put tonight, and I'll go to the cops tomorrow when Herbert R. Ellis can accompany me."

"Meanwhile, try to remember if other nursery staff members were upset with Loren Lee. Or if he argued with anyone on the phone during work hours. Whatever you can add to the knowledge about Loren Lee Suffield's last days will vastly improve your chances of sleeping in your bed for two nights in a row."

Sage braced her arms against the counter, a slow smile dawning on her face. "I hate ratting out anyone, unless it's Mary Nicole. She deserves a good setdown, and she's gunning for me, so why shouldn't I return the favor?"

"Atta girl," Auntie O said.

"Should I stay here with you tonight?" I asked my twin. "For moral support?"

"No need. I'm a big girl, and I won't put the kibosh on the big romance. You're our family's best chance for reproductive success."

"Oh, yes," Auntie O said, clapping her hands. "When can we expect a baby, Tabby?"

I like babies, and the idea of having Quig's baby appealed to me, but why rush that end of things? Heck, we'd only been dating for a few months. We were still working through our likes and dislikes. I needed to be firm about that.

"No time soon." I headed for the door. With the crisis averted, I wanted to be with Quig. "Everything is too new, too perfect. We're keeping it simple. We need to be *us* first."

"Don't wait too long," Auntie O said. "Your eggs aren't getting any younger."

Chapter Five

The next morning after my shower I still simmered over the negative comment about my reproductive organs. Quig noticed my distraction as he dressed for work. "What's up, buttercup?"

"Feeling moody this morning." I stood before the bathroom mirror looking to see if parts of my body sagged yet. "Do you ever feel time is running out?"

Quig turned from his closet and crossed to me, concern blazing in his eyes. "Did you find a lump or something?"

"No. Nothing like that."

"Talk to me." Hands on my shoulders, he gently rotated me to face him. "Tell me what's wrong so I can fix it."

"Relax. Aging is on my mind. I'm thirty. Won't be long until the other big years roll by. Trying to get perspective on my life span."

"What brought this on? Did someone call you ma'am again?"

I laughed and adjusted the towel I'd wrapped around my damp body. "It's okay. Something Auntie O said yesterday struck a nerve. As you know, she's keen on us twins adding children to the family tree."

Quig bowed. "I can help there."

"You'll make a great dad, but I'm not ready for kids. Someday, I'll do my part. Auntie O reminded me yesterday that my fertility is a ticking clock. The notion sobered me. All my life, I've been aware of the choices I could make. Now, through no fault of my own, some of those open windows are closing."

"You're young for a bucket list, but I'm curious. What else might time be running out on?"

"Being an astronaut comes to mind."

"Trekkie wanderlust invaded your soul?"

Our mutual interest in science fiction surprised us a few weeks ago. "A little. The idea of space travel appeals to me. On the other hand, I don't want to leave the planet or even this street. I want my feet planted firmly on the ground. Not just any ground. Bristol Street."

"The appeal of the *Star Trek* multiverse to me is linked to how other sentient life responds to conflict."

He looked so serious. And handsome. Couldn't forget that. "You are a natural born problem solver and fixer. You'd make an excellent starship captain."

"I'd do it if you were my first and only mate."

His words warmed me to my toes. Being with him expanded my horizon of experiences and adventures. No need to go to space for excitement when I had plenty at home. "Given that the universe is so vast, how'd you come to live on Bristol Street?"

"Easy." He grinned. "You live here." He closed the small gap between us and ran his hands down my bare arms. "I've always known you were the one for me. My dad said it happened like that for him and my mom. Once he realized my intentions toward you, he bought this place for me. Said proximity would make things easier."

That explained this apartment, but not everything I wanted to know. So far I'd discovered Quig had a few energy-related talents. Somehow he'd known from across town how distressed I felt before I confronted Blithe McAdam's killer. Also, I recuperated faster in his arms than alone, so he sped up my energy recharging process, though to a lesser extent than Bristol Street did.

With families on my mind, I had a few questions for Quig. I had to be careful how I phrased things because his science background made him smarter than the average bear. "Are your parents like me? Do they see auras?"

"Not that I know of. Mom's specialty is in weather prediction. She always knows better than the weatherman what will happen. My dad loves insects. We lived on a farm before we moved to Savannah. He has the largest insect collection outside of any museum. I spent most of my youth outdoors observing insects in nature."

I believed his parents had some extrasensory perception since their son had vestiges of it. "That's interesting. Did your interest in anatomy grow from those sessions? Or did you quite naturally follow your father's footsteps into the role of coroner?"

"Could be. Dad turned every experience into a teaching opportunity." He nuzzled my neck. "Now I'm fixating on your anatomy and your scent. I am addicted to how you smell."

My arms went around his neck. "You'll be late for work at this rate."

"Yep."

* * *

Both of us were late for work. Not even the cloudy day affected my fine mood. I floated on air into The Book and Candle Shop to find Frankie and Auntie O taking care of business. Earlier, Sage drove herself to the Law Enforcement Center with the plan of meeting Herbert R. Ellis there. Our shop clerk, Gerard Smith, had an early morning dentist appointment.

"Heard from Sage yet?" I asked my aunt.

She looked holiday festive today in a burgundy blouse and pants set, accented with a cream and burgundy scarf. Having Frankie here improved her self-esteem and brought out her sense of style. "Not yet, dearie. My, don't you look rosy today. You're glowing all over."

Living with Quig—heck, being with Quig—felt as right as anything I did with my special talent. "What can I say? Life is good."

Auntie O's head tilted to the side. "You thought more about having a baby?"

I glanced around the shop. For once, we had no customers. I hoped that didn't mean a slow Monday. "I appreciate your interest in our family's longevity, but I wish you wouldn't harp on it."

Even though we had privacy right now on the sales floor, Auntie O waved me into the stillroom. She talked in a low voice. "Frankie and I have been researching Quig's family for energetics in his line."

"That doesn't matter to me. I love him the way he is, and he understands that I am *quirky*. He accepts the little he knows about my other gears. He gets me. For you to be scouring records for his pedigree feels invasive. I wouldn't like it if his family did the same thing to me."

"It would be best if he has energetics in his family tree. We found no evidence of that, though he could have a spontaneous genetic mutation, which would explain why he bonded to you. We could only trace back two generations in the Quigsly family. They stay way off the grid."

Since I moved in with Quig, I'd met his parents once, and it had been beyond awkward. They volunteered nothing in the way of personal information, and his mom didn't cotton to me. "I figured that out already. So what?"

"We don't know what you're getting into."

"I love you, but please, let it go. These are modern times. If Quig and I have kids, that's on us. I'm more than a womb. I have an entire body full of organs, and no one tells me how to dream, hear, see, or anything else my other organs can do. I welcome your advice on everything else, so please don't take this the wrong way."

Understandably, Auntie O's hopeful expression shuttered. "If that's what you want, dear."

If I didn't stand my ground on this, she'd be tracking my ovulation cycle next. My reproductive ability stayed off the table as a family discussion topic. "It is."

"So be it." Auntie O nodded. "Moving on, I left you a note about a prepaid order by the register, but I'll tell you as well. Pour a double batch of votives in your new scent. A bride came in first thing and went gaga over your new fragrance. She needs votives for her entire wedding party, and she's coming back late this afternoon to get the remainder of the order."

"Wow. I'm jazzed about her interest in my new blend. I felt inspired making them."

"That's how it happened for me. The ones that came out *hot* like that always drew notice, as if they had built-in customer pheromones. Be sure to add this new recipe to the book, dear."

"I will be delighted if any of my blended scents withstand the test of time like yours have done."

"I'm proud of you, Tabby. You've pushed past your fear of using your energy abilities and embraced who you are, and your actions changed Gerard Smith's future. He has one now, thanks to you. You girls are making your mark on the world. Marjoram would be so proud." Auntie O radiated approval, then she sobered and pointed to my candle molds. "Those votives are your top priority this morning. If I'm not mistaken, Sage will leave that police interview steaming mad, and will tie up the rest of your day. Don't let her situation sour your good intentions."

"Will do on the votives." Making candles is what I wanted to do every day, so it never felt like work. I began assembling the supplies I needed. "Good guess on Sage's afternoon mood, seeing as that's how she fared last time around. One more thing. I've often wondered why Sage stays so angry and wound tight. Is there a way I can help her let that tension go without making it worse?"

"Oh, honey. You two are not from the same egg, though you shared a womb. Sage has smarts and good control of her energetic reflexes, but emotions are her Achilles' heel. She's always been so protective of you."

Another door chime. Another friendly customer greeting from Frankie. I shook my head to clear it. "Annoyingly so."

"Against my better judgment, I'll share another thought. Sage has tried hard to establish her independence from our family and our business, but the more she runs away, the more she's drawn into our midst." Auntie O picked up an essential oil vial and sniffed until a blissful expression filled her face. "Marjoram wouldn't approve, but I have a related observation along those lines. You're complete as an energetic, but Sage is not. She physically requires this building and you to fully function."

"Impossible. Sage went to Europe for months, and I stayed home."

"I didn't say she wouldn't survive without you. Remember how things went wrong for her overseas? She blamed her troubles on her love life, but it's deeper than that." Auntie O put the essential oil away. "Consider a rechargeable battery. It works fine until it loses its charge, then it fails. To return to that high level of performance, it must be recharged. Some chargers act faster than others. The latent energy in the apartment upstairs provides a continuous slow charge for you and your sister. You, on the other hand, function as Sage's quick-charge portal. When she's with you, I've noticed you share energy with her. Always."

"It's what we do." A niggle of guilt came through. Except for the time I refused to share after she'd drained Gerard to within an inch of his life. She'd gone way too far with him. I wouldn't condone that kind of behavior.

Auntie O held my gaze. "Because she needs you. The pattern is that you give energy, and she takes it. Never the other way around."

Her insight stunned me. How did I miss that? Sage siphoned energy from anyone she pleased. I'd criticized her scruples before, especially about stealing energy from our shop clerk. Only one explanation made sense. Sage acted like an energy thief, also known as an energy vampire. While I had the same ability to take energy from others, I rarely did so because of the invasion of privacy and because I recharged naturally overnight at home. I couldn't manage a full breath, but somehow I spoke. "Why am I whole and she is not?"

"I have a theory on that, but I'm not ready to share it. Make your candles, dear, and then be ready to help your sister."

Perversely, I wanted the day to myself to come to terms with what Auntie O revealed. When I called Sage a monster for nearly killing Gerard, I hadn't been that far off the mark. How could I look at Sage and hide what I'd learned? I'd rather avoid that.

"It's my day in the shop." That sounded weak, even to my ears.

"Gerard and I will cover this afternoon, don't worry about that. Your sister needs you."

I flailed around for another excuse to stay put. "Don't you want to spend the day with Frankie?"

"Frankie has other plans for the afternoon. Gerard and I are like bread and butter in the shop, so it's all good."

With that Auntie O headed to the shop. Rotely, I staged the stillroom for production, but I couldn't make candles while I felt so anxious. The energy would be wrong in the candles. I needed pure intentions, but how could I focus in the face of such dire news? My twin's energy deficit bound me in a way that severely limited my freedom.

I loved my sister, but energy transfers were finite in number. At some point, I'd have to stop augmenting her energy every time she demanded a quick charge. How would constant energy boosts to Sage and others affect my life? Further, if helping Sage energy-wise harmed me, I'd be forced to make an awful choice when I did one day get pregnant.

Yikes.

Harley and Luna padded in. I scooped a black cat in each arm and held on tight.

Chapter Six

When I read my sister's urgent text at noon, I let Gerard know I needed to spend time with Sage. I grabbed a sweatshirt and hurried out to the alley to join Sage in her new-to-her gold Honda Civic car. This puppy had twenty years under its belt, and it ran forever and a day on a tank of gas. "Thank goodness you're here," my twin said, accelerating out of our neighborhood once I secured my seat belt. "Take a ride with me? I am in deep trouble, Tabs, and I need your help."

As her words registered, I also felt the urgent demand from her for my energy. Maybe Auntie O and Mom had a point about keeping secrets. Some things were better left unknown, like how automatically Sage expected energy from me.

But she couldn't help needing constant tap-offs, so I pushed energy her way. Small swaps wouldn't hurt me, and I knew her experience had been unpleasant. "Talk to me, Sage. What happened in the interview?"

"Nowry stayed all in my face about killing Loren Lee. He claims I poisoned my boss to get his job. If I wanted to poison someone it'd be that snarky Mary Nicole, and I'd do it so no one would know she'd been poisoned. She's so full of herself now that she's acting assistant manager. I can't stand her."

Heavy traffic flowed on this overcast day, reminding me to keep information flowing from Sage so I'd know what we were up against. "I hear you, but let's focus on the police interview. What specifically did he say?"

Sage headed toward Tybee. "He said other nursery employees remarked on our argument last week. He said my aggression, anger management issues, and social isolation were red flags, and that implied criminal behavior. If not for Herbert R. Ellis and the camera recording the interview, I'd have socked him with everything I've got. The nerve of that man."

"But you didn't sock him. You were free to walk out of the interview."

"They kept hammering at me, both Nowry and Belfor. I expected that from the old school cop, but Belfor really showed her teeth today. She took a few sharp nips at me, quizzing me about plant poisons, even when I told her every plant could be a poison in the right concentration. She didn't like that."

I'd told the cops something similar on Saturday. "Why didn't Herbert answer the questions?"

"I knew the answers, that's why. I wanted to prove my innocence."

"Oh, Sage. Not a good idea. With all your chatting, you established yourself as an expert in the field of poisons, and they are looking for a poisoner."

She shook her head, fast. "You don't understand. If I kept my trap shut, I looked guilty. I will never go down without a fight."

"I understand your rationale, but in that interview room cops have the upper hand. They keep pushing buttons until a suspect breaks or pushes back. When that person cooperates, cops win.

Information is power. Not only that, but they can twist what people say against them. In this case, you should've said nothing."

Sage banged her fist on the steering wheel and yelped. "Ow. That hurt. This is frustrating, and I feel so testy these days, even more so than usual. I can't deal with cops and their ways. If we see a police vehicle, take the wheel because I'm likely to ram their car and get in even more trouble."

I ignored her outburst and kept digging. "Hopefully you used your super-snooper personality to grill them. Did they say what poison killed your boss?"

"A local plant is what they said, nothing more. Get this. They assume I use our mortars and pestles to make poisons. Honestly, why would I poison someone when I could get the same result with a total energy drain?"

"No one said the cops had to make sense to persons of interest. Their questions make sense to them. Can't you just imagine their expressions if they knew what we can do?"

"Yeah. Belfor would flash those long fingernails of hers in the air like a fiddler crab mating ritual and Nowry would drop his little notebook on the floor."

I laughed even though I cringed inwardly. The blowback from her chatty interview could be positively horrific. "So in the course of that interview, they established you had means, motive, and opportunity to kill Loren Lee."

"You're right," Sage groaned. "Good news is they didn't arrest me, though that could be next. Herbert asked if they were interviewing all of Loren Lee's employees. They said they'd already talked with everyone else, including Ms. Chatham."

We wound closer and closer to Tybee Island on a narrow ribbon of elevated road, salt marshes stretching out to creeks on both sides. The air already smelled less like city and more like life. With this much sensory stimulus, who cared about gray skies? I loved storm energy.

I couldn't get distracted by the scenery, not when I expected answers. "Recapping for clarity. Cops interviewed all of Loren Lee's work associates, and they didn't arrest anyone. Did they question his neighbors and friends?"

"I don't know."

"Do you know his neighbors and friends?"

"I do not. I didn't hang out with Loren Lee outside of work."

Sage sounded testy. I asked her the most important question point blank. "Did you set them straight about the argument?"

"I did. Nowry sent Belfor out to call a few of my coworkers to verify my statement while he kept lobbing loaded questions at me. Meanwhile, Belfor independently confirmed that I wanted to take him for medical treatment, and he refused to go. I thought Nowry would blow an artery when Belfor returned with that confirmation. He absolutely wanted me to be guilty."

Nowry and Belfor were partners on the force and, according to most sources, were well respected. My personal observations didn't jibe with that assessment. "Quig says Nowry's a good cop, but in my experience I've found him quick to judge people."

"He has it in for me. I can tell by the way he glares at me with those steely cop eyes. He doesn't believe a word I say."

We didn't have time for a pity party. Wait. That thought sounded like Quig, not me. Pity party had been Sage's middle name for some time, only I hadn't noticed until now. Maybe Quig's practical nature had rubbed off on me. "He looks at everyone that way, Sis. It's part of the job description."

"Maybe, but it sure feels personal. My intuition tells me he's got an axe to grind against me. He asked me to take a lie detector test."

With her variable electrical currents, no telling what that test result would look like. The extra spikes in her aura—mine too if I were being honest—would play havoc with the detector. "You told him no, right?"

"Of course. I'm not stupid."

Sage took the next curve too fast, and I held onto the armrest and console for dear life. "Did your lawyer push for it?"

"Not really. He sat quietly through that part. He spent most of the time looking at Sharmila Belfor and scowling as if he didn't believe his eyes."

"They're dating."

"That explains it. He looked unhappy with her. I hope they're breaking up. I wouldn't mind dating him. There's something about his energy that pulls me."

Air hissed through my clenched teeth. Now that Sage had dated and dumped our shop's lawyer, Brindle Platt, we needed a new attorney for business and personal reasons. "It worked out so well when you dated Brindle."

"We are not amused." Sage tuned the radio to a classic rock station, cranked up the volume, and effectively silenced our conversation. She shut down her energy draw from me too.

I settled back into my seat, glad for a sleuthing reprieve, and today her taste in music suited me fine. I longed to forget our troubles by flinging myself into the up-tempo drama of rock and the soaring vocals. Thanks to Sage, I knew many songs in this genre and even knew some lyrics. Except my brain wouldn't shut down on the likely threat to my sister. With Sage's competitiveness, razor-sharp wit, and supersized libido, she couldn't back down from a fight.

She and Mary Nicole would never get along, even if they were stranded on a desert island. She acted aggressively every time something bothered her, ramping from calm to all-out war in a heartbeat. I loved her fierce loyalty to our family, but ungoverned actions could jeopardize her future and our family's need to hide in plain sight.

Sage wouldn't hear anything I said right now. She needed to come to terms with whatever drove her to act out before her ears would work again. Thankfully we had that time now and an entire seashore at her disposal. The wind, waves, and weather bathed the coast in natural energy and infused our personal energy grids with a characteristic zest.

I'd often tried to understand that zest. Joy and cheer couldn't quite describe it, though they were side effects. Elation and "high" didn't begin to do it justice. The refreshment went soul-deep, more akin to a post-yoga glow magnified to a higher power. As it turned out, I needed this break in routine too.

At the beach, we walked beside the water, and tension ebbed away. I filled my lungs with ocean-fresh air, and it felt marvelous. However, despite December's mild, overcast weather, a brisk breeze off the ocean cut through my sweatshirt. Barely five minutes passed before I wished for a windbreaker, another ten before I wanted to dash back to the car.

My twin showed no sign of turning around. She kept going and going, like that battery-powered bunny of television fame. "Sage, I love an ocean recharge as much as you, but I'm chilled to the bone. I'm turning around."

"Don't be a wimp, Tabs. I need more time, much more. That jail-house vibe invaded every part of me. I have to work the dissonance out of my mind, body, and spirit."

"I want you to feel better, but I need warmer clothes to be your beach sidekick."

"I have no problem with the wind. Suck it up. Or create an energy blanket around yourself. This is my crisis, not yours."

Without knowing how much energy she might siphon off on the way home, a strong nudge of self-preservation whispered in my ear that I didn't have any spare energy right now. Managing an energy blanket and supplying Sage could get dicey. I'd exceeded my limit of energy sharing once and vowed never to do that again.

Today I had the attention span of a gnat. I came here to help my sister. She needed to vent her frustration, and I approved even if we were the only ones on this cold beach. "Hey, I'm on your side. I can't help if I turn into a popsicle. With your icer energy, you're used to feeling chilled. It is an unnatural state for me, and I much prefer warm over cold. I'll wait in the car. Walk as long as you like."

"Loren Lee won't ever feel hot or cold again," Sage said, halting and staring at the shallow crests of low tide. "His life is over, thanks to a killer."

About time she shared her thoughts. This breakthrough exceeded the personal cost of an energy-based wind barrier. I shielded us with my aura and felt warmer immediately. "Who do you think killed him?"

Sage tipped her head to the side as a wide vee of birds glided above the tidal zone. "Mary Nicole, of course. She's after Loren Lee's job, and she's thrilled the road ahead is clear."

"He have trouble with any of his employees?"

She didn't answer at first, just stared at the distant sea buoy. "With everyone but me. Not his fault. Just nobody else worked as hard as he demanded. They always griped about him behind his back."

The shells on the shore called to me. Not now, I told myself. Later. "Any of your coworkers have an apothecary hobby?"

"Not that I know of. For most of them, the nursery served as a temporary position on the way to the rest of their lives. Very few cared for plants or landscaping, but it paid better than fast food, and they had more autonomy."

"You like those things too."

"Sure, but I enjoy working with plants. My green thumb needs to be in the dirt."

I studied her carefully. Her color looked better, her shoulders less hunched around her ears. Beach therapy had worked its subtle magic. We could go home now. "Let's hope they stay nice and green. Race you back to the car?"

"You're on!"

Chapter Seven

Gas surged into Sage's gas tank. A text message chimed on Sage's phone. She checked the display, then swore and tossed her phone through the open window onto the back seat. More message chimes followed.

"What's going on?" I asked. "Brindle again?"

My twin huffed out a breath as she leaned down to glare at me in the passenger seat. "Not Brindle. Worse."

"What could be worse?"

"Alyss. That's what. She's bananas if she expects a reply. Hand me that phone. I'm blocking her right now."

I reached for the phone as Sage sat beside me. Her fingers rat-a-tap-tapped on the phone. "Done."

My curiosity stretched its sleek neck. "Not interested in knowing what she wants?"

"She can get sucked out to sea in a rip current, get swallowed by a whale, and spend the rest of her days in Davy Jones' locker for all I care."

So much for Sage's beach recharge. Her calm center had atomized quicker than heat radiating from twilight dunes. For the first time that afternoon, the dark gray skies weighed on me, filling me with lethargy. Why did my sister have such a hair trigger response? Why couldn't I press a button and reset my twin to an even keel?

From long experience, letting her fume worked best. "Gotcha."

Sage's rock and roll faves precluded conversation on the way home, giving me time to reflect. I loved my twin dearly, but her drama took a toll on me. I looked forward to parting ways with her in town, finishing up my day at the shop, and spending a delightfully quiet evening with Quig. My mood brightened with possibilities as we neared home.

Sage parked in our parking area and we walked in the thick twilight to our alley and our homes. We reached the stairs to Sage's apartment first. It would have been impossible to miss the bright yellow blouse on a woman perched midway on her steps. I drew in a sharp gulp of recognition. Ms. Alyss Carter, Brindle's secretary. The woman who most likely bewitched Brindle. As Alyss hurried down the stairs to intercept us, I wondered if she had a death wish. Given Sage's mercurial temper, the thought of her and the root cause of her shattered love life being in the same city block seemed a recipe for disaster.

I shot Sage a warning on our twin-link. *Remember we are out in the open. Don't do anything rash or consequential.*

Sage bared her teeth at me, then glowered at Alyss. "You're trespassing on private property. Leave or I will call the cops."

"I must talk to you. Brindle is—"

Energy pulsed off my twin like storm-fueled breakers rolling in from the sea. Dark currents pulsed between Sage and her nemesis. "Stop right there. I want nothing to do with you or that cheater. Leave me alone."

Alyss didn't flinch in the face of my sister's anger. She acted as if she expected this for wronging Sage. "He fired me once you left.

When he skipped work today, Mr. Everson called me at home to ask where we both were. I explained I'd been fired. He hung up on me. I just learned Brindle is in the hospital." She hesitated. "He asked to see you. I tried to visit him, but I'm not on the visitor list. You are."

Sage said nothing, her face pale as white wax.

"What's wrong with him?" I asked, giving Sage time to process Alyss's words.

"Don't," Sage said, her hands fisting at her sides.

"He took a bunch of pills is what I heard," Alyss said.

"Brindle?" The man who meditated while doing headstands in his office? I couldn't wrap my head around that. Something felt very wrong here. "I can't believe it."

"Call Memorial yourself."

"I hate you for ruining my life and for putting Brindle in the hospital," Sage said. "I bet you gave him those pills to take. Get lost. Scram."

"I'm sorry. I didn't know this would happen, but he cares about you. I kept hoping he'd notice me, and then he did and we went to his place. He is everything I've ever dreamed of. Then you showed up, and he freaked out."

"Are you still here?" Sage muttered.

Uh-oh. I heard the tremble in her voice, saw her aura flare. Those flashes of ultraviolet lightning could be deadly. If Alyss had a lick of sense she'd run for cover right now. *Go inside, Sage. I've got this.*

I want to squash her like a bug. She deserves it.

"He fired me and pushed me out of his house, in my bra, no less," Alyss nattered on, oblivious to her peril. "What a jerk."

My twin's invisible energy bolt arced out into the dusky sky. While I appreciated her not zapping a person, I knew she teetered on the brink of disaster. *Sage! Walk away. Please. For both of us. I'll get rid of her.*

The shriek of outrage that blasted through our twin-link nearly deafened me, but thankfully, Sage shoved around Alyss and raced up the stairs. I turned to the interloper, my voice harsh and heavy as my heart. "Get out of here. Right now. If you ever contact my sister again, I'll file charges for harassment and slap a restraining order on you."

Alyss flashed a haughty smile full of challenge. "I can do anything I want. This is a free country. You don't scare me and neither does your flaky sister."

Sounded like a dare to me. Time to show her she swam with the big dogs now. I brushed ghostly fingers across the nape of her neck. Her eyes bulged. "You're all crazy. The lawyers. The clients. Screw all of you."

I directed another micro-pulse of energy to her knees, causing her to stumble, then I stormed home. I shot Sage a twin-link message. *She's gone.*

Nothing. I tried again. *Talk to me.*

I called the hospital. Brindle is there. I need to see him with my own two eyes.

Not without me.

* * *

My name didn't appear on the visitor list, and Sage had to leave her phone with me when she entered the psych ward. I called Quig to let him know where my whereabouts.

"Stay put," he said. "I'm on my way."

I reached for a magazine and gave the appearance of reading it. All my senses were attuned to the emotions Sage felt. She'd gone in there with a belly full of fear and barely enough moxie to keep her feet moving. I tried to cheer her up. *You've got this.*

In the Wick of Time

I've got nothing but heartache.

You have a wonderful life, plus family and friends who love you. I'm proud of you for doing this.

I have to see him. To know he's alive.

Her voice sounded so fierce. *I'm here if you need me.*

Oh, Tabs. I see him coming to the room where they asked me to wait. He's slumped in a wheelchair. His face is so pale. He barely looks like himself.

He's alive. He made a mistake. Two, actually. He feels awful. Go easy on him. You can yell at him later.

You're right. No yelling today.

She shielded her thoughts from me, and I hoped and prayed she could be strong for her boyfriend in this moment. I didn't know what made Brindle overdose. Seemed like having two women fight over you would be every man's dream.

More like a nightmare for Brindle.

Someone sat in the loveseat next to me and slid his arm around me. I had to tamp down the cry of alarm that wanted to spring from my throat. In the next breath, I relaxed. I'd know this man anywhere. "Thanks for coming," I said, leaning into his embrace.

"Of course," Quig said. "How is he?"

"Not good if he's in the psych ward. Did your cop friend have any information about what happened?"

"Nothing about the lawyer. The receptionist is bad news. She has a history of restraining orders, from men and women. Seems her MO is causing trouble everywhere she goes. Steer clear of her and encourage your sister to do likewise."

"Trust me. I want nothing to do with that woman and neither does Sage."

"Umm." He caressed my hand. "I signed off on Dr. Chang's autopsy report this morning. The cause of Loren Lee's death is officially poisoning. The cops will make a move soon."

"Sage is okay, isn't she?" His face tightened and that scared me. "I mean she didn't do anything except try to persuade her boss to see a doctor. That's not an arrestable offense."

"I can't say."

"I'm afraid for her." I searched his face, wishing I knew what he knew. No way I could read his thoughts, but I'd had some luck sending him a mental image once. How could I show him I needed her to be free? I pulled an image from us in her car with the wind blowing her hair and shared it telepathically with him.

His grip on my arm tightened. "It would not look right if your sister took a trip right now."

Oh. Good idea but wrong concept. I tried again, with an image of her holding her hair in front of the breaking surf at Tybee. "She's not planning a trip as far as I know."

Quig shook his head. "I'm worried this will take a lot out of you. Should something happen to sideline her for whatever reason, you'd be solely responsible for managing your business. I know you two share the responsibilities, but have you done any cross-training?"

His question confused me. "I don't know what that means."

"It's where you each learn to perform the duties of the other team members."

"No. She manages our online orders and the inventory system."

"You can access those programs, right?"

"I . . ." My voice trailed off. After Mom passed and Auntie O wanted to move, my aunt trained each of us in various jobs and bugged out. We'd never had reason to learn what the other person did. "No. I can't do her part. Auntie O knows it, though. She and Mom ran this shop for years before it came to us. If Sage can't do it, Auntie O will teach me, same as she taught Sage. Only, Sage is a whiz with computer stuff. I'm likely to erase the entire data set when I log in."

"Definitely time for you to make notes on what she does and how she does it. She should also shadow you to see what you do."

I heard someone coming down the corridor, fast. "Easier said than done," I told Quig as I rose and caught Sage in my arms. "Easy. Easy does it. What happened?"

"I'm leaving." Sage swiped at tears on her face. "Come with me or stay, I don't care, but I can't stand being here one more minute."

I held on tight, keeping her tethered to me, surrounding her with soothing energy. "Sage, calm down. What's wrong?"

"Brindle. He's a mess. He's zoned out on meds, and he's a liar. He kept saying he would never hurt me. He broke my heart all over again."

"Sage."

He said Alyss must've bewitched him, that he doesn't like her. He claimed she looked like me and she sounded like me. How could he be so dense? It hurts all over again. Like a knife gouging my heart. It's too much.

Even though such a thing might be possible, I couldn't spare the time to think about it, not with Sage so upset. Grief and anger radiated from her in unrelenting waves, smacking me in the face like a sandy beach towel. No matter what the truth between Brindle and Alyss was, their betrayal crushed my sister and, by extension, me. As I stroked Sage's hair, she trembled and gulped in ragged breaths. My arms tightened reflexively around her. Heaven help me, Alyss and Brindle would pay for what they'd done.

Chapter Eight

B ack in Sage's apartment, I served her tea and peanut butter toast on the sofa, but not even her favorite comfort foods put a dint in her sorrow. I wrapped her in my arms and held tight as she cried. I did my best to anchor her during the storm of tears, comforting her with words, touch, and energy, though my eyes moistened with tears too.

We'd spent most of our lives within these walls, suffered through every scrape and heartache of growing up. Gazing at the primitive artwork Mom had framed from our elementary days felt as normal as anything, same as the rest of the dated furnishings. How many times had we sheltered from life's storms in this very room, on this sofa? More than I could count, that's for sure.

As I regained my peaceful center, my mind cleared, and I realized Brindle's words could be interpreted differently. Sage automatically leaped to the conclusion he'd lied to her. But what if he told the truth? Root doctors and occult practitioners thrived in our low country region. What did we really know about Alyss?

Finally, Sage calmed and her breathing evened. Both black cats watched from the coffee table. I ran my supposition past her through our twin-link since it seemed natural after being so deep in thought. *Sis, consider this. What if Alyss truly bewitched Brindle? If so, this isn't his fault. She charmed him to see what he wanted to see, you in his arms.*

Her grip around me tightened. *That is wishful thinking. I won't go that route.*

Is it? If we didn't know people like us existed, we wouldn't believe in us either. Alyss could be a witch, or she could've visited a witch to make him take an interest in her.

Sage dashed the moisture from her face. "Sorry. I couldn't hold it in any longer. I couldn't let Brindle see me cry. I didn't want him to know how bad he hurt me."

"Brindle's issue deserves a closer look, and we should focus on facts."

Her face darkened, then she drew in a shaky breath. "This sucks."

I felt proud of her for holding it together. "Of course it does. Your boyfriend cheated with another woman. I don't trust Alyss, and it is possible there are extenuating circumstances."

"I can't let hope in. It hurts too much."

"If a plausible explanation existed, you'd get your guy back, and all would be well again."

"The world takes, and it takes some more until it bleeds you dry." Sage sat quietly for a few minutes before adding, "You think she charmed him?"

"It is possible. Do we know anyone who claims to be a witch?"

"Mary Nicole at the nursery acts like something that rhymes with witch."

I scowled at her. "Not helpful." I reached for my cup of luke-warm tea. "What about that girl from your sophomore English class? The one that dressed like our art student customers."

My sister sipped her tea. Then she ate a bite of her cold toast. "Jeanine Acworth wore a lot of black and kept to herself. She never claimed to be a witch."

"Nobody picked on her. Not the jocks, the cool kids, the alternative kids. Loners are bullied. We experienced that. Somehow Jeanine went her own way and suffered no repercussions."

"Ah. Now that I think back, she navigated as if she had a repellant bubble around her."

"She has witch potential. Heck, she might even be an energetic like us. Is she still in Savannah?"

"Let me plug her name in several social media apps." Sage's thumbs flew over her phone. She made several considering noises before she turned to me. "Found her. Her page says she works at a metaphysical shop in town. It's off the beaten track, but I would expect no less from Jeanine."

"She's our age. Cut her some slack. Like us, she has no interest in climbing a corporate ladder."

"Okay. We'll ask Jeanine if Alyss mesmerized or cursed Brindle."

Sage studied a dark window as if it held compelling secrets. "Bad idea. Let's stay focused on who killed Loren Lee. We can't go chasing tangents. My love life is less important than my freedom."

Harley approached and circled my lap until he found the perfect spot. I stroked his sleek back, and he purred with feline contentment. "I will do both because you deserve a man who loves you. From all accounts, Brindle Platt is that man. Let's check his story and solve Loren Lee's murder."

"You know something more about that?"

My hands stilled on Harley's back. His head nudged me until I resumed petting him. "I might. His autopsy is now official."

"Quig told you?"

"Yeah. He won't tell me the plant responsible, but he believes you're in the hot seat."

Sage swore with passion etching her words. "The cops hate Winslows, and they have it in for me."

"They must have something solid. Let's brainstorm and try to figure out what cards the cops are holding. You had no extra opportunity to poison him because you were friends, but still acquaintances only. However, you work in an occupation that distills plant essences."

Our other black cat, Luna, regarded Sage steadily from the coffee table. My sister ignored the cat's invisible message, whatever it had been. "But I wouldn't hurt Loren Lee. Ever. I respected him too much. I talk tough, but I'm not vengeful, or I would've punished all the people who wronged me."

I thought how close I'd come to exacting vengeance on Brindle and Alyss for hurting Sage. I could barely back down from that emotional ledge. "I'm thinking like a cop. In your interview, you established yourself as a poisoning expert, so they must believe you could've poisoned him."

Sage chewed on her thumbnail. "It must be the actual poison, then, that has their attention. They must think I made it. What poison is it?"

"I wish I knew. Of the deadly plants you mentioned the other day, we don't have sago palms nearby, but plenty grow near here. In fact, anyone could harvest what they needed from a road median and be home free."

My twin sighed deeply, as if it were her last breath. "Except everyone isn't a poison expert. I'm an idiot."

Harley tensed and crouched as if he would run away. I drew him close until he relaxed. "Don't throw in the towel yet. Sago palms might fit the bill, but what about oleanders? Those grow in our alley."

My twin stared at me before shrieking, "Oh my God. That must be it. Thankfully, I've never picked oleander. Had no reason to, so there shouldn't be any oleander residue in our shop."

I shivered and then pulled cat claws from my arm. Harley twisted and bounded away. "Let's hope not."

"Hmm. I wonder if there are oleanders near Mary Nicole's house? She would do anything to win the assistant manager job."

"Good idea. You know where she lives?"

"Nope. Never cared until this discussion," Sage said. "But I will find out tonight because I need to do something."

I rose from the sofa to turn on more lights to quench the shadows in the corners. "Don't break into Brindle's place, okay?"

"I'd rather use my key to enter, but I threw the key in his face."

"Let me be crystal clear. Don't do anything illegal tonight. If it came to the cops' attention, Detective Nowry might leap to the conclusion that you're a criminal because criminals commit crimes. We don't know if he has an undercover unit surveilling you. We do not want to hand him extra ammunition to use against you."

She gave me The Look. Not as effective as when Mom peered over her glasses and hit us with it, but I got the point, especially when Sage poked my shoulder. "Killjoy."

"I'm being the big sister right now."

"Don't get used to that role. It's mine."

"You can have it back. While I'm in bossy mode, who else benefits from Loren Lee not being at the nursery?"

"Any employee. Loren Lee measured everyone's performance against his, and he never stopped working."

I perched on the sofa arm. "How many people work at the nursery?"

"A dozen, and all are part-time, except the manager and assistant manager. Ms. Chatham doesn't pay for our health care that way."

"Surely there were employees he rode the hardest?"

"Not really. He complained a lot. But everyone got moving when he cruised their area."

"Did he fire anyone recently?"

My twin examined her short fingernails. "Nope. Wait. Chris Kachuba. She got the axe two years ago. She excelled at chatting up customers and ringing up sales, but she never jumped when Loren Lee said to jump. She infuriated him."

"Your boss acted finicky and demanding. No wonder his employees disliked him."

"As I recall, Chris and Loren Lee got in a shouting match. Another employee taped it with his phone. Later, Ms. Chatham acted appalled at seeing the video on social media. She ordered Loren Lee to handle it."

I massaged a brewing headache in my temples. "I'm confused. An argument isn't grounds for murder. May I remind you that you argued with Loren Lee the day before he died."

"My argument doesn't count." Sage beamed a triumphant smile and scooped her kitty close. "Chris Kachuba's parting words to Loren Lee shocked me. I can't believe I forgot them until now, but when she didn't follow up on her threat I dismissed it as wild talk, something everyone does in the heat of the moment. After Chris, Loren Lee had four assistant managers, but Chris is the only one who threatened to kill him."

Chapter Nine

"What happened to this Kachuba gal?" I asked, my stomach growling for a meal. I'd forgotten lunch, and now dinnertime loomed on the horizon. I had no idea what I would make for dinner tonight, only that I needed to start cooking soon.

"Don't know," Sage said. "I didn't give Chris another thought until now. I mean who takes two years to carry out a death threat? I assumed she'd moved on. Personally, I viewed assistant managers as expendable because Loren Lee went through so many. For that reason, I never applied for the position until this month, and I only did so because Loren Lee urged me to apply."

"Let me try to connect with Chris online while I'm thinking about it." I picked up my phone, and Chris Kachuba had a social media page. I messaged her that we had mutual friends and that I'd like to talk to her. I pocketed the phone. "Okay. I messaged her. I'll let you know if I hear from her, and if I don't I'll find her another way. Getting back to Loren Lee, why didn't he hire people who matched his energy level?"

Sage made a chopping motion with her hand. "He didn't hire anyone. Ms. Chatham did the hires."

"Hmm. Any chance Ms. Chatham got tired of the revolving door of assistant managers and killed Loren Lee?"

"Have you met Ms. Chatham? She's a dithery sort. That's why she got along with Loren Lee. He stated his needs clearly, and she respected his insights. She needed his backbone and consistent delivery of profits. He needed her deep pockets."

The sofa arm under my bottom felt harder and harder with every passing moment. I eased back down on the sofa cushions and propped up my feet on the coffee table. "Okay, so far we've got Chris Kachuba on our suspect list. What about other nurseries? Assuming Loren Lee held All Good Things together and that the nursery's future is uncertain without him, what other nursery business stands to gain your customer base?"

"I hadn't considered that angle. You're good at this, Tabs. Your talents are wasted making candles."

"I love candlemaking. Investigating uses a similar mindset as crafting. There's an art and a science to each process. Come on. You must know who The Competition is."

"There are well-established nurseries like Gene's Nursery, Fancy Plants, and Hester and Zipperer, to name a very few, but we're no threat to them. The chain lumber stores carry plants, but they cater to their regular DIY customers. There are also florists who maintain a supply of shrubs and palms. Our nursery customer base includes the working class, neighbors, college students, and a few tourists. All Good Things has been in business for decades, Sis."

A dead end. I tried to think of someone else to investigate. "Hmm. What about Larry Rau or Mary Nicole Frasier?"

"What about them? They obviously love plants, or they wouldn't work at a nursery."

"Not helpful. What about their murderous tendencies?"

"Larry doesn't have a mean bone in his body. If he were a dog he'd be a mellow great Dane. Mary Nicole has a vicious tongue and acts like a rabid Chihuahua. I can imagine her poisoning the whole nursery staff if it suited her purposes. After working under her for a few days, I know she's every bit as much a tyrant as Loren Lee, but the things she nitpicks about aren't related to productivity or sales. She's never happy, even if people do her bidding."

As she spoke, I thought how nicely someone with Larry's calm temperament paired with my volatile sister would work together. Or would he be another mistake? If his personality didn't match Sage's, her volatile mood swings might make his life miserable. I tuned in to Sage's comments, catching tyrant and unhappy as descriptors of Mary Nicole, as well as several dog references.

Not sure I could add to that, so I went with a recap of information. "So far we've got Chris Kachuba and Mary Nicole as suspects who benefit from Loren Lee's death or might have wanted him dead. If we ask who benefits with you gone, Mary Nicole hits the list again, as does Alyss Carter. She wants Brindle. You had him. She broke up your relationship, but her plans derailed when Brindle rejected her."

Sage sniffed a few times before answering. "He rejected himself. Taking a handful of pills is a bad idea."

"If she bewitched him, by definition he didn't act normally. Brindle flirted with women, but it seemed like you and he were in a very good place. His seduction of Alyss is inconsistent with recent behavior, and he thought you were in his arms."

"I don't believe that could happen." Sage gestured emphatically with her hands. "I can't believe him. I saw him today because I couldn't not go, but he burned his bridges with me."

Anyone else would take some time before deciding. My sister's emotional response seemed typical of her. Out of long practice, I began talking her down from emotion-driven posturing to true listening.

"Really, Sis?" I asked. "If he acted under compulsion, you wouldn't extend an olive branch?"

"Damn straight I wouldn't. Getting in that mess indicates a weak character."

"You're making a snap judgment. Compulsion means doing something that's not your choice. If someone bewitched him, there are other choices besides witches. The offender might have consulted one of Savannah's root doctors or an occult practitioner. He could be completely innocent."

"Don't mess with my head, Tabs. He cheated. That's inexcusable."

"You're upset right now, but you and Brindle will decide if anything comes next between you two. My point is you were in Alyss's way. Killing your boss and implicating you removes you from Brindle's life. If you're arrested for murder, so much the better for Alyss and Mary Nicole. Heck, maybe even for Chris Kachuba. She could sweet talk Ms. Chatham into making her the manager due to her management expertise and familiarity with the nursery."

"Huh." Sage rose and paced the room. "Heck, maybe they conspired to get rid of me."

I took a deep breath because she was listening with her ears and brains now instead of her heart. "Perhaps, but it feels like someone working alone. If multiple people got involved, someone would've cut a deal with the cops by now. One thing is certain. Loren Lee didn't die immediately. How long did he suffer?"

"At least six weeks. That's when I first noticed his flagging energy and sunken cheeks. Whoever did this was intentionally cruel. They wanted him to suffer."

I considered that for a moment. Mary Nicole had a spiteful personality. Now that Mary Nicole served as acting assistant manager, she must believe she had it made.

Fingers snapped in front of my face. "Tabby! Where'd you go? This is my life we're talking about. Pay attention."

"Thinking about the case. We have a vindictive killer. When we add in Brindle's situation, whether he acted on impulse or compulsion, you're the connection. Someone is setting you up."

My phone buzzed. I glanced at it in alarm. Auntie O sent me a two-word message from downstairs. "SOS. Hurry."

Chapter Ten

Sage and I raced downstairs and into the showroom. My two least favorite people in the world, Detectives Nowry and Belfor, pulsed stern and unforgiving vibes in our shop. Worse, they locked Frankie Mango in handcuffs and led him away.

This was the worst Monday ever.

"Make the call, Oralee," Frankie said over his shoulder to Auntie O as he left.

"What happened?" I wrapped my arms around Auntie O.

Her eyes swam with tears. "They know."

Whatever she meant, it seemed prudent to have this conversation upstairs. "Sage, would you escort Auntie O to the apartment and make lunch? I'll be right behind you." I saw Gerard behind the counter. He'd returned from the dentist. "You got the shop?"

"I'm good here," he said, flashing his gleaming white teeth. "And no cavities, thanks for asking."

"Congratulations. Looks like Sage and I may be busy the rest of the day getting Frankie out of police clutches. Text me if you need anything."

"I'll be fine. Ramon is on his way over to keep me company. We're going out to dinner tonight to celebrate our two-month anniversary."

Our shop clerk enjoyed the social scene, and Ramon Hernandez caught his eye recently. They appeared to be a good match. "Congratulations. It's fine with me if Ramon keeps you company as long as he doesn't distract you." Another thought popped into my head. Ramon and Gerard were still in that flush of new love and couldn't keep their hands off each other. "No making out in the shop or my stillroom."

"Got it." He grinned, then schooled his features. "Hope y'all can spring Frankie. I like him. He tells interesting stories."

"About what?"

He waggled his eyebrows. "The good old days."

Interesting. Frankie had never mentioned anything other than his late wife's illness and death to me. "Tell me later. I need to get upstairs."

"Sure."

I hustled up the stairs and joined Sage and Auntie O at the kitchen table. Bacon flavored the air and I hoped that meant BLTs for our late lunch. "What's going on?"

Auntie O dabbed at her eyes with a tissue. "We didn't share this earlier with you girls, but given what I know about those detectives, Frankie's past will be used against him. They'll leak it to the papers too. This is awful."

"It can't be too bad," I said loyally. "Frankie is a nice guy."

"His history makes him a suspect," she said. "Much earlier in life, he hung with the wrong crowd, skirted the edge of the law, that sort of thing."

She acted circumspect, which frustrated me. I needed to nudge her along to straight talk, but Sage beat me to it.

"Are you talking about gangs or organized crime?" Sage asked as she poured three sodas, then rose to tend the bacon.

"I don't know the details, and truly I didn't want to know at first," Auntie O said. "It happened a long, long time ago, back before Frankie's marriage. He wanted out of his old life. He didn't take the feds' offer of witness protection. Instead, he vanished and started over with a new name in a new career in a new state."

Sage tossed cooled bacon bits to the cats. "He's been hiding from the law all these years?"

Auntie O took a moment to gather herself. "He's been an upstanding citizen for four decades, paid his taxes, the whole deal. This is beyond cruel."

Sage's dramas had already wound me tight today. I gentled my thoughts and voice so as not to vent my frustration on my aunt. "Tell us."

"You mustn't think poorly of him. Frankie did what he had to do to survive." Auntie O blinked furiously at the tears filling her eyes. "Times were tough back then. In his hometown, if you didn't affiliate with a group, you got dead right away. I want to emphasize Frankie is a survivor."

My curiosity meter pegged. "Why did the cops grab Frankie? What's he in trouble for?"

Auntie O wept in earnest, and I felt like a heel. Sage and I boosted her energy by laying hands on her shoulders.

What is she trying so hard not to say? Sage sent me privately.

She seems worried we won't help if we know the full truth, I shot back. Aloud I said, "Whatever it is, it can't be that bad."

Auntie O glanced up at Sage. "Did you know Loren Lee liked to research cold cases? So much is on the internet these days. Anyway, soon after Frankie moved here, Loren Lee recognized him from a cold case he'd studied. Months ago, your other car needed repairs so Frankie carried you to and from work, Sage, remember?"

Sage tapped her foot on the floor. "Yes. I remember. Last September, Loren Lee sat in the back room with me, and we were brainstorming about the possibility of a holiday tree booth when Frankie came to give me a lift home." Sage sat quietly for a moment. "I remember going to my locker for my purse, and when I came out Loren Lee said Frankie looked familiar. And then Frankie said he'd never visited the nursery before. I remember the exchange because Loren Lee then asked Frankie if he'd ever lived in Chicago. Frankie said he came from Florida, and we left."

"That's odd," I said, looking over Auntie O's head at my sister. "Did Frankie explain?"

"Let's eat before these get cold." Sage carried our plates to the table. "Frankie brushed it off as a case of mistaken identity. Said a lot of people look like him. I thought nothing of it until you just mentioned it. Why is that important?"

"Loren Lee nailed it," Auntie O said. "Frankie is the guy from Loren Lee's cold case."

A question welled up from my bones. I couldn't hold it in. I had to know the answer. "Did Frankie kill someone back in the day?"

Auntie O's spine stiffened. She took a bracing sip of her soda. "He did not. He's the youngest son of a powerful man in Chicago, though he's the son of this man's mistress. The legitimate family members barely tolerated him, but the boss insisted he be part of the family 'activities,' if you catch my drift."

"Did he hold a gun on anyone?" Sage asked after she chewed a bite of her sandwich.

"Nothing like that. They made him drive them around once he grew tall enough to see over the dash."

"Like a chauffeur or a getaway driver?" I chimed in.

"A little of both. He landed in trouble for driving without a license on those family excursions. The cops pressed him to turn on his family after he caught time for breaking and entering with his relatives, but he wouldn't flip, not even when he took all the blame. Then his mother died in the crossfire of a shootout. He had no full siblings, and by then he'd tired of being a second-rate brother. He couldn't see any way out of the family business unless he went in a pine box. So he bided his time, liquidated his few assets, and one day when he ran errands he took off. Abandoned the car in a parking lot and vanished."

"How'd he escape?" I asked. "They would've checked the planes, trains, buses, and used car places."

"Aren't you just the perfect armchair sleuth?" Sage asked.

I stuck my tongue out at her and then bit into my BLT. "This is delicious. Thanks for fixing lunch." I glanced over at our aunt, who twisted her damp tissue into a paper rope and stared ahead vacantly. My heart went out to her, but we needed to know what we faced. Sharing information would protect all of us.

"How does his history connect Frankie and Loren Lee?" I asked.

"Here's what I know." Auntie O glanced at her hands and sighed. "The men met privately a few times. Loren Lee asked about the old days, but Frankie wouldn't talk about his past. The upshot is Frankie's fingerprints turned up in Loren Lee's house because of those meetings."

"That's not a crime." Sage leaped from her chair. "They have no reason to hold Frankie. He needs a lawyer."

Auntie O hung her head. "That's what has me so upset. He wants me to call someone in Chicago, to get a *family* lawyer down here. I can't do it. I don't want him mixed up with those people again, and who knows what they'll do to punish him for running away the first time. He's better off handling this locally."

"Why can't Frankie explain the truth, that he knew Loren Lee due to him being Sage's employer?" I said slowly, feeling each word out. "If he only drove for his family all those years ago, they couldn't have much on him."

"True." My aunt rubbed her forehead. "However, there's another problem. His wife died a lingering death."

"Of cancer," Sage said. "Don't those detectives know anything? Why can't they leave Frankie alone? Why drag his dead wife into this?"

"Because she died at home and not under hospice care, an autopsy and tox screen were required by law," Auntie O said, her shoulders slumping even more. "Her blood test lit up for narcotics, including some not prescribed for her. The ME listed 'undetermined' as the cause of her death. Frankie couldn't get the life insurance payout because of that."

I jumped in before Sage could state the obvious conclusion that shone beacon-bright in my thoughts. "You're saying because his wife's cause of death is undetermined, and because she stayed ill for a long time, that the cops believe Frankie poisons people?"

Auntie O's lip trembled, fresh tears on her pale cheeks. "'Fraid so."

Chapter Eleven

Frankie needed a lawyer to beat the poisoner charge, and using his Chicago family's attorney begged for the wrong kind of trouble. Our regular lawyer slept in the psych ward after a bizarre personal encounter with his office receptionist, and our new lawyer, the mysterious Herbert R. Ellis, wouldn't represent him because he represented Sage in the same matter. Therefore, it would be a conflict of interest if he took Frankie on as well.

Herbert R. Ellis's law partner at Confidential Representation, Leland Oakes, declined taking Frankie as a client. The lawyers at Brindle's firm of Aldrich, Platt, Dixon, and Everson did not return my calls. Next I tried a reputable firm of criminal defense attorneys. The receptionist took down the basic information and said someone would get back to me today. Same story at two other firms.

My confidence flagged. Never would I have believed hiring a lawyer would be so hard. Frankie's representation options narrowed with each passing moment. If none of the big guns would take the case, the choices were a public defender or a slip and fall lawyer, neither of which might have the chops for a complex representation.

As the hour ticked closer to five o'clock, I glanced over at Auntie O on the sofa. She'd shredded multiple tissues and worry clouded her face. I hated to add to her stress, but we had to push through to hire a lawyer for Frankie. "Is there anyone you know in Savannah who might help us secure a lawyer's attention? Someone's wife, mother, aunt, or grandmother who shops at the store?"

"Oh. I don't know." Her entire body looked pinched in like she'd been run over by life. "Most of my acquaintances are blue-collar families. I should know a lawyer since I've lived here all but a few months of my life." She sat quietly for a few moments. "There might be someone. My hairdresser Jeanie has a sister in Atlanta who is a lawyer. Would that work?"

"The Atlanta attorney might collaborate with someone down here on a regular basis. It's worth calling your hairdresser for an introduction."

We waited while Auntie O called Jeanie and left her a message. I texted Quig to tell him I would be late getting home. I turned back to my aunt. "Who did Frankie want you to call?"

"His stepbrother in Chicago." She shuddered. "The one involved with the *Outfit*."

"We need a different solution. Frankie will be in more danger if we call Chicago. What's the Outfit?"

Auntie O sniffed into her tissue. "The name dates from Al Capone's time. His crew went by the name of Al Capone's Outfit. I agree that we can't contact Chicago. I don't want Frankie mixed up with people who operate on the wrong side of the law. He is a good man."

We had to save Frankie. Wouldn't be easy, no matter who we hired. "Frankie's involvement may go viral and spread elsewhere, including Chicago, especially if his family is still nefarious. Though he has a new name, he's aged well so his face is recognizable."

"No doubt about the facial recognition." Auntie O grimaced and clenched her trembling hands. "However, Frankie said the big players in Chicago now are of other descents. Regardless, his family remains a small cog in the crime syndicate world."

Sage stirred herself from cuddling her cat to ask, "When his relatives find out about Frankie, what happens? Is his life in danger, as in he'll be rubbed out?"

"I don't know. That's why Frankie wants to make first contact. So he would appear to need them again." Tears leaked down Auntie O's face. She drew in a few shaky breaths. "He's running scared, and I'm terrified for him. I won't call his blood relatives. He's wrong about this. I feel that deep in my bones. We must keep him away from those people."

"His logic sounds flawed." I moved closer to rub my aunt's back. Not surprisingly, the muscles felt as tight as boat lines in a swift tide. "Why should he be indebted to the mob?"

Auntie O stared at the shrouded windows. Evening approached in the sky and in our aunt's heart. Her shoulders sagged. I empathized with her. If someone came after Quig, I'd be devastated too.

With a shake of her head, Auntie O glanced over her shoulder at me. "Better than being dead."

"What happens to your building if Frankie dies?" Sage asked.

While I condemned her silently for even asking such a tacky question right now, I listened closely for the answer.

"We willed our halves to each other, and if for some reason we die together, then it goes to you girls."

My sister and I exchanged a look of alarm. "Let's hope nothing happens to you two. Ever," I said firmly. "First, I would hate to lose you for any reason. You're our second mom, have been all our lives. Besides that, I can't imagine running two businesses. It's hard enough keeping one shop afloat."

"We hoped for at least twenty years together. Frankie's so happy here. He's thriving, and then this ugly mess comes along." Auntie O fixed Sage with a stern look. "Your boss may have acted nice to you, but he brought fear back into Frankie's life. That man made Frankie dance on his command. He blackmailed Frankie for his silence. It tore Frankie up inside. He's spent his entire life hiding from his relatives. Loren Lee's blackmail hurt Frankie as much as if the mob found him. Now his background will come out in the press. We can't stop it. One way or another, Frankie's gonna lose his freedom. I feel awful for him. He doesn't deserve this. His whole life he wanted a family. He found that with us. I thought we could keep him safe."

I didn't want trouble to find Frankie either, but I couldn't see how I could stop this train wreck from coming. Everything I tried left me grasping at smoke. My heart sank at how helpless I felt. "Given our lack of luck in hiring a lawyer today, odds are we can't bail him out tonight. Will he be able to manage if he stays overnight? Is he claustrophobic?"

"Not that I know of." Auntie O's face tightened even more. "He'll do whatever he has to do, but I don't want that for him. He needs to be home. With me. I'm sending good vibes out into the universe so he can catch a break. He deserves it."

I hugged her close, showering her with positive energy. "I'm all in. Good vibes only."

Sage joined us on the sofa. "I'm in."

"I love you girls," Auntie O said in a strangled voice. "Never forget that."

My phone rang, and we jumped. An independent criminal defense lawyer had returned my call. Hope sparkled in the air. Good vibes threaded through that hope.

Eagerly I listened, and supplied answers to additional questions. A few minutes later I hung up, a flower of hope blossoming in my heart. "This is the lucky break we wanted. Attorney Joel Pollard is taking the case. He's on his way to Frankie now."

Chapter Twelve

Frankie came home at midnight.

A dark SUV discharged him in the alley, all of us spilling out of our respective upper-story apartments to our back steps to greet him. I hadn't wanted to leave Auntie O alone for a minute, but she insisted she needed the time to compose herself. I glanced her way, and she looked radiant. Positivity in action.

On the other hand, Frankie looked pale, gaunt even. As one, we hurried down to hug him, a feat made harder because he wouldn't let Auntie O go. Or maybe she wouldn't let him go.

"Come upstairs, all of you," Auntie O said. "I've made dinner for Frankie and have dessert for everyone else."

"I'll start with dessert," Frankie grumbled. "I do not like jail. I like those detectives even less."

"I totally get that," I said. "I've sat in their hot seat before, and it ranks the same as a root canal."

"Two root canals," Frankie said.

We gathered around their table, pulling extra folding chairs from the coat closet. Frankie tucked into the plate of stuffed shells and marinara Auntie O pulled from the oven. By the time he'd finished eating dinner and her chocolate chip cookies, his color looked better.

"That tasted delicious, Oralee," Frankie said. "You are a fine cook."

"Glad you liked it. Glad you're home." Auntie O closed the dishwasher and sat in the vacant chair next to him. "You had a close call."

"Very close. At least I found out I'm still in the system."

"We need to hire a hacker to get you out of the system," Sage said.

Frankie barked out a laugh. "That'd be nice, but I don't want you dragged into my mess."

"Your lawyer must be a smooth talker to pry you out of their clutches," my twin continued. "I sat in that hot seat for four hours, and I hated every minute of it."

"My lawyer did great. Joel Pollard got their attention. He threw around words like model citizen and community volunteer until I felt like Savannah couldn't function without me, even though I've only lived here a few months."

Sage helped herself to another cookie from the platter of sweets. "How'd you explain the fingerprints at Loren Lee's house?"

"Easy. I met Loren Lee through Sage at the nursery, and I explained we shared an interest in historical events."

"That covers a lot of territory." I worried about his vagueness. If he phrased something wrong in even the slightest way, the cops would be relentless. "Did they quiz you about that?"

"Sure, but the lawyer prepped me first. I stuck to the script and gave them no openings." His eyes narrowed. "My personal life isn't their business."

In that instant, affable Frankie looked like a mobster. I'd never seen that hard edge of him before, never worried my aunt might be in any danger from associating with him. His aura darkened and pulsed ominously. It happened so swiftly, the transition from kind Frankie to gangster Frankie, I couldn't speak of it, couldn't even share it with Sage, because saying it might give the thought wings. I didn't want that. I wanted the loving man who treated Auntie O like she walked on water to remain.

"Any problems on the inside?" Quig asked.

Quig had been so quiet I'd forgotten he sat beside me. So when he spoke, my head swiveled his way then back to Frankie as if I were viewing a ping-pong tournament. Obviously this had been a long day for everyone, especially a morning person like me.

"No. They held me in a cell with other guys while I waited for representation." Frankie finished his decaf coffee and set the empty cup in the saucer with care. "Two guys were sleeping off a drunk. One guy tried to set a speed record on I-16. A coupla guys came and went. I kept to myself, didn't speak to anyone. Long ago I learned nothing could be gained by talking in that situation. One of the guys, though . . ."

"What's that, Frankie?" Auntie O asked, patting his hand. "Tell us."

Frankie laced his fingers through hers and smiled at her before continuing his tale. "One of the in-and-out guys tried to chat me up. Something about him gave me the impression of undercover cop. Didn't say a word to him."

"Smart," Quig said.

A painful silence followed. I couldn't take the pins and needles sensation of waiting when action seemed prudent. "What do we do now?"

"We ride out the storm, that's what," Frankie said. "Sadly, I've walked this road before."

"Take some time off from the shop," I suggested, thinking it might be easier on his nerves if he didn't become a public spectacle. "Until things cool down."

"I'd climb the walls. Nope. The best thing for me is to keep busy doing things I enjoy. Being with Oralee, managing the T-shirt place, filling in at The Book and Candle Shop. That's how I want to live. Besides, hiding would make me look guilty. I didn't do anything. The fact that they brought my wife's death into this is beyond wrong. She had terminal cancer. My lawyer reamed them out for exploiting my pain."

When Frankie's voice broke on the word cancer, the hurt he still felt about his loss pulsed in his aura. I ached for his loss. "Good for him. Those cops should be held accountable."

Frankie shook his head. "They were doing their job. I had a record, I visited the dead man's house, so I get it. Not that I liked it. Mr. Pollard did me right. Thanks for hiring him."

"Of course," Auntie O said. "I would never rat you out to your blood family. You're our family now, and we intend to keep you."

"I like that," Frankie said. "Thanks, all of you, for your help. We are both grateful for it."

We talked for a few more minutes, then Quig and I returned to our apartment and Sage went to hers.

"You believe Frankie, don't you?" I asked Quig as we got ready for bed.

"I believe he's a darned good liar."

"What!" I moved in front of him and grabbed his shirt. "Explain. Right now."

"Frankie's got some miles on him. That's understandable, given his life path."

My fingers tightened on his shirt. "He's not guilty. He said so."

Quig caught my hand and kissed it. "We don't know the whole story, and Frankie will never tell us. He's street tough, but he knows a good thing when he sees it. He's part of our family now, and he'll do everything in his power not to mess that up. Whether he killed Loren Lee or not doesn't matter."

Of course it mattered. A wave of anxiety crested. "Is my aunt in danger?"

"Oralee knows more about Frankie than we do, and she's got mad skills at reading people. She's in no danger from him."

"Wait. Are you implying my aunt killed Loren Lee?"

"Again, doesn't matter." Quig went through his nightly routine of checking the door and window locks.

It took everything I had not to dog his steps. I planted my bare feet on the floor and crossed my arms. My stomach churned until he returned to our bedroom. "It matters to me."

He ran his fingers through my shoulder-length hair and caressed my scalp. "Don't shoot the messenger, sunshine. I meant it in the nicest way. I would joyfully murder anyone who threatened you, and I'd do it in a manner that would never be traced."

"You would? Even though it's wrong?"

Quig caught my chin and angled it so our gazes met. "I would. You are my everything." He kissed me. "My sun. My moon. My stars."

I melted into his embrace as strong emotions blazed.

Chapter Thirteen

The next day I tried to interest Sage in cross-training in regard to our shop responsibilities.

"Forget it." She strolled around the stillroom checking on this plant and that one as I prepped for candlemaking.

Plants soothed her, and our shop had plenty to keep her busy. By contrast, creating useful items comforted me. Demand for my new candle scent had been steady, and that pleased me. My actions yielded a positive impact on the shop, on our customers, and on our bottom line. I helped the shop, and the shop helped me by providing a viable creative outlet. Symbiosis at work.

"I'm not going anywhere," Sage continued, "and neither are you. Our shop requires two Winslows. I'd know if it were our time to die. And it's not. We should enjoy every minute we've got on this planet. I suck at candlemaking, and you're good at it. Let's conserve resources and leave well enough alone."

"You *know* how to make candles," I countered as I pulled out a rack of our house blends of essential oils. "I don't know where the passwords are for all the accounts you manage for the shop. I have no idea how to fill an online order."

"I hope you never need to do it. It's job security for both of us. I don't write down my passwords. Too easy for them to get ripped off. It's all good. Say, did you hear from Chris?"

"Not as of this morning. Can you get her phone number from her employee file at work?"

"I doubt it. Loren Lee probably threw it out when he fired her. There's an equally good chance Mary Nicole dumped the files out of spite. Since I haven't worked there in days, I don't know. And if it's Mary Nicole's office already, I don't want to be caught snooping in her lair."

"Could you ask someone else to search for it? Would Larry do it?"

A smile dawned on Sage's face. "He will do anything I ask of him. Great idea. I'll text him now."

I swallowed wrong and hiccupped as I waited for her to finish. Quig's midnight words resurfaced in my thoughts. "At bedtime last night, Quig said he'd kill anyone who harmed me. Joyfully. Whatcha think about that?"

My sister laughed and laughed like she would never stop. Her profound glee annoyed me. My hiccups became more pronounced.

Finally, Sage wiped the happy tears from her eyes. "That's priceless. I totally take back every warning I ever had about Quig's suitability for you. Hang on to him. Brindle would never kill for me."

"How do you know?"

"Easy. He didn't come after me when I saw him with Alyss. He didn't fight to stay in my life. Instead, he tried to end his. I want someone who cares for me as deeply as Quig cares for you. I hoped Brindle would be my Quig, but he broke my heart."

"But if Alyss somehow forced his attentions, his behavior is and was abnormal. He enacted her wishes in that kitchen seduction scene, not his."

Sage shook her head vehemently. "If he were strong, she couldn't have gotten to him. Our personal relationship is toast. I feel less inclined to cut him any slack. I'm back to square one for dating."

"Brindle is different, but he isn't weak." I paused for another hiccup. I knew Sage's protests were too much, that she couldn't walk away from Brindle. Her pride spoke loud and clear, though I had high hopes she'd see the light soon enough. Regardless, it wouldn't hurt to nudge her in the right direction.

"I wouldn't write him off just yet," I said. "Maybe we can find out which magic-wielder Alyss used and unspell him, if unspell is even a word. Then you'll have the real Brindle back and can make a better decision."

"It would be good to remove her workings, as I'd hate for him to go through life thinking every girl in the world is me. How many times do I have to say it? I don't want him back. Seeing Brindle with Alyss cut me to the quick. I can't do that twice."

I hiccupped again. This time I saw a flash of white light, and my stomach rumbled a warning. Not now, I thought. I didn't have time to be sick, not when the holidays were upon us and my family needed me. "Why don't we visit Alyss today? You can apologize for being rude to her the other night."

"You're kidding. Apologies aren't my style. Besides, she pulled a fast one on my boyfriend. She owes me an apology and more."

When I glanced down, my water glass moved on its own. Strangely, the glass felt solid in my hand. "What the heck?"

My twin chuckled. "Wondered when you'd notice. When you began hiccupping, you started phasing in and out. You're visible until you hiccup, then you disappear and gradually become yourself."

"You should've told me." I hiccupped again and sure enough, my hand and body vanished. The primitive need to hide until this passed thrummed in my veins. "No one can see me like this. Close the showroom door, please."

"Done." Sage trotted over and shut us inside.

"This is embarrassing." I gazed over at my sister. "Any ideas on what's causing this?"

Sage brightened. "Ask Mom."

Good answer. Lousy timing. "I wish."

"We could ask Auntie O, but she stayed up late last night with Frankie, so she gets a pass. She's gotta be so relieved Frankie's home."

"For now. Those cops glom onto suspects like barnacles on a dock piling." I glanced at my twin. "You know where Alyss lives?"

"Nope." She glanced down at her fisted hands. "And I don't want to know."

"Would someone at the law firm tell you?"

"Doubt it, though perhaps Brindle knows."

"If you visit him at the hospital again, we should contact a woman of knowledge first, so you can help him right away, assuming he's under a magical compulsion. What a chicken or egg conundrum."

A brisk knock sounded on the stillroom door. Gerard peeked in. "Everyone okay in here?"

Sage screened me with her body as I hiccupped again. "We're strategizing. Know any spell casters?"

"Wait just a minute." He pulled out his phone and tapped on the screen. "My phone lists twelve sympathetic magic practitioners in Savannah. Some say they cast spells, some claim they're love specialists. What kind of help do you seek, Sage?"

I drew my invisible hands to my face and cupped my nose, trying desperately to stop the hiccups. No way I could draw attention to myself by talking.

"We believe someone put the whammy on Brindle. I want it removed," Sage said. "Thanks for your help. I didn't think to search online for answers."

"People who manipulate luck wield a two-edged sword. Be careful as you proceed."

After checking my visibility and finding it satisfactory for the moment, I leaned around my sister between hiccups. "You know anyone who afflicts others with serious setbacks?"

He hesitated. "I've heard MawMaw mention something about that before."

If she could help us understand what happened, that would be a big leg up on solving Brindle's problem. So helpful to have access to someone with expertise. "I'll check with her before we go very far down this road. Thanks."

The front door chimed. "Gotta go." Gerard closed the door and called out a cheery greeting to the customer.

I glanced at Sage and burst out laughing. "Who knew help was at our fingertips this whole time?"

"I thought these practitioners would ply their trade in secret. Boy, was I wrong. They might be as upscale as we are." Sage stopped talking to tap rapidly on her phone.

She scrolled through several screens before glancing my way. "Many who offer spells and charms aren't located in Savannah. The award-winning love specialist is in California. One person is in Savannah, but we must book an appointment through her scheduler. Looks like it'll cost at least a hundred dollars or more per practitioner depending on appointment length. That's a lot of cash to shell out on an ex-boyfriend."

Since she'd gone silent for a few minutes before she spoke, I got distracted thinking about today's candlemaking. Then I quickly replayed Sage's words in my head. What a bad time to zone out. Helping Brindle was the right thing to do. "I'll pay the fee."

"No," Sage said firmly. "Our relationship landed him in this trouble. I'll pay."

My curiosity about her attitude reversal overcame all else. I twisted to look over Sage's shoulder at her phone display. Users of light and dark magic sought out herbs, roots, and more to tend to their customers' needs. "Any intuitive sense on who to contact?"

"No idea." She handed me her phone. "See for yourself."

I took the phone, but none of the names or websites listed looked more promising than the others. "I believe the right person is in Savannah and relies on word-of-mouth advertising instead of online ads. We need Auntie O's advice."

"Not my day in the shop," my twin said. "I'll go knock on her door."

I turned on soothing music and deepened my breathing. Soon, I felt under control and emoted good spirits. Best yet, my hiccups ceased. I had begun the candle melt when Sage raced into the room, eyes open wide.

"They're gone," she said.

"Gone?" I switched off the burner. Even as I tried to make sense of her words, an uneasy feeling wormed through my gut. "Gone, as in they went to Carey Hilliards for a late breakfast?"

"Gone as in no suitcases or toiletries are in their apartment."

Alarmed, I trailed her next door to Auntie O and Frankie's place, where Sage used her key to unlock the door. The only odd thing, besides no one being home, were the two mobile phones on the hall table. I picked up Auntie O's phone and opened it. Nothing happened. The display remained dark. "They left their cell phones."

"Smart. Cops track people through their phones."

In the Wick of Time

Thoughts zipped through my head. Last night Frankie said he'd stay, that he needed his everyday routine to be the same. He'd gazed at Auntie O with love, and she him. They loved each other. Now they'd left. Vanished like sea foam on the sand.

Would they be safe?

Where did they go?

How could I find them?

Though numb inside, I made myself ask, "Why'd they run? Nothing says I did it like taking off."

Sage looked at me, her face pale. "They must've feared something else more than the cops."

Chapter Fourteen

With a heavy heart, I returned to the shop to finish out the day. Nothing brightened my outlook, not even Sage's claim that Larry would sneak into Loren Lee's files to get us Chris Kachuba's number and address. Why did life throw multiple curve balls our way?

Try as I might, I couldn't figure out how to find Auntie O and Frankie; however, I trusted them to reach out when they felt safe. Nothing I liked about that realization, but I couldn't do anything about it.

Now I had three related problems: my aunt's disappearance, Frankie and Sage topping the police suspect list, and Sage's boyfriend's likely brush with dark magic. Though with the suspect focus squarely on Frankie, that might mean Sage moved off the person of interest hook.

That sucked for Frankie but rocked for my sister. Even so, I couldn't stop investigating the case. Once the police cleared Frankie, they might focus on Sage again. I had no choice but to continue to investigate the murder.

With only one current lead, I decided to shift gears and focus on helping Brindle. At day's end, I hitched a ride with Gerard to his place to talk with MawMaw about the world of magic.

In the Wick of Time

The octogenarian wore her Sunday best as she watched television. When we entered, Gerard's cousin, her daytime caretaker, left for the night. The tidy house smelled of witch hazel. I sat down beside her and took her small hand. Often this time of day confused her so I started slowly. "I'm Oralee's niece Tabby, MawMaw. Oralee left suddenly on a trip this morning. I wondered if you knew about that."

"I remember you." MawMaw nodded congenially. "Oralee's been worrisome of late. Her man got a troubled past an' it done him wrong. Slapped him smack between the eyes, it did."

"I heard about that. She mention taking a trip to you?"

"Sho' didn't. We had a nice lunch a few days ago, and everything looked so pretty and tasty. That Oralee always has a way about her in the kitchen."

"She sure does. She's been cooking nonstop since she got back, and we're thankful for her many talents." I stopped to clear my throat, conscious of Gerard moving pots and pans on the stove and preparing their dinner. "I have another question. A friend of ours is acting strange. Best we can figure, someone used magic on him, possibly dark magic. Do you know who can help us fix that?"

"Lawsy, I can help with that. What kind of strangeness he caught?"

"He mistook another woman for my sister and romanced her until Sage interrupted them."

"This other woman, she wear a little sack around her neck?"

"Not that I heard about."

"Could be in a pocket or such. Hidden, you know? She likely took somethin' of his. Might be a bit of fingernail, a hair, or even his clothes. If you find that sack, bury it at a crossroads."

"Noted. However, we don't know where this woman lives. Is there a way we can undo her actions?"

MawMaw made a clucking sound. "Unless you know how powerful the magic is, more harm than good might happen. Try sprinklin' holy water on him instead."

"Where do I get that?"

"Gerard will get you some." She waved toward the kitchen. "While you're in there, ask him for the letter Oralee left this mornin'. I needs to rest my eyes now. Been a busy day."

Her comments eased the tightness in my lungs. Holy water and an explanation from my aunt awaited in the kitchen. Exactly what I needed to help Brindle and news I desperately coveted. Luck favored me today. "Thank you, MawMaw. You've been a big help."

I padded into the kitchen and spoke softly to Gerard. "You hear what she said?"

"Most of it. Sage's latest is laid up by conjure work?"

"We think so. How's your grandmother know about that stuff?"

He put a lid on some mouthwatering corned beef. "She's from a different generation that sought out 'extra' help. I didn't mention her knowledge about this to you before because of how she is now. You caught her on a clear afternoon. Those are becoming rarer with each passing day."

"It's okay. I expected a referral to someone else, so I hit the jackpot because I'm going home with help right away. MawMaw said you could hook me up with some holy water and a letter from my aunt."

Gerard scowled at me. "How much holy water?"

His sudden bad mood didn't faze me. I had to do this for Sage. "Enough to sprinkle on Brindle, however much that is."

Gerard reached in the cupboard and pulled out a dark bottle about the size of a cough syrup flask. "This is our supply. It's a precious commodity. Bring back whatever isn't used."

In the Wick of Time

After he carefully decanted holy water into a vial and capped it, I punched him lightly in the bicep. "You made me think I asked for something hard to come by, and you have a stash in the cabinet?"

"Don't tell anyone, okay? MawMaw's been out of the biz for years. I don't want people coming around here to see her again. It's too hard on her. Too hard on her family. We don't want her to be stressed. That makes her feel worse."

I pocketed the vial and motioned as if I were zipping my mouth. "My lips are sealed."

"Good. Solve this case fast. We need Oralee and Frankie in the shop. You'll burn out working there every day."

"I can do it. You know where they went?"

"Didn't even know they were gone until you said so just now."

His sour tone put me on the defensive. "Sage and I needed to ask her something before lunch, and when we went over, they had packed up and left. We kept the news quiet so they'd have all day to get away."

"You coulda told me. Thought we were friends."

"You are my friend. It isn't personal. We needed to contain the news. You talk to a lot of people over the course of a day. Something might have slipped."

"Talking to customers is my superpower. What cover story are you putting out there to explain her absence?"

"We didn't think of that. Too focused on them getting away today. Do you have a suggestion?"

"Let's see. Few would believe they left to join the circus. We could say they eloped."

"Except if they came back unmarried, that wouldn't work."

"Good point. What about visiting family, taking a vacation, or going on a cruise?"

I mentally tried on each suggestion in turn before I spoke. "The cruise would be hard to prove. I like visiting family, only I don't know how far that will stretch. They wouldn't visit Frankie's family, and we don't have any family beyond what's right here."

"Maybe something came up in Orlando that they needed to address. People know they came here from Orlando. That sounds like your best bet."

"Maybe we don't need to invent a cover story. Where's that letter from Auntie O that your grandmother mentioned?"

"She didn't tell me about it, but she always puts important papers in the bread box." He turned and opened a vented drawer.

We both peered inside. There among the loaf of bread and package of rolls rested a small envelope with my name on it. Auntie O's old-fashioned handwriting flowed over the front like melted butter. I wanted to reach for it, but I couldn't. I didn't want to know if it contained bad news. Until I read the letter, I could easily believe they were safe and sound.

Undeterred by my hesitation, Gerard handed it to me. My hands trembled as I opened the seal and withdrew the small notecard. "My darling nieces," I read aloud in a whisper. "Frankie and I regret the trouble we've brought to your doors. It will be worse if we pretend nothing is wrong. For everyone's safety, we're leaving. Don't try to find us or our sacrifice will be in vain. Do what brings you joy every day and know you're always foremost in our hearts. With all my love, Auntie O."

I sagged against the counter, feeling the keen loss of my aunt all over again. The hole in my heart felt as empty as when she moved to Orlando, only worse. This time I couldn't reach her. I didn't know if I would see her again. Sage and I were truly on our own.

In the Wick of Time

The trouble she referred to must be from Chicago and Frankie's old life. Would a gang of men show up here and demand Frankie? How would we handle any threat from his family?

Gerard wrapped an arm around my shoulder. "You all right?"

Tears fell like summer rain. I couldn't speak. He held me until the storm subsided. MawMaw joined us in the kitchen hug. Then she led me over to the table.

After we sat, she reached for my hand. "I know you gonna miss Oralee. She's a force in this world, a force for good. She done saved that man of hers, and now she's doin' her best to save you churren. Be happy for her, you hear?"

It took me a moment to digest her words. "What if I never see her again?"

"Pshaw, girlie. You goin' to see her again and that's a natural born fact."

I dashed away the fresh tears. "I'm afraid, for all of us. The law and bad men from Chicago are after Frankie. How can we fight them and at the same time find Loren Lee's killer so Frankie's name is cleared?"

"Do it the same as everythin' else. One step at a time."

"You make it sound easy."

"Didn't say movin' on is easy. Likely to be hard." MawMaw nodded. "You gotta be careful and choose your battles wisely. But you can take one step, and then another. That's the way of hard times. Don't look for more trouble. Storms come no matter what you do. The way people fight trouble is takin' one step. One step is easier than many steps. It will save your life."

I had a feeling her advice applied to much more than my pity party. MawMaw and Auntie O were wise beyond their years. I had to pull myself together. "Thank you. Those words are now part of me. I will keep taking single steps, and I will get our family back together."

MawMaw surprised me with a hearty laugh. "You got it, sistah."

They insisted I stay for dinner, then I helped Gerard get Maw-Maw bedded down for the night. His cousin returned to sit with her so Gerard could drive me home. Through it all, I felt Gerard's glance more frequently than usual.

"What?" I asked as he pulled up behind the shop.

"You're different now."

I snorted out a laugh. "I have always been different."

"Not that," he said earnestly. "You seem more . . ."

"More what?"

"More everything. More compassionate. More in charge. More loving. It's like you had a dimmer switch on all this time, and you're suddenly switched to the brightest setting."

"I know what you mean." I couldn't tell him I actively used my energetic skills these days. "I feel more connected to everyone now. Being with Quig and feeling like my contributions matter at the shop, those boost my confidence."

"It shows. Quig is a lucky man."

"We're both lucky. Gerard, about tonight—"

The car door opened. Quig. How much had he heard? I beamed a smile his way, then I turned back to Gerard. "Thank you for dinner and the holy water. I couldn't have gotten through this trying evening without you. Give MawMaw an extra hug in the morning. I'll never forget her words of wisdom."

I squeezed his hand then stepped out of the car. Gerard sped away, and Quig seemed stiff. "Is something wrong?" I asked, fearing the mob had already arrived.

In the Wick of Time

"About *tonight*?" he repeated and then stared at me, his eyes unreadable behind his glasses in this light. "Should I be worried?"

"You should not be worried. Let's go upstairs so I can tell you what happened."

He fell into step behind me. "Something happened?"

"Oh yeah."

Chapter Fifteen

I showed Quig the letter from Auntie O and shared the highlights from MawMaw's pearls of wisdom. He listened without interrupting, a skill neither Sage nor I had ever mastered. We sat side by side on the sofa in our living room. One of these days I'd add some color to this place, but for now I accepted his stark color palette of gray, black, and white.

"I'll protect you," he said simply.

His pledge warmed me everywhere, especially in my heart. I kissed his fingers, which were intertwined with mine. "Thank you. I don't know how quickly Frankie's Chicago people will get here, but we need to be on high alert if that happens."

"Your sister too."

"Yes. If it's all right with you, I might invite her to stay over on the couch for a few nights if it gets ugly. The thing is, we don't know what's coming, or what level of force they'll bring against us."

"That's true about most things in life. I'm fine with your sister staying over for a bit."

Inwardly I let out a sigh of relief. Technically, I had a free ride here, though I'd offered to split the rent. Our block consisted of four conjoined buildings, each with a shop on the bottom and an apartment on top. Mr. Sawyer owned the liquor store. Quig owned the building and shop where he lived. Sage and I co-owned The Book and Candle Shop and Sage's apartment. Auntie O and Frankie owned the building and apartment in between Sage and Quig's place. Our place, I silently amended.

In any event, I'd wondered how to protect Sage if things fouled up even more during this investigation. Inviting her to stay here would increase her safety. Our locks were newer, and she wouldn't be alone. I felt comfort knowing she'd be safer with us.

My thoughts drifted to the case. "Everything is a mystery now. We don't know who killed Loren Lee. Both Sage and Frankie are suspects, with Frankie at the top of the list and Sage hopefully near the bottom. Sage's boyfriend most likely had a curse put on him by his receptionist, Alyss, only we don't know how to remove it or where she lives, though I got Sage a flask of MawMaw's holy water to sprinkle on Brindle. And now Frankie's notorious relatives or their proxies might show up and raise sand, ending Frankie's freedom and likely his life. With Auntie O and Frankie on the lam and Sage working more shifts at the nursery's Christmas tree booth, I'm in the shop almost every waking hour. I'm in way over my head. Feels like crosswinds are hitting me on every side."

He smoothed my hair away from my face. I hoped I never got used to the amazing tingles from his touch. "No one could handle all that," Quig said. "Take it easy. You'll flame out trying to save the world."

The weight of the day tugged on my bones. A yawn slipped out. "Possibly, but I have no choice. Detective Nowry is quick to form an opinion of who did it, and then he's good at convincing the DA to prosecute a circumstantial case. The clock is already ticking. Heck, several clocks are ticking here."

"We'll figure it out together." He pulled me into his arms. "I vote we sleep on it."

"Good idea."

*   *   *

Quig's alarm went off as usual the next day, and he headed to the shower. I rose and started our breakfast, though my shift in the store didn't start for three more hours. As I puttered in the kitchen, my thoughts turned to ticking clocks. Only two weeks remained before Christmas arrived. Would I celebrate the holiday with my sister this year? Or my aunt? For that matter, what gift did one buy a live-in boyfriend? I couldn't imagine him ever wearing a holiday sweater. What I'd really love is to create a soap especially for Quig.

In my spare time, of course.

No pressure there.

Quig emerged from our bedroom fully dressed and looking darned handsome. He presented a scrap of paper with a grand flourish. "Here you go."

"What is this?"

"Alyss's phone number and home address."

My energy surged. "How'd you get it?"

He rocked on his toes. "I'm a man of many talents and also numerous friends on the force."

"Thank you. This is a big help." I pocketed the slip of paper. "Once I have the name of the magic user Alyss sought to harm Brindle, then I can help him and in doing so help Sage. With any luck, I can scratch Brindle's mental health off my to-do list today."

We ate a hearty breakfast of oatmeal topped with apple chunks, walnuts, and raisins. Before Quig left for work, he reminded me he'd made a dinner reservation for us tonight. I made a mental note of the time and place as I dressed for work and headed to Sage's apartment. I found her hunched over a cup of coffee and staring into its dark depths.

"Morning," Sage managed.

I joined her at the table, sliding the scrap of paper from Quig over to her. "Look what I have."

She glanced at it, then picked it up to study it, hope filling her face. "Where'd you get this?"

"Quig made a call. Pretty cool, eh?"

"Great, but I have a hitch. Ms. Chatham texted me this morning and said that until further notice, I am running the waterfront Christmas tree booth. That leaves Mary Nicole running the nursery. I have confidence I can sell all the trees. I don't have confidence in Mary Nicole running the nursery."

"Sounds like a good strategy for the boss to see which of you rises to the occasion. It's sink or swim for you ladies."

Her expression clouded. "You're right. My goal is to sell out of live trees, today, tomorrow, and every day, but that leaves you on shift every day, all day here, with Gerard's backup on weekdays. I won't be much help on your investigation either. Working outdoors all day saps my energy."

"Don't worry about it. Auntie O and Frankie will return once I determine who killed Loren Lee, if Frankie's Chicago relatives don't come after him for deserting the family. Meanwhile, I'll work at the shop through the lunch hour rush each day and let Gerard solo for the last three or so hours on weekday afternoons. That way I'll have time to work in the shop and investigate."

"Maybe some evenings I can help with sleuthing. In fact, we should have a go at Loren Lee's place tonight."

"Uh." A big roadblock loomed in my head. With Quig being a stickler about my safety, he wouldn't approve of our trespassing in her former boss's place. I wouldn't lie to him, so my options were limited. Fortunately, I had a ready-made excuse. "Can't tonight. Quig and I have a dinner reservation. Apparently having a three-month anniversary is an occasion to celebrate."

"Lucky you," Sage sighed, then brightened. "I mean that, though it sounded snarky. You and Quig are good together. You should celebrate your happiness. I want you to be happy, and I need to do a better job of boyfriend selection in the future."

"You'll find somebody who's perfect for you. Gotta keep that hope alive. Meanwhile, I'll track Alyss down this afternoon and ferret out what she did to Brindle."

My sister bolted upright in her chair. "Don't let her touch anything of yours. If she's trained in magic, she might curse you too."

I blanched, having not considered that before. "I'll be careful." I pulled Auntie O's letter from my pocket and pushed it toward her. "I should've led with this, but I know you've been worried about Brindle's health."

Sage grabbed the envelope. "Where'd you find this?"

"I went home with Gerard last night to ask MawMaw questions about the dark arts. Apparently Auntie O left this over there before she left town."

"You had this since last night?"

I winced at the accusation in her tone. "I should've mentioned it right away, but when I got home I got . . . distracted and then I fell asleep. Nothing personal, and I didn't intend to slight you. I just ran out of oomph. The note is a goodbye letter."

I fiddled with my cuticles and studied her face as she read and reread the note. "How come you aren't bawling?" I asked. "I cried my eyes out when I read that."

"I'm sad, but she didn't have to be all cloak-and-dagger. She could've told us. I wonder why she bothered to write a note. Is there a code hidden between the lines? I've tried first words, last words, and skipped words, but I can't find a hidden message."

"My brain didn't go there. I've never known Auntie O to use coded messages."

Sage drained her coffee mug. "I tried it. It didn't work. Let's move on."

"Hard to do that when I wish they didn't leave. We're safer together."

"They'll be all right. So will we. Let's solve this case and fix Brindle."

"Speaking of which," I said, stopping to withdraw the vial from my pocket. "This is holy water from MawMaw's stash. Sprinkle it on Brindle. It will help. Oh, and Gerard wants us to return any unused amount."

My twin clutched the vial to her heart. "I'll do it today."

"All right then. My work here is done." With that I headed to the shop and explained the December staff situation to Gerard.

He shrugged off my concern about his being stuck alone in the shop at nonpeak times. "We can both step up because solving the case will allow Oralee and Frankie to come home. They can't return until the case is closed. I'm in a hundred percent."

Cheered by his enthusiasm, I bustled around, doing my routine shop things. I dusted the shop, chatted with customers, and made bars of soap. Nothing experimental today, just routine scents. The work soothed me so that I drew deep breaths and relaxed my hunched shoulders.

However, as one thirty rolled around and I covered the shop while Gerard took lunch across the street with his friend, my unease about today's investigation grew. If Alyss used spells, I could be in big trouble. Would my energy-wielding skills be enough protection from her?

My trepidation boiled down to one question I couldn't answer. *Alyss, who are you?*

Chapter Sixteen

I motioned for the ride-share driver to drop me off a few units down from Alyss Carter's building in midafternoon. When she worked at the law firm, she'd always been dressed like a lawyer appearing in court, but with her very feminine curves on display. I'd had the sense that she invested heavily in her appearance. Nothing wrong with that, but her polished exterior ran counter to my perception of a root doctor client.

My work attire of houndstooth plaid pants, a lightweight pull-over sweater, and a festive scarf didn't scream law office receptionist. However, I looked exactly like a small business owner. Setting aside the undercurrents of unease, I bolstered my aura to fight off any spiritual attack she might have in her back pocket and strode briskly to her door.

I knocked.

She opened the door in her dressed-for-success look, crossed her arms, and glared at me. "What do you want, Tabby Winslow?"

"We need to talk. Mind if I come in?"

"I do mind. State your business out here."

She wouldn't make this easy for me. "First, I came to apologize for Sage's rudeness. Brindle's cheating and subsequent mental breakdown hit her hard." I cleared my throat. "About that, Brindle is not improving, and I am deeply concerned for him. Will you clarify the sequence of events that led to his hospitalization?"

"Go away." Alyss tried to close the door and shut me out.

I pulsed enough energy to hold the door open. "Please, I must understand what happened so I can help." I glanced at the corridor of doors behind her, hoping no one else could hear our conversation. "I promise not to take much of your time."

"Why would I relive the worst humiliation of my life? I loved Brindle Platt."

"But you didn't feel an abiding love. Don't you see? My sister is still in in love with him even though he broke her heart. Her well-being is tied to his."

Alyss barked out a laugh. "You think I should help them reunite? What is this, third grade?"

My hands clenched, and I mentally kicked myself for being too open. "No. This is two, maybe three lives derailed because you used magical help for self-gain. Please, can we do this inside? I'm sure you don't want your private business discussed in the corridor."

Much to my amazement, she stepped back, and I took that as an invitation for me to enter. The apartment smelled musty, as if she hadn't run the air or cracked the windows in a while. No pets rushed out to greet me, and her living room looked showroom sterile, with no personal touches and an overabundance of taupe. Even the sofa set and the drapes were the same gray-tan color.

I met her level gaze. "Thank you. This must be as difficult for you as it is for me."

"You have no idea." She huffed out a breath and perched rigidly on the sofa.

I took the chair across from her. Nothing about her place indicated a trickster or someone who made mischief. There were no candles, no decorative bowls, no bunches of roots. This place felt hollow, like a shell of an apartment.

Though the emptiness here and in Alyss echoed within me, she didn't expect or want me to fix her. I needed to stay on task because she'd surely kick me out. My intentions to gain her confidence welled through my aura. "I barely know you, Alyss, but it must be awful to have your dreams misfire. Trying to win Brindle cost you a job and more."

"I can get another job," she said, running a hand over her big hair. "I'm an excellent executive assistant."

"There's always a cost."

"I've been in this game for a while. Men are attracted to me, except experience has shown looks aren't enough. I'm seeking a successful husband. I do everything right, but every time it turns to dust."

"Men date pretty women," I began slowly, feeling my way. "However, men who settle down usually seek a deeper connection. Have you tried being open with your dates? Do you tell them what you like?"

"I do what they like. It's easier that way."

My image of her as a successful businesswoman shifted to one of a porcelain doll. "Vulnerability can be painful."

"At this point, I'd settle for someone twice my age, but the pretense of affection would never end. I've made a mess of my life. I barely know where I begin or end. I don't know why I'm telling you all this."

"I have an idea of what happened. You reached a point where you couldn't keep the emptiness inside anymore. Perhaps Brindle's breakdown opened your eyes." I chewed my lip, needing to elicit the truth from her. "I have to ask . . . did you use extra help to try to catch Brindle?"

She stilled and stared over my head. "I have no idea what you're talking about."

The wobble in her aura indicated I was on the right track. "I've known Brindle Platt for three years, and he served as my mother's attorney before that. He's a stable individual, not prone to mental breakdowns. Plus, he and my sister were good together. Anyone in the room with them could sense the strong emotion they shared. He didn't stray of his own accord. Did you entice him with mesmerism or magic?"

Her breath caught. Fear, anger, and remorse flashed across her face. Her aura pulsed more and darkened.

"It's eating you up inside, isn't it? More so than losing your job." I pressed harder. "You ruined a good man. Broke him by forcing him to betray his commitment to Sage. He told my sister he thought he held and kissed her, but when the real Sage walked in the room he couldn't believe his eyes."

"Magic?" Alyss backhanded some innocent air. "What do I know about that or mesmerism? There aren't witches in Savannah."

The spikes of angry energy in her aura told me more than her lies. "No telling what's in Savannah these days," I countered. "And magic in and of itself isn't bad. My guess is you've sought a little help before to try to catch a rich husband. Only this time it blew up in your face."

"The information store is closed." Alyss looked at me through partially lowered lashes.

Maybe so, but I still needed information. "I apologized for my sister's rudeness toward you when you told her Brindle had been hospitalized. The pain you inflicted on Brindle hurt my sister. Sage will recover from this emotional wound in time, but Brindle must get rid of the *affliction*, or whatever it is, to have a ghost of a chance at healing. Who crafted the help you used to trap him?"

Alyss stilled like a lioness who'd sighted prey. "You have some nerve coming in here and accusing me of anything."

"You messed with his karma, and it backfired. Your chance at redemption is making this right for Brindle. You crushed his heart. You broke him. You ruined a good man."

Alyss blinked away tears. "You can't pin his issues on me."

I gestured toward her with an open palm. "You're doing that to yourself. Will you set things right so you can heal as well?"

She regarded me in stony silence. I mirrored her expression until a grandfather clock chimed the hour, shattering the moment. With nothing left to lose, I changed my approach. "Brindle will never put you on his visitor list. If you have feelings for him, this man whose life you shattered, share the information so I can help him. You owe him that much."

"I owe him nothing, which is exactly what he gave me."

The edge to her voice indicated my gambit had failed, so I rose. "I'll see myself out."

I pulled up a ride-share app, but I couldn't bring myself to request a ride yet. Alyss had been up to no good. I also learned that the bad karma she'd brought upon herself made her situation worse. Until she righted her wrong, trouble would perch on her shoulder.

Standing across the street, I watched Alyss storm out of the building and hurry to the parking lot with numbered spaces. She roared out a moment later.

If I only had a car.

Chapter Seventeen

Alyss drove off, and without transportation, I could only watch her rapid departure with regret. I didn't know if she saw me standing on the sidewalk or not.

Frankly, I didn't care.

Her lies hurt people. Only she could break herself out of that cycle. Alyss needed to solve her problems before she tried something new again. Bottom line, she wouldn't help me.

But I knew someone else who might have the knowledge I sought. Jeanine Acworth. On a whim, I asked my ride-share driver to take me to the New Dawn store where this girl I knew of in high school allegedly worked. Though I hadn't seen Jeanine in twelve years, I immediately recognized the black-haired woman dressed in black behind the counter. Jeanine still looked the same and apparently still wore the same color clothing.

The store had no customers right now, so I walked to the counter. "Hey, Jeanine, Remember me from high school?"

"Tabby Winslow, as I live and breathe. What brings you to my slice of the pie?"

In the Wick of Time

"I'm seeking advice for a friend. You were . . . different . . . in high school, and I'm hoping that's still the case."

She flashed white teeth at me. "I'll bite. What's this about?"

"A friend is in trouble. He had a mental breakdown after being spelled or cursed. The woman who did this to him won't tell me how to help him. I'm hoping you can help me, or you know someone who can help. Are you familiar with these kind of tricksters?"

Jeanine stared through me for a long time. I decided to leave, but she spoke first. "If anyone else walked in here and asked me that, I would've sent them on their way. You were . . . different . . . back in the day and seem even more so now."

The hair on my arms stirred. I created an energy barrier to block whatever murky fog Jeanine sent my way.

Her expression tightened. "Why should I get involved?"

"I'll pay for your services, of course. What are your rates?"

"You can't afford me, and even if you could, I wouldn't work with your kind."

Her words baffled me. "My kind?" The energy barrier held, but it felt like pins and needles stabbed my head.

"You're a leech, same as your sister."

Oh, glory! What had Sage done to this woman? "I don't understand."

Her face burned red. "Liar."

"Look, I don't know what Sage or I did to offend you. High school was a strange time, especially for those who weren't mainstream. I'm sorry for whatever happened to you back then, but I truly am desperate to help my friend. Desperate enough to seek out a classmate who might have the knowledge I seek."

In the edgy silence that followed, I noticed her items for sale. There were squatty candles, dried plants and sticks. A huge sprig of fragrant rosemary was tied over the cash register, with ceramic frogs and owls, incense, tarot cards, and tie-dyed shirts arrayed on shelves. The shop smelled of patchouli.

Her gaze became gunslinger tough. "Exactly who needs this help?"

I focused on Jeanine, having the feeling that I'd just failed a test. "A nice lawyer. Brindle Platt."

"Don't know him, but I hate lawyers. You stay on your side of town, Winslow, and I'll stay on mine."

My shoulders sagged. "You won't help?"

She waggled her fingers at me, and I found myself on the street outside her shop. Dang. She wielded power, and a lot of it. Though tempted to wipe the smug smile off her face with an energy display of my own, I realized theatrics wouldn't help Brindle.

Unfortunately, Jeanine Acworth proved to be another dead end, and a problem for another day.

I had the driver drop me off behind our shop. Back at home, I hurried upstairs to dress for our anniversary dinner date. As I did so, I connected with Sage on our twin-link, surprised that I could reach her so easily at the waterfront. *I'm short on time today. Here's my update. Met with Alyss. She did something to change Brindle's perceptions, but she wouldn't talk. The only consolation is that bad karma is eating her up.*

Good, Sage replied. *She deserves those bad vibes for what she did to him and to me.*

How's it going at the waterfront live Christmas tree booth?

We're selling trees right and left. You wouldn't happen to have any extra ornaments tucked around and about would ya?

I have nothing. I never put up a tree when I lived on my own, and Mom only ever decorated the tree in the shop.

Darn. If you get a chance when you're out with Quig tonight, I need more tree lights and cheap reflective ornaments. Keep the receipt, and I'll reimburse you.

Don't count on me for this. I can't promise Quig will want to go to a big box discount store on our romantic evening.

You never know.

I'll ask.

Appreciate it.

Also, I went by and spoke with Jeanine Acworth. She's got serious hidden talents, but she refused to help Brindle. Get this, she's furious with us. Called us leeches.

Oh. She's still mad about that.

What?

I may have borrowed energy from a friend of hers a long time ago.

Sage! Mom told us never to do that at school.

Mom didn't know everything, and this kid kept bugging me. If you recall, I tried to steer you clear of Jeanine earlier. I only risked an energy grab that one time. Looking back, I'm embarrassed at my clumsiness. I didn't want you to know. Anyway, that's all ancient history.

Not for Jeanine. Changing the subject, did you use the holy water on Brindle?

I did, but I don't know if it worked.

We'll know soon enough.

Right.

When we close the tree booth tonight, I'm coming home and crashing. I am dead on my feet, and my face hurts from smiling at strangers. Plus, I need to remember not to drink so much hot chocolate tomorrow. Bladder is full to near bursting, and I'm not feeling the port-a-potty vibe.

Too much information! Will let you know if I score lights and ornaments for you.

K.

* * *

Dinner at the Cotton Exchange on River Street exceeded my expectations. After starting with a glass of white wine for me and a draft beer for Quig, I ordered a Caesar salad and Tybee crab stew, while Quig requested spinach salad and Cajun tortellini.

Then Quig placed a jewelry box on the table in front of me. "For you. Happy anniversary."

My jaw dropped. A gift. "We didn't talk about exchanging gifts. I didn't get you anything."

"Not necessary. You are all the gift I need. Open it."

I glanced down at it, not moving otherwise. The box looked too big for a ring. I gave an inward sigh of relief he hadn't asked me to marry him, and then one of regret for the same reason.

"Nothing will jump out and scare you. I promise."

A nervous laugh came out. "Not even on my radar. I'm distracted by the thought no one ever gave me jewelry before."

He beamed. "Perfect. Go on."

My hands trembled as I removed the gold bow and ribbon and then lifted the lid. The most beautiful heart locket I'd ever seen in white gold gleamed in the box. Delicately engraved flowers and curlicues bordered the locket's edge. The fragile linked chain looked to be the perfect length as I held it up and met his gaze. "It's lovely. Truly, perfect for me."

"Check the back."

I turned it over, and the engraving read, "All my love, Quig." My heart did flips. "Thank you so much. I will treasure it always."

Clutching the necklace in my palm, I half rose to kiss him. "I love the necklace, and I love you."

"That's the way it's supposed to be, you and me, together."

"How are you so sure about us?"

He shrugged, flashing me an unrepentant grin. "I've always been into you. Maybe we paired in a past life as well. Our connection feels soul deep."

"I can't say about past lives, but I've always felt happy and comfortable with you."

"Like an old shoe?"

"Like the ocean and the shore, a bird in a tree, or the kindling in a fire." I warmed to my analogies. "Like we fit together naturally. I didn't realize the depth of my feelings for you until recently. I knew we would always be friends."

"And lovers."

His intensity shot heat clear to my toes. "That too." I traced the lettering on the hand-warmed locket.

"May I put it on you?"

"Yes." I handed him the necklace, everything tingling when his fingers brushed my hand. I lifted my hair, and he rose to connect the clasp. "How's it look?"

He kissed the back of my neck before returning to his seat. "Perfect. Like you."

"Ha! I'm not perfect, far from it, but I will wear this proudly."

As the evening progressed, my hand strayed to the new necklace, wondering how he knew my preference for white gold. Another mystery of Quig.

I shared my meeting with Alyss Carter, ending with, "It's maddening. She isn't telling me everything. Some of what she said were lies. I had no leverage to make her want to help Brindle get his life back. Far as I could tell, she's glad he's messed up now."

"Seems harsh."

"She's a harsh person. I spoke with her, but she wouldn't divulge anything about the magic she used on Brindle. I still don't know how to resolve it."

"If not for your sister, I'd say the lawyer isn't our problem, but Sage is into him, so I get your concern."

Our conversation drifted to mundane topics. After dinner, we strolled River Street holding hands. Loud music spilled out of bars, boat lights twinkled on the water. All around us, people were laughing and happy. The evening felt just right.

I didn't plan to visit the nursery's live tree booth, but that's where we ended up.

"Can I interest you in a live tree?" Sage asked as she closed her booth.

We hadn't put up a tree, hadn't talked about decorating at all. "Do we need a tree?" I asked Quig. "It's up to you," I said. "I'm good either way."

The Winslows weren't devoutly religious. Growing up, we'd been exposed to mainstream Christian churches, but formal religion hadn't stuck with us. I believed in the principles of being kind to everyone and doing unto others as I'd like to be treated, and so did Quig. Owning a Christmas tree didn't move us closer to religion or further from it.

Before he could answer, Sage's gaze riveted on my new locket. "Your necklace is stunning."

My twin and I shared a love of white gold jewelry. I beamed with pride. "Quig gave this to me for our three-month anniversary."

Sage's expression soured. "Lucky ducky." On our private twin-link she said, *You can't take that off until he puts a ring on your finger.*

I plan to save it for special occasions.

In the Wick of Time

He'll have a heart attack if you don't keep it on.

How do you know this?

Lots of boyfriend-jewelry experience.

Quig broke the silence to say, "We'll take a tree. The five-footer with lights."

"Yes, sir," Sage said as if she'd been waiting patiently all this time for him to make up his mind. "That one is such a good choice. Cash or charge?"

He handed her a credit card, and she completed the transaction. After his purchase, she had exactly four trees left. "You have more of these at the nursery?"

"We've already ferried the reserve trees over, much to Mary Nicole's chagrin. Seems all I do is mention the trees to passersby, and they buy one, if not for themselves, for a parent. It's so sweet."

"Will you still participate in the luminary celebration for the Festival of Lights if the booth is empty?"

"I will. I'll bring some of our other stock down here if Ms. Chatham agrees, or I'll find a tree farm nearby and work a deal."

"What about Loren Lee?" I asked. "Any waterfront customers quiz you about your poisoned boss?"

"More than you would think. He'd been with All Good Things for so long that his name is synonymous with the business. He knew a lot of people. Most are sad he's gone. One person who stopped by the booth is former assistant manager Chris Kachuba. She kept going on and on about trying to get her job back now that Loren Lee's gone. Doesn't that give her motive? She hated Loren Lee. They butted heads from the start."

"Should I interview her next?"

"Perhaps." She narrowed her eyes at me. "She bought the wreath Larry made from tree scraps. I'll shoot you a picture of her check.

It has her phone number and address on it. Speaking of interviews, anything you forgot to mention about your interview with Alyss Carter today?"

I made sure no one else could hear us and spoke softly. "She lies, and she won't remove the spell on Brindle. I don't trust her at all."

"Me either. However, it finally makes sense why she treated me like dirt at Brindle's office. Jealousy."

"Still is jealous of you, far as I can tell." My shoulders bowed from tension. "I don't know how to help Brindle other than the holy water. We're running blind on our goals of healing and springing him from the psych ward. We could do more damage inadvertently as we try to help him."

"Haven't had the chance to do more than swing by there on my way to work. His parents must be so worried about him," Sage added with a heartfelt sigh.

My head jerked back at her revelation. She'd never mentioned meeting Brindle's parents before. Her emotions for Brindle ran deeper than she claimed, just as I'd thought. "You know them?"

"Yeah. I met them a few weeks ago when they were visiting from Arizona." Her voice faltered. "Brindle introduced me to them as his girlfriend. His mom really liked me."

"This is news to me. Meeting the parents is a big relationship step."

"You already know Quig's parents," she pointed out.

Noting that Quig and Larry stood by the river talking about tree care, I leaned close and said, "I've seen them exactly once since we've become a couple. We drove over to Hilton Head for dinner with them. I told you about that."

"Yes, you did, and you two have his parents' blessing. You've got it made. He's already giving you jewelry. I predict he'll have a ring on your finger soon."

The wistful tone of her voice tugged at me. In our entire lives, she'd had many boyfriends but I had few. Now our roles had reversed. I sought another topic to avoid getting bogged down. I nodded toward Mr. Tall and Mostly Silent. "How's it going with Larry?"

"He has no idea who killed Loren Lee, but he's happy our boss is gone. He considered Loren Lee a tyrant."

Not what I expected to hear. If Sage dated Larry, I'd learn of it after the fact, since she didn't appear to be enamored with him.

"He's not a dud, though," Sage said. "These long shifts at the waterfront have given me time to get to know him. There's no endless jibber-jabbering about sports, fishing, or hunting. He's more of the strong, silent type, so we're compatible, but there's no flash, if you know what I mean."

I shivered at the fresh breeze off the Savannah River. Quig must've noticed. "Ready to go home?" he asked as he joined us again.

"Yes."

"I'll carry our tree to the car."

I barred my arms close to my chest for warmth as we walked. "How should we decorate it? Are we shooting for a theme?"

"Why make it complicated? Let's collect items we like. Maybe we could find some candle-shaped ornaments."

"More likely to find lights shaped like a candle taper," I said, "Though we may have to shop online for those."

"Let's make a deal. Since lights came on the tree, we'll each find twenty ornaments or so. The catch is that the ornaments should mean something to you or me."

Much to my surprise, ornament ideas flowed into my head immediately. A black cat. A coffee mug. A book. A starfish for my love of the beach. A miniature replica of Quig's Hummer. Something heart-shaped. Or even one of those "our first Christmas" ornaments. As for the rest, they'd come in due time.

Meanwhile, my to-do list hadn't changed. I needed to unmask Loren Lee's killer, spring Brindle from the psych ward, work in my shop, and shop for Christmas ornaments. And buy a Christmas gift for Quig. He wouldn't upstage me again, not if I had anything to do with it.

Chapter Eighteen

I missed Auntie O terribly and hoped she and Frankie were safe, wherever they may be. My aunt's competency and loving acceptance made me feel like I had a safety net. I knew what to do because I had experience, but I preferred through Auntie O.

More than that, though, Auntie O showered us with her love, and that tangible outpouring charged me with positivity. We'd been spoiled, having such a tight family unit for so many years. Then Mom died, and now Auntie O was who knows where.

In any event, I remained available to work at the shop, and thus picked up the slack from our staffing reduction. That meant physically being there every day. Maybe all this weekday exposure to Gerard's super sales ability would rub off on me so that I replicated his sales levels on the weekends.

Already I'd learned that he employed personalized greetings for each repeat customer. Many of whom were looking for Christmas items from our shop, and they loved the personal touch. Gerard kept the music tuned to wacky Christmas songs, and even though I preferred more reflective music, I found myself humming along and smiling more. Note to self: play upbeat music in the shop.

Gerard noticed my new jewelry right away. "The big guy gave you a locket?"

"He did."

"Sweet."

Some Savannah College of Art and Design students entered the shop, including the gal with blue hair who had a crush on Gerard. Blue Hair enjoyed being on the Gerard train but not in a stalker kind of way. I believed their nearly ten-year age difference kept Gerard from considering her as an after-hours friend.

I kept busy in the stillroom creating a new scent, blending peppermint and cedarwood to create a personalized bar of soap for Quig. The combination appealed to me, uplifting me and making me feel like I stood in a fragrant forest. I then mixed up a fifty-drop blend in the same proportions and set the essential oils mixture aside.

Because I wanted to try this as soon as possible, I grabbed a clear melt-and-pour soap base, the sample-sized seashell soap molds, and a medium-sized glass bowl. I followed the step-by-step process. I cut the base into small uniform cubes, tossed them in the bowl, and melted them in twenty-second bursts in the microwave, stirring between reps. I added my essential oil blend, stirred the soap, and filled my molds. These needed to sit for a day before I removed them.

Once I washed, dried, and stored my utensils for next time, Gerard sauntered back into the stillroom. "I sold every Christmas soap in the shop. Need to check the storeroom closet for more."

Our storeroom resembled a glorified broom closet, where floor-to-ceiling shelving on all sides and cabinets held our inventory. Over the years, the storeroom product reserve shrank since we could restock in a day from local consigners. Maintaining the right amount of inventory to balance reserve and sales every month kept us on our toes.

Gerard returned with a scant handful of items. "News flash. We're out of holiday soaps along with most $5 everyday soaps and scraping bottom on the $10 size. How quickly can you restock?"

"Let me see what supplies are here." I opened the raw materials cabinet and held my breath at the voids. Not enough melt-and-pour bases here for the soap I should make today, but I could get started at least. I could make several larger batches of the hot-process soaps because those needed a week's rest after making. I pulled down all the melt-and-pour bases we had. "I wish I'd thought to check on our inventory and supplies before now. I would have been making soaps and ordering supplies all week."

"Not entirely anyone's fault," Gerard said. "Everyone is so busy right now. You've got the investigation and daily shifts here. Sage has the tree booth to run and a dead boss to mourn. As for me, I've been distracted of late trying to decide if Ramon is the guy for me. He wants to take our relationship to the next level."

"You'll figure it out." Wait a sec. That sounded harsh, and I didn't mean to hurt Gerard's feelings. "I have full faith in you knowing what's best for you, but I am here if you want to talk about anything."

He beamed. "I'm good."

Whew. Glad my distraction about the inventory didn't inadvertently cause friction with Gerard. Sage should've done the inventory, but when would she have had time? How could I fault her lapse when her boss had been murdered and ever since she'd been stuck working full-time at the nursery's holiday booth? Her grief and extra responsibilities consumed her every waking moment.

Bottom line, though, with Sage busy elsewhere I ruled the roost right now. The oversight of all aspects of our business rested on my shoulders. I returned Gerard's grin. "Don't beat yourself up about our inventory goof. I'll make three batches of the peppermint swirl soaps, and three batches of our best sellers this afternoon. If I go cold process, we can sell them tomorrow. I will also prioritize restocking supplies on my to-do list."

"Works for me." Gerard leaned close to my brim-full molds. "This soap smells divine. I would love to product test these."

With cupped hands I raised the scent to my face. The woodsy notes with that kiss of mint filled my lungs and made me smile. "These are for Quig, but I definitely can spare one for you to try."

"Great. I need a lunch break at Southern Tea. You mind taking over out front?"

"Have at it. I'll cover the shop." I trailed him to the counter, where a customer had been standing for a while. I quickened my steps. "My apologies for your wait. Did you find everything you need?"

We chatted, and the customer added two more multi-packs of lip balm to her purchase stack. "You have any of those little candy cane swirled soaps?"

I tried not to wince, but I hated disappointing a customer. "We will have more tomorrow."

"Good." The woman schooled her features and used a deep voice. "I'll be back."

After that woman left, a young couple checked out, grinning about their finds in the store. The taller of the pair purchased one of Norman Googe's mini-dragons and couldn't stop raving about how much his sister would love it. His joy reminded me of why I loved my job. Connecting people and items that made them happy gave me satisfaction.

As customers ebbed and flowed, my thoughts turned to the case. The cops were stymied in their investigation. I needed to solve Loren Lee's murder for Sage to have closure. From his austere living space, possessions didn't bring him personal joy. He thrived on control, about unilaterally lording his authority over the nursery staff. That caustic management style won him no friends, but only one former employee voiced her discontent at his tactics. Chris Kachuba, a redhead with a temper. I now had her address and phone number. I should use them soon.

Gerard returned a bit later, a goofy smile on his face. "What happened?" I asked.

"I've got a hot date tonight."

"That's wonderful."

The door chimed again, and a man I didn't know entered the shop. However, I recognized him as often being pictured in the paper for public drunkenness. With a sniff of the tainted air that wafted in with him and a glance at his unsteady gait, I didn't need to be psychic to know trouble followed. I murmured to Gerard, "Call the cops. Unruly customer."

Gerard's eyes rounded, but he did as I asked while I intercepted the man near the door. "Can I help you?"

"Just looking," he said, catching his balance on the frame of our industrial shelving. Thank our lucky stars we'd bolted that rack to the wall. "This floor is dangerous."

Nothing wrong with my floor, just his blood alcohol level. Even so, I gave him the benefit of the doubt, though I shielded my aura against his dark vibes. "What are you looking for?"

He squinted at me. "Got any liquor-scented candles? Would love to give 'em as gifts."

"Sorry, we don't carry those. Is there something else I can help you with?"

The man rocked from heel to toe, chest puffed out. "Yeah. Outta my way so I can go sit with those sweet chickadees."

He pointed to the art students over in our book nook. Blue Hair watched him warily, same as I did. His aura seethed, radiating his likelihood to cause trouble.

The man didn't look homeless, but anyone with a nose knew he hadn't bathed recently. "How about one of our peppermint candles or an aromatherapy product?"

"Girlie, you bug me. Outta my face," he snarled, his voice increasing in volume and intensity. "This is a free country."

Memories of schoolyard taunts rang in my ears. I clamped down on my simultaneous urges to run and to hold fast. Time to be an adult. "Please keep your voice down or leave."

"I know my rights."

"So do I. This is my shop. Customers are expected to be polite and treat others with respect."

The guy swatted overhead and struck three windchimes, all keyed to different harmonic scales, and the discordant noise inflamed him more. He gave an evil laugh and juked right to go around me. The sudden movement proved too much for his balance.

He fell to the floor, and I cushioned his head with energy so it didn't strike the floor. The art students hurried our way. The drunk's face turned florid. "What you looking at?"

"Nothing," Blue Hair said defiantly. If her eyes were lasers, the man would be dead.

"Give him space," I said, using a hand to shoo the students back. Perversely, their feet rooted in place. Great. A customer I didn't want. Onlookers who would notice if I messed with his energy. Plus, in this central location, the shop camera recorded my every move.

I gazed down at the man. "Are you hurt?"

He beamed a megawatt smile. "Nothing wrong with me a little Chivas wouldn't cure. You have any?"

That brand of scotch didn't come cheap. "How about a cup of coffee?"

"Nope." He rolled as if to get to his feet and instead banged into the table leg of one of our round display tables. I grabbed a pair of wobbling glass candle globes in the nick of time. Whew. So far so good.

"Let me help you." After moving the glass items out of harm's way, I knelt beside him. "Perhaps fresh air might clear your head."

He muttered something about a gal lying to him that made no sense. Then he stared at me wide-eyed. "Don't touch me."

I raised my hands in mock surrender. Where were the cops? I noticed a set of keys on the floor, so I picked them up, intending to hand the man his keys, but the fierce energy of rage coating the keys caused me to drop them.

He must've heard the keys jangle. His aura spiked with anger. "You stealing from me?"

"Your keys are on the floor. I accidentally dropped them when I tried to return them to you."

"Well, we're even cuz I accidentally fell down." He belched, reached up, and snagged the tablecloth with a beefy paw. To my dismay, he pulled everything from the table down on his head. Loud cussing ensued and finally, finally, a patrol officer arrived.

Officer Willis breezed through the door, quartered the room, then glared at the man on the floor. "Jerry, didn't we agree you'd go home a few minutes ago?"

I rose and stood on shaky legs. "He made trouble in another shop?"

"Yes. Come on, Jer. You know the drill. Up and out."

"Not going. Need to shop for the holidays. They don't have candles that smell like booze. I want them for every family member to remind them of me year-round." He grabbed a toppled evergreen pillar candle with a cracked midline. "I'm taking this one for my trouble."

"Little help here." Officer Willis motioned Gerard over from the counter, and they muscled the man outdoors.

I followed, aware of the mess on my shop floor, and the stares from passersby. Keenly aware of the financial loss the shop just suffered from broken and now stolen items, I asked, "Who's compensating me for the mess he made, and the candle he stole?"

"Give me a minute," Officer Willis said as he wrangled the man into his cruiser.

The man started belting "Grandma Got Run Over By a Reindeer" and giggling between choruses.

When Gerard joined me on the sidewalk in front of the shop, I gave him a sisterly hug. "Thanks for helping."

"Any time."

"I'll write out a complaint against Jerry." I nodded to the shop, where our regulars were picking up the mess. "See what you can do in there."

"Will do." He beamed at me. "You were brave to confront that guy. I want to be you when I grow up."

"Thanks, I think." Gerard had a few years on me, but he'd motored through several careers already, searching for his true path. We were lucky he enjoyed working here.

I wrote out a statement saying that Jerry Meldrim destroyed property in the shop. I listed broken items formerly on the table and their value: a set of tapers, four pillar candles, and Norman's rainbow frog statue.

"He's headed for the drunk tank," Officer Willis said as he accepted my paperwork. "Tried to cut him a break earlier today because of the holidays, but he didn't heed my advice to move along. Just so you know, they'll only hold him overnight for drunk and disorderly conduct. Best scenario for your business is if you come in and swear out a restraining order. It's not a great solution, but it will give you leverage to get him out of here faster next time."

"Next time?" I asked, my heart sinking to my knees.

"Oh, yeah. Jerry Meldrim is a hot mess. Gets in a rut and repeats his mistakes."

"What about his family?"

"Daughter's in there. Fawn Meldrim." He pointed at Blue Hair. "His ex-wife kicked him out and disowned him."

Good grief. Poor kid. I didn't want to rain down more trouble on her family, but what could I do? If our shop failed, I would lose my home too. Even though I felt compassion toward our unruly customer, he'd been bent on destruction. I hoped I never saw him again.

Jerry Meldrim had burned his bridges here.

Chapter Nineteen

Sage and I met at the station, and we were shown into the conference room to work on the restraining order for our drunken customer. We weren't there two minutes before Detectives Nowry and Belfor joined us.

"Ladies," Belfor said, sliding into a chair opposite us, her expression cop-tough. Her partner stood by the door he'd closed. Did he plan on stopping us if we tried to leave?

The tag team approach to police questioning always left a sour taste in my mouth. Looked like Sharmila Belfor would be first up. She looked like a pushover due to her stylish clothing, but experience had shown she could be as painfully direct as her partner.

I'd only filled in the name and address part of the form before they arrived. I set my pen on the table, certain I'd best give her my full attention. "Afternoon, Detectives."

"Why are y'all here?" Sage asked.

Belfor smirked. "Oddly, the chief notifies us anytime your names cross his desk."

I kept silent, and Sage did the same. No point in giving law enforcement any ammunition to use against us. They came up with plenty of that on their own.

Behind me, Nowry growled. "Your shop draws a bad element."

I swiveled my neck to face him. "It does not. Officer Willis said Jerry Meldrim does this all over town. Today he picked our shop and others."

Nowry moved to stand beside his partner's chair. "If the shoe fits . . ."

"The majority of our customers are tourists," I said. "The rest are local citizens who prefer our products. If tourists are a bad element, why does the city court them?"

Nowry ignored me and glowered at Sage. "Why are men falling apart when they come near you? Are you a modern-day Siren luring men to their doom?"

Sage's eyes flashed heat, and her throbbing aura became more pronounced. I felt certain she wanted to zap Nowry hard with dark energy. At his age, his chances of surviving that attack weren't good. I reached out to Sage on our twin-link. *Easy, Sis. He's riling you on purpose. Ignore that last bit and tell him you were working.*

I hate Nowry. If we were alone on a midnight road, I would go all Siren on him without a second thought.

He's fishing for information, hoping you'll react. Stick to the truth, and they'll back off.

This sucks. Sage dialed back her emotions and cleared her throat. "Better check your facts. I worked all day with Larry Rau at my nursery job. We're selling potted Christmas trees at the waterfront this year."

"I want one of those," Belfor said. "I love the smell of a live tree, and if I get one with roots, then I won't have to keep buying trees every year."

"We've got a few trees left. Come over at lunch tomorrow or sooner if you want one."

"Duly noted," Belfor said.

"Knock it off about the trees," Nowry said. "You Winslows are a nuisance. It would be better for everyone if you didn't darken our doorstep."

Just when I thought Sage had been exercising tremendous restraint, she glowered at Nowry. "We wouldn't be here if you kept the actual bad element off the street."

"Per the captain's order, Meldrim is en route to the hospital for a psych evaluation. Bail will be set, unless he's found to be a danger to himself or society." Nowry studied us like we were roaches on a garbage heap. "I can't prove it, but somehow all hell breaks loose around you two."

An unfortunately true accusation. Sage's aura darkened again. The energy in the room roiled until my arm hairs snapped to attention. I didn't appreciate his snide remark one bit, and for a few intense seconds I considered blasting him out of his shoes. Then I realized I should heed the advice I'd given Sage and ignore his loaded allegations. He won if I lost control or yielded to emotion.

Darn it, I said to Sage via our twin-link. *How'd they make this about us? It isn't fair. We're protecting our business by filing for a restraining order.*

The justice system isn't perfect. Let's hope Jerry Meldrim gets the help he needs.

The man wouldn't stop drinking, and if his troubled aura meant anything, he might be drinking to block his own energy. Besides detox, the man needed an energetic intervention, an aura cleanse, and a new lease on life.

Fat chance of that.

Our entire silent exchange happened before the detective drew a second breath. I glared at Nowry. "My family has lived in Savannah for generations, and our shop is a reputable, established business. The Winslows are on the same side of the law as you are."

In the Wick of Time

"We're watching you," he said, and then both cops left.

By outward appearance, Sage and I silently finished filling out the paperwork for the restraining order. Privately, we kept the twin-link buzzing.

The nerve of that jerk, Sage began. *We saved his bacon a few months ago by solving a case for him, and he acts as if we're trash? If I possessed killer singing talent, I would've lured many offensive men to their doom by now.*

Let's finish before he tries to intimidate us again. This place gives me the willies, even this conference room, and it's huge compared to the tiny interview room we usually see.

Sage shuddered. *Never want to go there again.*

Me either, but given Nowry's bias toward us, we're living on borrowed time.

Oh joy.

Say, is it okay if I borrow your car? I want to visit Chris Kachuba before another day goes past.

No need to borrow it. I'm coming with you.

* * *

The double-wide where Chris Kachuba lived looked spacious, but it needed pressure cleaning. The evergreen wreath hanging on the door, the one she'd bought from Sage's tree booth, brought a touch of cheer to the place. I turned to Sage. "Note the landscaping."

"What landscaping? She's got a lawn of weeds and three clusters of out-of-control azaleas." Sage surveyed the yard with a practiced eye. "This doesn't look like the yard of someone who loves plants."

"Another strange fact in this case." My sister switched off the motor. "Please let me do all the talking."

She shrugged and then exited the small sedan.

I knocked on the door and a small dog yapped in reply.

Footsteps approached from inside the trailer. "Go away," a woman said. "Whatever you're selling, I don't want any."

"Chris, it's Tabby Winslow. I'm not selling anything. I want to talk with you about All Good Things Nursery."

"I want nothing to do with that place."

"Please? I won't take much of your time. I wanted to hear your opinion of the former manager, Loren Lee Suffield."

The door swung wide. Chris stood there with her hands planted on her hips. The dog barked from another room. "I want nothing to do with that man. He hates me."

"He's dead," Sage said, speaking instead of letting me handle the interview. "And you threatened to kill him."

"Sage." Chris startled visibly. "My association with him was a long time ago. He fired me. I spoke in anger at the time because I needed that job. Doesn't mean I killed him."

"But you still sounded upset before you heard he was dead," Sage said.

"I was going through something else then. That was not an easy part of my life. It stirs up old memories to think of those dark times. Loren Lee didn't do me any favors, but I'm not that person anymore. I got help and I turned my life around."

Her voice sounded familiar. "Do I know you?" I asked. "Do you shop at The Book and Candle Shop in Savannah?"

"I shopped there recently. I keep a big candle supply in case of hurricanes. When I'm downtown, I run multiple errands at once."

"Have you been to the nursery lately?"

"No reason to go." Chris pointed to her wreath. "Although I did buy this wreath from their riverside booth."

"You bought it from me," Sage said.

"If you say so."

I viewed Chris's aura several times during our exchange. Nothing looked horrific. In fact, her aura looked normal, if a bit murky here and there. How disappointing. I had hoped there would be a flashing neon sign over her head proclaiming her guilt.

The silence lengthened. "I hated that place," Chris said. "The nursery, I mean. It's the scene of my most embarrassing moments. The only time I've ever been fired. The cops already questioned me and ruled me out as a suspect in that man's murder. I got nothing more to say to either of you."

The door slammed in our faces.

When Sage made no move to leave, I turned and went down the short stack of steps. "Let's go."

"She's guilty as the day is long."

The winter solstice approached, so her comment didn't make sense to me. "The days are getting shorter by the minute."

"You know what I mean."

"Actually I don't. Her aura looked okay. She said she didn't do it. And the cops cleared her."

"So she says. I don't trust her."

"You barely trust anyone."

"I trust you, Sis."

"I trust you back."

Afterward, Sage headed to the waterfront. I stuck with her, though I could've just as easily hiked back to the shop. Since Sage had taken some time off, she offered her coworker, Larry, a chance for an extended break, so we were alone in the booth under sunny skies and sixty-degree temperatures.

I gestured to the empty space in the booth. "Your big boss must be pleased with your efforts here."

"Not sure my performance matters in the grand scheme of things." Sage shrugged. "Ms. Chatham and Mary Nicole speak the same business language. I am one hundred percent sure the assistant manager job is hers. And you know what? She won't do a bad job."

"She won't do the superb job you'd do either."

Sage tried to hold back a smile, but it brightened her face. "That's true. She'll kill the store's momentum with her mediocrity. I should warn Ms. Chatham. But the truth is I'm reconsidering everything. Taking a full-time job will lead to constant staff shortages at our family business, and I'll always be darting from one place to another, trying to keep up. I've barely had a moment of peace since Loren Lee's murder. We've covered shifts in our shop so far for December, but we'll burn out working seven days a week all the time. Neither of us wants that."

I felt fine now, but I privately conceded burnout could happen. "I thought you wanted the nursery management job?"

"Loren Lee flattered me by encouraging me to apply. I believed he saw management material in me." She gazed over the river and sighed. "In hindsight, he had a private agenda. When Mary Nicole applied first, Loren Lee told me he didn't want to work with her. I now know he encouraged me to apply so she wouldn't bother him. He intended to use me as a buffer."

Her insight turned my former assumption on its head. First, her late boss sounded self-centered. Second, Sage deserved the promotion because of her knowledge and experience. Third, this line of thought could change the order on my suspect list. Hmm.

I began to think out loud. "I agree everything goes back to Loren Lee. Since he had no social life, his interests aligned with job satisfaction at work. There's a strong possibility he got himself killed by pitting you against Mary Nicole. She is my new prime suspect."

"Where are we on our suspect list?" Sage asked. "Frankie and I are innocent. That leaves Mary Nicole, Chris, and the big boss."

"Ms. Chatham? She owns the whole shooting match. If she wanted Loren Lee gone, she could fire him. No need to kill him." I took a moment to gather my thoughts. Out on the river a tugboat chugged by. I wished this case had the steady momentum of a tug. Instead, our sails flapped in slack wind, and we were going nowhere. "Earlier I heard the drunk guy mutter something about someone telling him to come to our shop. What if we add him to our suspect list? Or the person who steered him our way?"

Sage dismissed the suggestion with a wave of her hand. "I don't recall Jerry Meldrim ever darkening our doorway before. Given his problem with booze, I don't trust his memory. He could be hallucinating or living in his own alternate reality."

"Perhaps Meldrim is an opportunist more than a strategic thinker," I said. "Since the killer used poison as the murder weapon, access to a food or drink item in Loren Lee's house is all he or she needed to dose him. However, I doubt Meldrim could manage that more than once. Loren Lee's illness persisted for weeks before he passed."

"If you consider the drunk guy's volatility and Loren Lee's intractability, those two would not have gotten along for a second. Both men are control freaks."

"So that brings us back to nursery employees."

"Most nursery employees thought Loren Lee acted like a jerk," Sage said.

"Everyone has baggage that might be related, but we'd be short-sighted to rely solely on that approach. Even so, the drunk guy isn't a murder suspect in my book."

My phone buzzed, and I was alarmed at the display—Gerard's text message read: "SOS."

Chapter Twenty

"Gotta run. Another emergency at the shop," I told Sage after I sent Gerard a quick text with an acronym for on the way. "Maybe the cops are right. Trouble is sure finding us."

Her eyebrows rose as I hurried away. "Wait. What kind of trouble?"

I called over my shoulder. "SOS. Our second one this month."

Though she shouted for me to wait again, I ran the six blocks from the waterfront like the hounds of hell were after me. Quig's locket beat on my chest with every stride. Terrible possibilities pounded in my head, each more horrific than the last. Frankie's Chicago relatives could've hit town. The cops came to arrest Frankie. Our aunt defended Frankie with her talent. Something happened to MawMaw. The poisoner struck again. I tried to shake off the dark thoughts, but they hummed with malignancy.

Lungs burning as I zipped past people, dogs, baby strollers, and cars, I vowed silently to be better about exercising in the future. I prayed my family and friends were safe from harm, and I tried to block the fear that iced my gut. It wouldn't go away.

Pausing outside the shop, I mentally prepared for this encounter. A dark-haired stranger in black stood near the sales counter, sniffing my candles. Gerard stood behind the counter, arms barred. This trouble did not come from cops, Ramon, MawMaw, Auntie O, or Alyss. Probably someone from Frankie's long-ago life in Chicago then. I looked to see if the man carried a gun. No jacket, so probably no concealed weapon.

In any event, waiting outside wouldn't clarify matters. I strode in with more bravado than I felt and joined Gerard behind the sales counter. "You okay?" I whispered.

He gave a slight nod and squeezed my hand briefly. "I'm better with you here."

"What happened?"

"This guy is looking for his cousin *Paulie Vinci*."

I silently mouthed the unfamiliar name. Was that Frankie's birth name? I switched to my other vision to study the stranger's aura. The pulsing blend of dirty crimson, murky brown, and black smacked down my energy probe. This guy reeked of Trouble. I pushed out an energy barrier to protect me and Gerard.

The stranger turned to face me at that moment, his expression warming as if I wore a low-cut dress instead of trousers, a button-down blouse, and a red sweater. "You are the shop owner, *Bella*?"

The man called me beautiful, and his accent caressed the air around me. I smiled at the stranger in the name of customer service. "One of them. I'm Tabby Winslow. How may I help you?"

A scowl darted across his face, as if he had expected me to do more than smile. Then he nodded curtly as if we were sparring partners. "Vito Morelli. I heard my cousin Paulie is here."

He didn't expect my energy barrier. Good thing I thought ahead. "We don't have a Paulie on staff. Sure you have the right address?"

His dark eyes bored into mine. "This is the place. Paulie left before I was born, but Big Tony says he's here. On this street and in this shop." He paused briefly and glowered. "Big Tony is never wrong."

Oh, dear. Vito believed he'd found his elusive cousin. I couldn't miss the alarming solar-like flares in his aura. All that fiery energy made me uneasy. To be frank, danger throbbed in his energy field.

Worse, his agitation flared as I viewed his aura. I struggled to stand my ground, when I wanted to run far away from this man. "I don't know anyone by that name. However, I see you're interested in our candles. Perhaps you have a question about them or our other wares?"

The smile on his face looked genuine, worrying me further. "I am indeed interested in your candles. They are excellent for setting the mood, no?"

Another customer approached the counter with a basket of items to buy. I waved Vito aside so that Gerard could make the sale. "Is there a particular scent you're interested in?"

He edged closer. "The one that makes you smile, sweet lady."

Ooh, seductive words, but deceptive ones. His energy lanced through my energy barrier and wrapped around me like a boa constrictor. I shoved at the pulse, hard, until it retreated. "I am with someone. Save your charms for another."

"Ah, but the game has just begun." He sighed. "You are a heartbreaker."

"You just met me." That came out squeakier than I intended. To ground myself, I ran through the standard spiel about our candles.

He gazed upon me with rapt fascination until Sage dashed in the door. She headed straight to us, and for a moment I thought she would bowl me over.

Vito caught her easily, set her on her feet between us and grinned. "This is my lucky day. Welcome, lovely."

Why didn't you wait for me? Sage demanded on our twin-link.

Because you were working. I can handle this guy.

You want all the fun for yourself. I'll take care of this Romeo.

Careful. There's something strange about his energy field, and he's after Frankie.

I can handle him.

Seriously, he tried to ooze his energy all over me, I said silently.

Kinky, I like that in a man.

It felt suffocating. Shield yourself right now, Sage, or something awful might happen.

All right, spoilsport.

The playboy grinned at Sage. "I'm Vito Morelli. I did not catch your name, *Bella.*"

"Sage Winslow." Vito kissed her offered hand and lingered over it way too long. I tried to swing the conversation back to our merchandise. "About the candles, you can't go wrong with Southern Lites. That scent is a perennial best seller."

"Enchanted," Vito said. "May I take you ladies to dinner?"

This guy powered through like a runaway freight train barreling down the track. "No. As I said when you hit on me a few minutes ago, I'm with someone."

"I'm free tonight," Sage said.

"My hotel is on the river," he began.

"Sage." I tugged on her arm. "May I speak to you privately?"

Not now, Tabs. Busy.

In the Wick of Time

Tough. Stillroom. Now.

"Excuse us," I said to Vito as I dragged my twin to the back room. "What is wrong with you?" I asked quietly. "This guy is from the mob. He works for a man called Big Tony. With his trickster energy, he can manipulate people. He tried to seduce me five minutes ago. Within seconds of meeting me. Unreal."

Sage glanced at him over her shoulder, waving her fingers his way before turning back. "He can seduce me if he wants. I'm a free agent."

"So he can find out everything you know about Frankie."

"I don't know where he is and neither do you. I don't see a problem."

"Frankie is with Auntie O and is family. Vito is not family. He might hurt you or all of us. We know nothing about him."

"I'm going out with him tonight. My life's been hell lately. I need a sexy distraction."

"It isn't safe. Bad idea."

"What if I take Gerard?" Sage asked, waggling her eyebrows.

Gerard could chaperone them. "Works for me, but don't be disappointed if the guy rescinds the invite if you drag along another guy."

Sage shrugged. "It's all good."

I felt uneasy about her plan. "Report in during dinner, please. Quig and I will take care of MawMaw tonight for Gerard if he wants to accompany you."

Surprisingly, Vito had no issue with Gerard coming along, but Gerard begged off because he had a date planned and coverage for his grandmother this evening. Smart guy.

Hours later, no Sage and no message from her either. I sent my sister a "where are you" message on our twin-link. No response.

I checked the hotels along the waterfront for a lodger with Vito's name. Nothing. Quig and I settled in for the night, my thoughts racing. After a restless night of tossing and turning, I awoke to the new day rumpled and out of sorts. Quig went to work, and I headed over to open the shop, deeply troubled.

What had Vito Morelli done with my sister?

Chapter
Twenty-One

Though Sage's radio silence bothered me, I had to go to work. I puttered around in the shop stillroom until I heard someone moving around overhead. Finally. I ran up the inside stairs and unlocked the apartment door, except I didn't encounter Sage in the kitchen. I found Vito instead.

"What are you doing here?" I asked.

He grinned all over. I could tell because he didn't have on a stitch of clothing. "Amore."

Love? This day got stranger by the second. "Where's my sister?"

He propped against the island, regarding me with cool calculation, his regard drifting down to my locket. "You are the boss of her?"

"No, I am not."

"Ah." He turned to the cabinets, unerringly opening the glass cabinet, then filled a glass with tap water and drank thirstily. Without another word, he padded to Sage's bedroom.

What? Our conversation had barely begun. Miffed at being snubbed, I started to yell after him, but I followed him instead. I wanted him gone.

I stopped short in the doorway, the intimate scene forever etched on my retinas. Sage and Vito were kissing and . . . more. Yikes! I covered my eyes and backed away. My sister would be mortified if she knew I saw her in such a private moment.

I tried reaching her on the twin-link again, but she didn't respond. Something blocked our silent communication, and I had a very good idea what caused the problem.

Vito's energy. I glanced at the pair again, with my other vision. His energy pulsed around the bed. In fact, it coated her bedroom. It glowed in Sage's closet, on her computer, and all over her wad of keys.

Her keys? I got a sick feeling in the pit of my stomach. Vito had made no bones about his reason for being here. He expected to find his cousin, the man I knew as Frankie. Had he used Sage's keys to enter Frankie and Auntie O's apartment? I hurried next door, entering with my own key. Vito's energy signature resonated here as well, along with the mess he'd left as he searched the place. No telling what the man had learned about Frankie.

I marched back to Sage's kitchen, filled a gallon pitcher with cold water, and splashed it on the bedmates.

Neither one noticed. What kind of stranglehold did Vito have on my sister? My anger turned to fear for her safety. I dared not touch them for fear I'd be drawn into the fray. Or electrocuted.

Crap.

Sage! Wake up! I tried on our twin-link.

No response. Sage had never been in this much trouble. Vito held her in thrall. He commanded her mind and body. Beings that could do that belonged in fairy tales, not my sister's bed.

"Out!" I clapped my hands loudly and shouted to Vito. "Out, out, out."

In the Wick of Time

"You wish to join our party?" he said lazily, at last addressing me with his attention.

"Leave now and I won't call the cops."

"The cops? I am a welcome guest."

"Don't go all innocent and big brown eyes with me. I know you did this. Get out."

"She invited me, so I do as I please, and I am pleased to stay."

"Wrong, bucko. I have authority here, and you will heed it. My name is on the property deed. I am the co-owner of this apartment and the shop. Leave before I do something I regret."

"Ah, you do wish to join us."

That did it. Deep concern for my sister prompted me to wipe that smirk off his face. I shot an energy spear at Vito, another at Sage.

Sage passed out. Vito yelped, leaped off the bed, and reached quickly for his pants. Finally. I silently rejoiced at his discomfiture. "What did you do to me?"

I reveled in his discomfiture. "I see I deflated more than your ego."

"You are messing with fire, woman."

"You're a hypnotist."

He scowled as he jammed his bare feet into his shoes. "Not my fault lovers fall into my bed on a regular basis."

His boast rang false in my ears. With that realization, I figured him out. "Not of her free will. You dazzled her first."

"Nothing she did not want," he said coolly. "She is a consenting adult."

His skin radiated a healthy glow, whereas Sage looked exhausted, confirming my thinking. Vito was a powerful energy vampire and a para-hypnotist. My energy spear barely stunned him. He could've hit me with his full power or worse.

"Not anymore. I speak for Sage, since she can't speak for herself right now." I summoned courage and righteousness and pushed them forward as a shield. "Stay away from my sister. I will hurt you if you ever try this again."

As before, he acted as if I hadn't spoken, though my words must've sunk in. He tossed his shirt over his shoulder and left. I locked the alley door behind him, hoping that small precaution would keep him out. Then I hurried to my sister's side, praying I could save her. With a touch I confirmed her energy ebbed dangerously low. I shared energy full-force, laying hands on her shoulder and heart between our bodies.

I prayed to all higher powers to spare my sister. After a while I reached my automatic stop point, energy-sharing-wise, and I kept going, heedless of the danger to myself. I wouldn't let my sister die, no matter what the cost. *Come back to me, Sage. You can't leave yet.*

Finally, her spark of life glowed again. Tears blurred my gaze. She could rally.

"Sage. Wake up. Time for work."

She groaned and shoved me away.

I tried the twin-link. *Sage. Wake up. You spent the night with an energy vampire, and he is much more powerful than anyone we've ever met.*

She cracked one eye. "What are you talking about?"

"Last night you were with Frankie's cousin Vito from Chicago. I couldn't reach you all night. I came here, and his energy is everywhere. In your closet, in the drawers, on your keys."

"What?" Her chin dropped. "I have no recollection of last night. Now that you mention his name, I remember seeing a handsome man at the shop at closing time. That's it."

"You're starting to sound better," I said, finger-combing her hair. "How're you feeling?"

"Like I got run over by an eighteen-wheeler. Everything aches. Need more energy."

"I believe he hypnotized you and stole energy from you all night long in between him sneaking around and trying to find Frankie. He made a huge mess in Frankie and Auntie O's place. From all appearances, he took advantage of you, though he said you wanted to be with him."

"I don't remember him. Not even his face." She grimaced. "But that does explain my exhaustion this morning." She patted my leg. "Share energy with me?"

"I already did, and I can't spare any more now. He drained you to within an inch of your life. I've done everything I can, or you'd still be unconscious. Rest is what you need now, and I need to recharge."

"Have to go to work." Sage tried to sit up but slumped back onto the pillows. "Mary Nicole will fire me if I give her any reason."

"Tell you what. I'll get Gerard started downstairs, then I'll head to the tree booth to help Larry. If we're lucky, Mary Nicole will never know you missed the morning shift."

"You'll cover for me?"

I handed her the phone. "Of course, but call Ms. Chatham first to let her know you forgot a doctor's appointment, and I'm filling in for you this morning."

She made the call, then sagged into the bed, eyes closing. "Thanks, Sis. I'll be a few more minutes."

I set her phone alarm for eleven and returned to my apartment for a light jacket. Though we had a mild sunny day, when the tide turned, the wind would shift direction.

Gerard volunteered to cover the shop this morning, and he encouraged me to help Sage. I issued a warning about the man from

Chicago, ending with, "Don't let Vito in the stillroom or our apartment. I don't trust him."

He grinned as if he had a secret. "Gotcha. You cover for your sister, I've got the shop."

I'd get to the bottom of that smile later, but for now I needed to hustle. "Thanks. You're one in a million."

I hurried to the waterfront, and there my luck ran out. Mary Nicole glared at me from inside the treeless booth.

Chapter Twenty-Two

"Where's Sage?" Mary Nicole barred the booth entryway, fists on hips, her face scarlet. "She should've opened the booth thirty minutes ago."

Oh boy. Sage's interim boss was livid. Just what I didn't need this morning. "She forgot about an appointment, but she will be in by noon. I am filling in for her until then. As a volunteer."

I'd power walked the entire way to the waterfront, proud I wasn't gasping for air like a beached sea bass. Not having a car would keep me in shape, for sure. I peeked around the angry woman to see Larry Rau looking wary behind her. "Morning, Larry."

Larry gave a curt nod, his stoic features reminding me of a young Lou Diamond Phillips.

"This is unacceptable," Mary Nicole ranted. "First she killed our boss, and now she can't be bothered to come to work? She should've called instead of acting like she's the Queen Bee of Savannah."

Her accusation stung. Defensive words tumbled out in a rush. "My sister had nothing to do with Loren Lee's death. I advise you to consider your words carefully. Your defamatory statements about Sage in public are so noted. I heard you slander my sister, and so did Larry."

Larry got busy looking at the Savannah River. I took that to mean he couldn't get involved in this hen fight. Probably worried he'd get fired. I had no such qualms. "Further, she did call in. She spoke to Ms. Chatham this morning."

Mary Nicole sputtered and made a frustrated sound. "She should've called me. I'm her direct supervisor."

"She doesn't have your cell number programmed in her phone. So she called the nursery, and Ms. Chatham answered."

"Hmph." Mary Nicole gazed at the empty booth behind her. "What's happening with this empty stand? This is an embarrassment. It looks pathetic with nothing for sale here. We can't pay these two to twiddle their thumbs."

"I may have this wrong, but at one point Sage mentioned she might ask Ms. Chatham about moving some of the nursery's plant stock here."

Anger radiated from the woman like heat waves off a dune. My aura protected me from her negative energy, and Larry didn't show any adverse effects. This caustic woman would be vicious if she ever controlled her energy, so that counted as one blessing of the day. If she weaponized her aura, our entire city would be in a heap of trouble.

She advanced on me, hands on hips. "Our inventory stays at the nursery. It's mine. Sage can't have it."

I thrust out my arms to physically block her from entering my personal space. If she happened to get a jolt of my energy, so be it. "Y'all work that out. I'm merely a proxy."

Mary Nicole sniffed and eyed my puny-appearing defense with disdain. "You're not even on our payroll. You shouldn't be here. I have the authority to throw you out."

I reminded myself that Sage wanted this job. If I retaliated the way I wanted to, this woman would fire Sage in a red-hot minute, no other provocation needed. I drew in a deep, centering breath. "I've volunteered at the nursery many times in the past few years. How is this different from me helping Sage with the luminaries in the nursery?"

Anger flared in her eyes, and I thought she'd order me to leave. Instead, she gave a malicious smile that bothered me more than her palatable emotions. "Suit yourself."

She strolled away as if she had a leisurely lifestyle. *There blows trouble*, I thought silently, unsure if Larry shared my sentiment. I turned to find Larry watching me.

"Good for you," he said. "Mary Nicole goes down like a bitter pill. Three of our seasonal hires at the nursery quit this morning. Nobody wants to work for her. Nobody stands up to her—well, except Sage."

"She's something else," I said, not wanting to get caught defaming her in public.

"You're right about Sage talking to Ms. Chatham about our outstanding sales here. That's probably why Mary Nicole is harassing us this morning. She sees Sage as her rival."

"She's the acting assistant manager. I figured she'd keep the job."

"She would like that." He looked up and moved forward because a couple of thirty-somethings had stopped at the booth. "Can I help you?"

"We wanted to get a tree here," one man said.

"We're temporarily sold out," Larry said. "Check back this afternoon. We will be restocked by then."

The other man nodded. "Great. We should've bought our tree yesterday when you had only a few in here, but we had too much to carry already. We live around the corner, so we'll return later."

They wandered away, and I nodded at Larry. "They left happy, and I believe they'll be back."

"Lots of downtown folks are into the shopping-local-vendors-and-local-products mindset."

"We benefit from that effect in our shop on Bristol Street." The foot traffic pulsed here, heavy one minute, thinner the next. Our shop's traffic faintly echoed that pattern. "What should we do this morning with nothing to sell?"

"We wait for the delivery from the Christmas Tree Farm down in McIntosh County." He grinned. "They promised to bring twenty small trees nicely potted sometime this morning. Seeing that it's almost noon, I expect them any minute."

"Ah. You knew the plan, but you kept Mary Nicole in the dark?"

A muscle twitched on his face. "It's what Sage would've done."

The deadpan way he said that made me snort with laughter. "True, but she's probably not the best role model."

"She's easy to work with. Her vision for a project is always clear, and she knows how to get stuff done. Mary Nicole, not so much. She's full of bluster and anger all the time. Who needs that? It's Christmas, for Pete's sake."

"So it is." That counted as the most I'd heard Larry say, ever. "How'd you come to be working at the nursery, Larry?"

"Always had a green thumb, and I prefer outdoor jobs. I've worked a couple of places now, learning from different nursery managers. Loren Lee acted like a jerk at times, but he knew the business."

Someone like Larry, who kept their opinions guarded, might be a keen observer. This opportunity might yet yield pure investigative gold. "What are your thoughts on Loren Lee's death?"

He stared at his work boots for a bit. "Can't say as I'll miss him. At All Good Things, his way ruled, which led to high staff turnover.

Sage and I survived several employee purges. I really hoped she'd get the assistant manager job."

Two moms with four kids and a baby stroller between them rolled by, making so much racket I couldn't hear myself think. Finally they moved out of earshot. "Sounds like you've got the experience necessary to handle that job too. Is there a reason you didn't put your name in the hat?"

"Giving orders is not my thing. Besides, I'd never go against Sage."

"Gotcha." Hmm. This guy had a mega-crush on my sister. Did she know?

"Did she talk to you about our fishing trip?" he asked after a bit.

I turned my face up to the sun, enjoying the winter warmth on my face. "She mentioned it. She had a good time."

He radiated happiness. "Great."

I had more questions. "What about your coworkers? Any rumblings among them about Loren Lee's passing?"

"Most were happy he wouldn't be in their faces for B-level work when he demanded A-plus performance constantly. But now that Mary Nicole is in their grills all the time, yelling about everything, they gripe about her. I wouldn't be surprised if everyone quits by the first of the year."

"You included?"

"I'll follow Sage's lead." He nodded at the pickup truck wending its way toward us. "Our trees are here."

A crowd gathered round as we unloaded twenty Murray cypress trees into the booth. Three were table-top size and planted in one-gallon pots, three were six-footers in large pots, while the remainder, which rose about four feet in height, were in three-gallon pots. I loved the scent of these evergreens. They smelled like the holidays.

Larry signed for delivery, and we were off and running. Three customers swooped in immediately for trees, including the two gentlemen from before. We'd barely attended to the gathered customers when Sage stalked up. If she'd been a tugboat, there would've been a plume of smoke swirling from her head.

Chapter
Twenty-Three

"Why'd you sic Mary Nicole on me?" Sage demanded, red-faced. "She called and blistered my ears. I couldn't get a word in edgewise. You'd think nobody ever came to work late on her watch. She did everything but call me a serial killer on the phone."

"Not to worry," I said. "I didn't sic her on anyone. When she blistered our ears a bit ago, we heard her outright state you killed Loren Lee. She can't talk about you that way. I called her on her crap."

"Great gravy, she's a piece of work." Sage waved to her coworker, who'd retreated to soak the new trees with reserved jugs of water. "Morning, Larry."

Ever the man of few words, Larry gave her a hello nod.

"Everything okay with your unexpected appointment?" I asked, reminding her of the cover story I'd used for her tardiness.

"I'm good," she said. "Thanks for filling in for me. I apologize for unloading on you. It's just . . . that woman punched all my hot buttons this morning. I don't want to be around her negativity."

"Totally understand that." I checked my watch. "I'm glad you're here. It's close to lunchtime. I'll swing by the morgue on my way back to the shop."

As I gathered my purse from underneath the counter space, I saw Sage and Larry with their heads together. They were plucking a few wind-damaged branches from the trees. Larry looked the happiest I'd seen him all day, and his aura sparkled. Sage seemed oblivious to his affection for her. Business as usual with those two.

I hurried up the steps to street level and then darted a few streets over to the morgue. I knocked on the door, and an Asian man I didn't know answered. The scent of disinfectant wafted out to greet me. Could this be Quig's new assistant? I took a chance that it was. "Dr. Chang? I'm Tabby Winslow, and I'm looking for Quig, I mean Dr. Quigsly. Is he here?"

"Stuck in a meeting last I heard, but he should return shortly. Nice to meet you, Ms. Winslow."

"Please call me Tabby. May I wait for him here?"

His gaze sharpened. "You like spending time in the morgue?"

I gazed at the bank of cold lockers along the walls behind him, wondering if Sage's late boss, Loren Lee, still rested in a storage unit. Not sure if this new guy would allow me to cruise the wall to see if the body remained here, but I had an opportunity to snoop that I shouldn't let slide. "I sometimes visit Quig at work, like today, when I am near the morgue."

He motioned me inside the room. "You are an unusual woman."

I didn't know what to make of that odd hitch in his voice, so I ignored it and walked into the morgue. My nose wrinkled at the antiseptic smell. "And you're a smart guy. Quig told me about the diagnostic tests you ran on the Suffield case and how that locked in the cause of death. You are truly the man of the hour in my book. My sister worked for Loren Lee, and his murder hit her hard."

"I enjoy the process of seeking the truth."

Quig kept mum about open cases. Maybe this new guy would let something slip if I asked the right question. "Did the evidence point to one particular suspect?"

"Nothing specific, though the killer had great knowledge of poisons to pull this off."

I sighed. "Anyone with an internet connection is an expert these days."

"Perhaps."

Dr. Chang's sour tone implied annoyance, and I had barely started. "Could he have been saved if Sage talked him into going to the hospital a few days before he died? Would they have given him activated charcoal or induced vomiting at the emergency room?"

"Treatment depends on how quickly they identified the poison, and then treatment would be poison-specific. The attending physician would have assessed the patient's condition and history as well as his airways, breathing, and circulation, all of which play into treatment selection." He paused for a moment, then nodded curtly. "Given his weeks of illness, it is unlikely they would induce vomiting. That's most often used for a recently ingested toxin."

"My sister and I wondered which local toxin caused his demise. We considered sago palm, pyracantha, and oleander. Are we in the right ballpark?"

Unfortunately, Dr. Chang had one of the best poker faces I'd ever come across. Not a single muscle twitched. "Ongoing investigation," he said. "Can't discuss it."

Rats. Another stickler for the rules. He wouldn't let anything slip. I checked my watch again. Already a quarter past noon. I couldn't hang out here indefinitely. Places to go, other people to bug. I'd see Quig tonight in any event.

I said goodbye to Dr. Chang and detoured through the restroom, selecting the stall farthest from the door out of long practice. While I sat there, the restroom door opened and closed. I heard talking and froze at the sound, wanting to hear the conversation.

"He's weird, Pat," a gal with a squeaky voice said.

"He's brilliant," a deeper voice woman replied. "Everybody knows smart people have less walking around sense."

"His eyes are cold," Squeaky continued. "Don't get your hopes up with him. Just because he figured out that poison doesn't make him a hero."

Jackpot. I held my breath and didn't move. I even contemplated lifting my feet and rejected the idea, It would be humiliating if I fell off the john. I could go invisible, but if the women stayed in here a long time I'd be in trouble from the extended energy drain.

"You're jealous because he didn't show you his vegetarian sausages."

"Only you would call that flirting," Squeaky said. "I'm telling you, Mr. Oleander is not worthy of you or your cookies."

"That's Dr. Oleander to you, and I don't agree. He talks to me now. The cookies are working."

"He talks to you about autopsies. It isn't the same thing as him dating you."

Toilets flushed as the ladies exited their respective stalls, and then water splashed in the sinks. I hoped like anything they didn't notice my presence.

"At least he notices me. Dr. Dreamy never does," Pat said. "I used to fantasize about taking his glasses off so that he only saw me."

"He's got a live-in girlfriend now. You missed your chance with the ME."

In the Wick of Time

My eyes narrowed. She referred to Quig. My Quig. She'd hoped to date him? Not happening. The urge to zap her with laser-hot energy welled up like a July storm. *Easy does it.* From this overheard conversation, I surmised oleander fatally poisoned Loren Lee.

Once the room cleared, I finished and left the morgue. My phone chirped as soon as I stepped outside. Text messages from Quig. He had lunch for us at home. I texted a quick reply and hurried his way.

Were our biorhythms synchronizing? Or our auras? The longer we stayed together the more I sensed that intangible harmony. I'd never felt that before, except with Sage. Whatever the cause, our cohabitation prompted something energetically profound and new. And scary as all get out.

Chapter
Twenty-Four

Quig met me at the door with a rose between his teeth and all his everything showing. Thoughts of lunch vanished. I'd never dreamed of having such a close romantic connection to anyone, and yet Quig's currents interweaved with mine. His need for me felt as tangible as mine for him, and our vulnerability cut both ways.

After a lovely interlude, we ate deli sandwiches at the kitchen island, sitting side by side. I grinned as he wolfed his down. "Worked up an appetite, did ya?"

"I'm getting plenty of exercise these days, but that's not the whole story." He paused to drain his glass of water. "You make me feel so comfortable in my own skin, and I reach a deeper state of Zen around you."

Upon reflection his words described what I'd observed about myself. I touched his arm. "Me too. I mean, you do that to me as well."

"Good." He lifted my chin so that his eyes bored into mine. "Where were you this morning? Gerard said you went to help Sage, but when I called her she said you'd left a while ago."

Okay. Did not like his tone or his proximity while he made that accusation. Pulling away and defending myself seemed reasonable, but I shouldn't overreact. I had to make myself clear. I wouldn't stay on a short leash and constantly reassure him of his number one status in my world. He should trust me.

I flashed a smile, though his eyes narrowed, so it must have looked fake. His aura darkened. Oh, to heck with trying to finesse anything. I knew how appearances weren't always what they seemed. "Let me remind you I'm walking everywhere, so it takes me longer to get anywhere. However, after covering for Sage this morning at the tree booth, I detoured by the morgue to surprise you. That's why I didn't receive your messages right away. As you know, there are weak phone signals inside your building."

"Still, I worried about you. You're always quick to respond to my texts and calls. Not getting bored with me, I hope?"

"Quite the opposite. You're becoming so necessary I can't imagine doing without you." I stumbled mentally, groping for the right words. "You fill my heart, Quig."

He drew me into his lap, his fingers threading through my hair. "I have literally waited twenty years for you to say that. From the first moment I saw you, I knew we were meant to be. You're smart, beautiful, and kind. Tabby, you're everything I've ever dreamed of."

Overwhelmed and unable to speak, I kissed him. He kissed me back.

* * *

Since I showered first, I decided to check on Gerard in The Book and Candle Shop before I started my afternoon sleuthing. Quig promised he'd stop by the shop on his way to work. As I walked downstairs, I realized I'd have better luck snooping in Loren Lee's place with Sage, and that I might as well finish the workday in the shop. Sage and I could have an evening adventure.

Gerard took one look at my glowing skin and grinned. "Nice lunch?"

Heat rose to my cheeks. "The best."

His nod and raised eyebrows implied he wanted details. Not happening. I grabbed the duster and made a quick circuit around the shop, hitting the highlights. "How are you doing?" I asked airily.

Gerard glanced at me over the decimated display of dragon sculptures. "Healthy as a horse. There's so much I love about my squeeze."

I stopped futzing around. "I'm surprised in a good way. I had the impression that things were at a crossroads with you two. You didn't break up with him?"

"Heck, no. Ramon's a fab boyfriend as long as he keeps his jealousy in check."

"His possessiveness would be a deal breaker for me." Ugh. Quig shared that trait, but we'd figure it out. I shouldn't have mentioned possessiveness.

"Not all of us are destined to fall in love with our childhood sweethearts and have every day be a happily ever after. I'm lucky to have him."

Something about the way he said that last bit clanked in my ear. I wandered back to the sales counter, stowing the duster and focusing on my clerk. "He's never hurt you, has he?"

"Not the way you mean. He isn't violent, though his tongue can be wicked sharp."

I rested my hand on his shoulder. "Verbal abuse counts as abuse. I'm concerned for you, Gerard. Ramon hasn't always honored your best interests."

Quig interrupted us by entering the shop. I got a hug from my squeeze. "See you tonight," he said.

"About that." I cleared my throat. "Sage and I need some sister time tonight. Is that all right with you?"

"Of course. I'll make a late dinner for us." He took his leave.

"Be still, my beating heart," Gerard said, fanning his face. "That man has buckets of sex appeal. I see why you're with him now."

"I'm lucky. He's easy going."

"Umm. I don't know about that, Tabby. He's protective of you, but that's nothing new."

His words puzzled me. "And you know this how?"

"Sage said he's been looking out for you ever since you met, nearly two decades ago?"

"Something like that." We were friends as kids. Seemed like we'd always been friends, even though he hadn't made any romantic overtures until this year. I remembered him saying I wasn't ready until a few months ago. I didn't push him at the time to explain, because everything between us felt so new and fragile. I didn't want to jinx it. Still didn't want to rock the boat.

However, the biggest change to me in recent months occurred when I fully embraced my energy talents. Did he sense that? There were times when he acted like a sensitive, and others when he seemed oblivious to what Sage and I did with energy.

"Does he know you and Sage are snooping tonight?" Gerard asked.

"No. It isn't a secret, though I'd rather he didn't spend the evening worrying about us."

"Can I go with you?"

"I'm flattered and appreciate the offer, but no. You are MawMaw's main caretaker. If we get caught, we can't protect you. We're putting our lives and reputations on the line. What we're doing would be risky for you . . . and MawMaw."

Gerard changed the music to a moody and dramatic channel. "I hate it when you use logic on me. I only wanted to have fun."

"Fun is enjoying the holiday lights, seeing the luminaries and boat parade at the Festival of Lights, that kind of thing. Sage and I snoop alone because the added burden of what discovery might do to your life would break us. However, you're welcome to attend the luminary festival with Quig and me on Saturday night."

"I'll think about it. Ramon hasn't expressed interest in the luminaries."

Ugh. I didn't care for his boyfriend's sharp tongue. "To be crystal clear, Ramon is not invited."

"Ouch, but I get it."

"To change the subject, have you heard anything from Auntie O or Frankie?"

"Not a peep."

"I'm worried about them. Frankie's cousin might have extra resources to find their hiding place."

"For all his affability around the shop, Frankie has a solid core, and he grew up with people like his cousin. He's no marshmallow of a guy. He'll keep Oralee safe."

I didn't want her to be in danger, but darn it. I'd lost my mom this year. The holidays were a time for family gatherings, no matter if you were religious or not. I missed Auntie O. "I want them home for Christmas."

"Me too. Speaking of Christmas, we need more votives in your new scent. They're flying off the shelves. The inventory supplies you ordered arrived this morning while you were out."

"I'll make candles right now. Can't disappoint our customers."

In the Wick of Time

As I melted wax, added scents, and poured a double batch, I infused the candles with good energy, though I couldn't help wondering what we would find in Loren Lee's place tonight. I hoped to find a lead to his killer, and this would all be over.

Unfortunately, high hopes left a lot of room for human error.

Chapter
Twenty-Five

Sage and I parked a block away and skulked through the evening shadows to Loren Lee's house. My sister took only a minute with her lock pick to open the back door of the single-story cottage. "You're getting good at that," I said softly as we stepped inside the house. The refrigerator hummed softly in the background of a very quiet house.

"We all have our talents," she replied, closing the door gently so it didn't make a noise.

As if we were synchronized swimmers, we pulled out small penlight flashlights with our gloved hands, careful to keep the light beams aimed away from the windows. The air smelled stale in here. The indoor temperature felt brisk, so no need to remove our dark hoodies.

Sad to say, we had something of a knack for sneaking into people's homes. If we ever lost the shop, we had a new skill set and built-in wardrobe for our résumés. Hopefully, our investigative days should be a flash in the pan, and we'd return to normal soon, whatever the heck normal looked like now.

"What are we looking for, Madam Investigator?" Sage whispered.

Sometimes when I entered a space it felt happy. This kitchen felt brooding, pensive even. I couldn't tell if the sensation came from my anxiety level or if the emotion persisted from the former resident. I knew Sage hoped we wouldn't find anything bad about her erstwhile mentor here, but murder rarely happened for no reason at all.

With that in mind, I opened the nearest cabinet and saw a jumble of mixing bowls. "Anything that shows he interacted with someone other than you and Frankie. Phone records would be nice. A hidden safe would help because that would reveal what he valued, though neither of us knows how to crack a safe."

"I'll learn that skill next," Sage said. "There may even be a stethoscope in Mom's bathroom closet."

"I said it as a joke, but maybe this added skill set could turn us into private eyes."

"A safer career choice than a life of crime."

I glanced over my shoulder at my twin. "Why didn't he have a funeral? What about his family?"

"Sadly, I know about his lack of relatives." Sage closed the grimy oven she'd been examining and gave a tragic sigh. "His parents predeceased him, grandparents too, and he had no siblings. Is his body still at the morgue?"

"I didn't find out because Quig went home for lunch, and the new guy is a stickler for the rules." I pawed through a box of covered single-edged razor blades, expired coupons, twist ties, and every size of spatula known to man. Everything looked kitchen-drawer appropriate. No clues jumping up and down saying "pick me, pick me."

"I should hope not," Sage said, wryly. "I keep meaning to ask, are you doing all right over at Quig's place?"

"Never better." Bending, I studied the undercounter cabinet of mismatched pots and pans and then one of big bowls. Loren Lee's plates and dishes were an unappealing shade of gray, his drinking glasses a mash-up of old beer steins and mason jars. His coffee cups were chipped refugees from a thrift store.

Sage spoke from across the room. "Glad you took my advice about his necklace. I never see you without it."

"You gave good advice, but I wear it always because I treasure it. I love him, Sis."

"Figured your feelings ran deep. Here's the big question. Do you love him enough to bear his children?"

"Yes." I opened and closed the boring silverware drawer. "Do I seem different to you?"

Sage stopped. "You're already preggers?"

I turned to face her. "Not that. I am happy. He's the One. I'm a hundred percent certain. If he asked me to marry him today, I would say yes."

"His persistence won you over?"

"More like he fills all the empty places in my heart and soul. I've never experienced that before. I'm *more* with him."

When she didn't respond, I stood on tiptoes to open the over-the-refrigerator cabinet. Stacks of paper plates, plastic cups, paper towel rolls, and an unopened box of sugar-coated cereal. I closed the cabinet door and moved on.

"Sounds like he has his hooks in you," Sage said.

Her voice sounded strangled. I stopped searching and faced her again. "Trust you to describe Quig in a way that sounds creepy."

"Don't you feel a loss of identity? Don't you wish you could do whatever you wanted whenever you wanted?"

"That's not an issue. I don't feel lost in any way, and I can do what I want. Those questions sound like constraints you might have felt in a relationship. Why can't you be happy for me?"

She didn't answer for so long my skin prickled. "I don't know."

My emotions shifted into second gear in the next heartbeat. I backed into the kitchen counter. "What?"

Her hands tightened into fists. "You saw what happened when Brindle got charmed. What if Quig mesmerizes you? And he reinforces it every time he touches you."

"I would know. Trust me. My feelings for Quig are my own. My thoughts are my own. I am still me, a separate identity from him."

Sage drifted closer. "You always hurry home to him."

I finally understood. My relationship threatened her in some way, but to be sure I asked point blank. "Are you upset because I moved in with him?"

"No. Maybe. Okay, yes. I miss you. I know that makes me sound childish, and I should be handling it better. You deserve happiness after putting up with me and my moods all these years."

"I haven't *put up* with you any more than you've put up with me. I'm your sister, your twin. I want you to be happy same as you want my happiness. That hasn't changed. I'm only two doors down. For the record, Quig didn't replace you in my heart. There's room for both of you. He's expanding our family. My living with him isn't a disaster. I view it as a midstream course correction."

"Everything changed, Tabs." Sage shook her head sadly. "Mom's gone. Auntie O's gone. Now you're gone."

"Oh, Sage, honey, I am right here." I went to her and hugged her close. She wept softly in my arms, and my tears fell in empathy. I stroked her hair and surrounded her with loving energy.

My world narrowed to my sibling, the one person who knew me best. "You're not alone, Sage. I'm here. I will always be here for you, whether I have Quig or kids or whatever. I am forever your sister and best friend."

Sage let out sobs that welled up from deep inside. Perhaps we'd never grieved enough for Mom, but it sure felt good to free this pent-up emotion. Mom and Auntie O had always been our anchors. Now the two of us were adrift in the stream of life and learning the truth about adulting. Both concealed lots of warts and speed bumps.

"I believe you." Sage dashed her tears. "And I'm happy for you. It's about time you had romance in your life. I should've said that before now. I apologize for my pettiness. I know I always tease you that I'm the big sister, but I've known the whole time that you're the grounded one. You are the best of us."

"You're grounded in different ways than me, that's all. For instance, among the elements of air, earth, water, and fire, I'm earth. You're air. By their very definition, earth is tethered and air is free-floating. Neither element is better than the other. They're both unique. I don't have all the answers, but I can make more sister time for us."

"I would love more sister time." She squeezed me tight before stepping out of my arms and blotting her face with her sleeve. "My thoughts are mixed about the nursery job now. I love plants, but Loren Lee turns out to be the reason I enjoyed the nursery job. I detest Mary Nicole, and I don't respect Ms. Chatham for passing me over. I'm waffling on my future, and that is disorienting." She looked me straight in the eye. "I don't know what I want to be when I grow up."

"You want to know a secret?" Sage nodded, and I continued, "No one knows what they want to be. We do what we can, when we can. That's as good as it gets."

"I wish we were kids again. Life was simple then."

"Perhaps, but we didn't know how to control our talents. Now, we're happier when we use them, so that's what we must do. There's no going back to being kids again."

"And we have to live on Bristol Street."

"True. Does that bother you?"

"Actually, it doesn't. Bristol Street is home in a way nothing else has ever been, except for you. You are *home* too."

"Same for me."

"Wow, I didn't expect to cry like that, but I needed it," Sage said, gathering herself.

I dried my face. "Seems both of us needed that release. We need each other. We mustn't forget that."

"I'm so lucky to have you. If I'd been an only child, I couldn't have stood it when Mom and then Auntie O left. I don't know what I'd do if anything happened to you. I can't do this alone."

"Nothing's going to happen to me. However, right now we have a job to do. We're going to search this man's house to make sure nothing untoward happens to your future, got it?"

Sage let out a ragged breath. "Got it."

"All right. Let's finish the search and get the heck out of here."

"Roger that. I'll start in the living room and work back this way."

I'd missed our sister bond in recent days. I liked being her anchor and having Sage as mine. As I sifted through the relics of Loren Lee Suffield's life, he struck me as depressingly average. Nothing seemed remarkable, nothing seemed out of place, and certainly nothing seemed worth killing over.

Everything about this man's home echoed those soldier-straight lines of cans in his pantry. Everything had a place. But something nagged at me.

Something I'd seen didn't fit the pattern.

The cereal box.

Chapter
Twenty-Six

There were no cookies, cakes, or pies in this house. No mixes for those treats either. Loren Lee had a surplus of bottled peppers, pickles, and spices. Savory items. Nothing sweet.

I dashed to the refrigerator and retrieved the cereal box from the upper cabinet.

"What is it?" Sage asked behind me. "I heard you running. Did you find something?"

I shook the unopened box, and it sounded like cereal. And yet, this box had to be important. My intuition chimed like an insistent doorbell. "This cereal doesn't fit the pattern. Did you ever see him eat anything sweet?"

Sage looked puzzled in the thin light. "I didn't eat with the guy. We grew plants together. No desserts were involved."

"What about company parties? He ever eat cake or ice cream?"

"We didn't have company parties. I stayed busy all the time and never once ate lunch with him."

"Oh. Guess that's not unusual." Some of the air leaked from my sails. "Maybe I'm making something out of nothing. We don't have company parties at our shop either."

In the Wick of Time

"Because our family members and Gerard keep us afloat. We see each other and eat together all the time. Why did you get so excited about this cereal box?"

"It contains the only sweet in this kitchen. The man doesn't even have jelly in his refrigerator."

Sage snorted. "What a travesty. Imagine that." She studied the box again. "Open it. Loren Lee is dead. He won't mind."

"I want to, but we might be tampering with evidence if I'm right."

"Not our fault the cops missed it." Sage picked up the box and examined it. "I want to know what's inside."

"Let's think for a minute before we commit to ripping the box. What would Loren Lee hide in plain sight like this?"

"He didn't confide in me. He kept his own counsel."

I eyed the box with suspicion. "Something inside that box might be the motive for Loren Lee's murder."

"Or not. I'm going for it." Sage yanked a knife out of the butcher block and slid it under the bottom edge. "Somebody glued this sucker before. I can feel a thick bead of glue. Something important is inside, I just know it. You're brilliant, Tabs."

The box popped apart with no discernible damage. Loose papers and an unopened bag of cereal slid out when Sage hefted the box.

I stood beside my twin staring slack-jawed at the top page. A faded photo of a younger version of Frankie smiled at me. Yellowed newspaper clippings told of Frankie being the alleged wheelman for his mob family. Since this had been hidden, chances were Loren Lee used them to get leverage on Frankie.

A vise clamped down on my lungs. Loren Lee tried to shake Frankie down. But seeing the proof made it horribly real. I fought for a breath. "We don't want the cops to have this blackmail evidence.

Frankie can't return to his quiet, unassuming life if this becomes public knowledge."

"The cops may already know about it through their contacts, but everyone in Savannah doesn't have this level of detail. We should take it," Sage said. "Take it and burn it."

"Can't do that. It belongs here."

"You think Frankie killed my boss?" Sage asked.

Prior conversations with Frankie rolled through my head. "No. I doubt he'd know how to do it, anyway. Frankie never showed any interest in our stillroom where we grind up plants. He never said one word to me about plants. It's unlikely he'd distill a natural plant poison in his apartment without Auntie O's knowledge. He is very direct. If he wanted you dead, he'd come at you head-on. Repeated poisoning of a victim and a lingering death doesn't fit the man Frankie is today."

"Unless someone planted that evidence here for us to find."

"That's a possibility, but the clippings are yellowed with age. Loren Lee had a known interest in cold cases, so I believe they're his. Anything else in those papers, anything that incriminates someone else?"

Sage rifled through the pages. "Only other thing I see is this string of numbers penciled on the back of a page."

I took the page from her hand, shined my penlight on it. A nine-digit number. "What could this be? Too short for a phone number."

"Could be a Social Security number," Sage suggested.

"We have to put this stuff back. But first, I'll snap pictures of the pages, including the number sequence. While I do that, look for glue. Let's reseal this box and scratch off."

"Sure, but snap the pics in the bathroom so the cell phone flash isn't visible to anyone who is watching the house."

"Good idea."

I photographed the clippings and returned the pages to Sage in the kitchen. A bottle of a white glue sat on the counter next to her.

"Mary Nicole used to tell anyone who'd listen that Loren Lee had the hots for me, and that's why I got deferential treatment from him," Sage began slowly. "I never believed her. He respected my strong work ethic. Plus, he never gave me deferential treatment. If anything, I had a heavier workload than most because I'd get the work done. Mary Nicole never knew how much I did because, unlike her, I didn't run around complaining about my workload. However, now that I'm sitting in Loren Lee's bland house, I wonder about his passions. Besides plants, cold cases, and blackmailing Frankie, I mean. I'm getting a different picture of Loren Lee now."

"So much about him is still a mystery." My thoughts veered immediately to companionship. Hanging my clothing in Quig's closet is the first thing I did when I moved to his place. "There's no indication of a female occupant in this house from the closets or dresser drawers, no female products in the bathroom either."

"I noticed the same thing. Also, I checked the size of the male clothing I found. I recognized his work clothes, and everything else matched his size. So, no long-term sleepover friends of either gender."

"Unless his killer removed his or her belongings before killing Loren Lee, though I didn't see gaps in the closet or drawers."

"You know," Sage said as she stuffed the pages and cereal in the box and then glued it, "Loren Lee was a liar. There's not a single plant in this house, and the few in his yard are old stock. He has no recent plantings, no landscaping at all. That is odd. If I had this much land, I'd install hundreds of plants, inside and out. There'd be plants in every room of this house."

Very odd indeed. Sage had filled our apartment and shop with plants and herbs. Why didn't the man with the greenest thumb around have any plants at home? "I agree, and good catch. I didn't consider that aspect. We are a great team."

"Most definitely."

Carefully, I replaced the cereal box back in the upper cabinet. "With luck no one will know we were here."

We left through the back door. Nothing stirred in the starry night, not even a blade of grass. Then a car rolled slowly down the street. We hid behind a large palmetto cluster. Though we made minimal noise, a neighborhood dog barked. Others joined in. Lights flared in houses down the street.

Sage shot me a quick twin-link message. *Run!*

Chapter Twenty-Seven

My heart raced as we scurried though the shadows. Thanks to my invisibility talent, I drew energy from the shadows to blur the air around us. Even if someone saw us running away, we wouldn't be clear images. This kind of invisibility had the lowest energy drain because I didn't totally remove our images. I merely obscured them as we dashed through natural shadows.

Even so, I couldn't draw an easy breath until we returned to Sage's car undetected. We hunkered low in the seats until the dogs quieted, then we eased out of Loren Lee's neighborhood, free and clear.

"What a rush. I'm buzzed on adrenaline," Sage said, motoring through neighborhoods and zigzagging our way to Bristol Street.

With another glance over my shoulder to check for flashing police lights and finding none, I felt amazed that Sage knew her way through this maze of neighborhood roads. I'd never even been on some of these streets.

I focused on the road before us. "Remind me why we're breaking into places we shouldn't be and risking our necks."

"So neither Frankie nor I spend the rest of our days behind bars. We're doing this for the family, Sis. It's for a very good cause."

"Be that as it may, my heart nearly leaped out of my chest for a few minutes. I went from slight awareness of the danger to a full-throttle panic attack in the snap of a finger. Holy cow, I'm not used to this level of excitement."

"You're fine, and we're both safe, plus we discovered two facts about Loren Lee. Well, one fact really. His life was fake, just like him. Since those clippings were concealed, he hid them and likely blackmailed Frankie. He didn't have a true passion for growing plants. Though I respected him at the time, I feel betrayed to my marrow. Loren Lee pretended to be a high-caliber person, but he played everyone."

"I'm discouraged as well. It's easy to forget people show us a fraction of who they are. Case in point, most people don't know our true nature. As for Loren Lee, he had dark secrets, and they colored our perception of him. Perhaps his alleged passion for plants came through his passion for a paycheck. Since you love working with plants, your passions temporarily aligned."

"I'm uncomfortable talking about Loren Lee and passions. If you're right, he used me like a straw horse to make the other employees feel like slackers. How did I not see this? If he'd berated me the way he did the others, I'd have quit in a lightning flash."

I warmed to my theme as Sage pulled into her parking slot. "My rationale makes sense. He kept you highly motivated by overloading you with work. Because he rewarded you with work you loved, you hustled to fill your assignments. He chastised the others for being slackers, but he never gave them enough tasks to stay busy. They enjoyed complaining about him and didn't worry about getting fired. The man's Machiavellian strategy suited everyone."

Sage banged the steering wheel with her hand. "He used everyone. He deceived us. The nursery employees endured his verbal abuse, and he blackmailed Frankie. He was evil."

"I agree, but I saw you working with him. Your compatibility felt genuine. He respected your natural affinity for plants. Anyone could see that."

"My desire to please him temporarily blinded me, that's my excuse. But not any longer. He used people, and if I could erase his memory in my head I would. He manipulated me, and I won't kill myself working for another controlling boss."

I listened to her vent, but I knew the truth. Sage could fuss all she liked. She had enjoyed working at the nursery under Loren Lee. Soon as she calmed down, she'd realize that good came with the bad.

My thoughts darted to Mary Nicole. She manipulated people, but she lacked Loren Lee's finesse. Plus, she would self-destruct without the nursery workhorse to carry the load. From what I'd observed, Mary Nicole would fail if she forced Sage out. Then Ms. Chatham would have to restaff her business, if it hadn't already foundered.

I sighed out a long breath of relief at having returned home safely from our snooping. "Did Loren Lee have a will? What happens to his estate?"

"Don't know and don't care. Something should be done with his house, but that's not my problem."

"The will could be relevant, especially if someone on our suspect list inherited, but I'm sure the cops are chasing that lead." The gears in my mind whirled. "I'll ask Quig if his body is still in the morgue. I'm frustrated our snooping tonight didn't reveal his killer. Truthfully, I'm ambivalent about most of our suspects. I have the sense we're in that fraught lull between washing machine cycles. Not quite in limbo, but not truly in motion either."

"Speaking of limbo, Brindle called this afternoon. He's getting released from the hospital tomorrow and asked me for a lift."

I shot her a speculative look, remembering how she'd spent a wild night with Frankie's cousin. "Is that wise? Didn't you recently, er, move on?"

Sage punched me in the shoulder. "That didn't count. Brindle needs a friend. I'm his best friend. Don't know if I'll be his girlfriend again, even after he overcomes this peculiar trouble. He needs to be himself before I make that decision. Alyss is no longer in his life, so she isn't a threat."

"Let's hope." I rubbed the sting from my shoulder. "Don't take this the wrong way, but why didn't Brindle call his parents or law partners to come get him?"

"His parents moved to Arizona earlier this year to be near his sister and her kids. Brindle doesn't want his law partners to see him when he's weak. He's already afraid his strange conduct will prompt them to force him out of the partnership."

The dimly lighted parking space faintly illuminated her car, reminding me of when we'd shared a bedroom as kids and would climb into bed together for late night talks. Those shared confidences were the best. "I wish we knew what spell Alyss used, but she's a dead end. What happened after you sprinkled Brindle with MawMaw's holy water?"

"I couldn't tell any difference, but the nurses say he quit hitting on all of them. I surmise that it's working."

I hoped Brindle could get on with his life. "With Frankie, Auntie O, and you out of The Book and Candle Shop's shift rotation, Gerard is handling a lot of weekdays solo, and I'm covering both weekend days solo. That hasn't left any time for holiday planning or shopping. I haven't even thought about Christmas presents. I have no idea what to get Quig for a gift."

"Tie a red bow on yourself. He'll like that."

Heat suffused my face. "Probably, but my goal is a wrapped present under our tree. I need time to shop before Christmas, but I'm super busy until then."

"Gift-giving isn't compulsory, you know. I'm skipping Christmas this year, so don't buy me a gift. It's been a crappy year, and I'll be thrilled when it's gone."

"You don't mean that. Why don't we shop downtown tomorrow evening when the luminaries are in full swing and the stores are open late?"

"Can't. I'm working an extended shift at the nursery booth during the nighttime festival. Mary Nicole will surely visit and find fault no matter what."

"If she's there, I'll analyze her aura to learn more about her."

"Now you're talking. Will Quig fuss about you taking two sister nights in a row?"

"I'm multitasking. Quig and I plan to attend the festival. I'll check out Mary Nicole's aura and keep an eye on you."

"Now who's the control freak?"

I caught her hand before she punched me again. "Takes one to know one."

Chapter
Twenty-Eight

O ut on the shop floor, Gerard chatted with our Friday customers, as I finished wrapping bar soaps I'd made in my new Savannah Sunshine scent. Carefully, I tucked two in my purse as Christmas gifts for Quig.

"What's going on?" I asked my sister when she marched in the stillroom with Brindle hard on her heels. I had a sinking feeling I knew why they were here. She intended to leave Brindle with me.

Sage looked militant, as if she expected a fight. "Brindle and I talked it over. Neither of us thinks he should go home. Since we believe Alyss deliberately caused his problems, who knows what other mischief she wrought at his place? He runs the risk of falling under her control again and returning to the psych ward. That would be bad. He needs time to recover completely, so he's staying upstairs with me. That way, someone he trusts will be in earshot. Okay if he bunks in your old room?"

Brindle jerked a thumb toward Sage. "What she said, if it's not too big of an ask."

He looked good for someone who'd been locked in a psych ward. Those dark circles under his eyes would vanish when he got solid sleep. His pale skin could be a function of reduced sunlight in winter. Best of all, his energy looked right. Nothing appeared warped or deadened in his aura.

"You're welcome to stay in my former room." I gestured to the counter of ingredients behind me but continued softly so only Sage could hear. "We keep selling out of products. This is me restocking the shop. Bottom line, I'm too busy to watch over anyone."

Sage shrugged and spoke in a normal tone. "He's fine now. It's quiet upstairs, and he'll sleep all day. Being at the waterfront booth with me wouldn't be restful. You don't have to keep an eye on him. He's potty trained."

"Not funny," Brindle and I said at the same time.

The wry smile he sent my way reminded me I'd always been comfortable around Brindle. "Whatever y'all decide is fine with me. I'll be right here."

"Thanks," Brindle said. "Definitely need to crash, and I can't afford to lose my marbles again."

"I understand."

As they climbed the interior apartment stairs, I sent Sage a message on our twin-link. *The holy water must've worked. Brindle didn't hit on me.*

He didn't hit on me either.

That's good, right? That's what you wanted.

Maybe.

It's not like you to waffle once you've made up your mind.

It's easier to be mad at him when he's not around. He looks lost and tired. I want to hug him and nap with him. If my job felt secure, I'd play hooky today.

Another tide is turning. What happened to the sister who wanted to rub her colossal tree booth success in Mary Nicole's face?

I had a reality check. I've been in a pressure cooker all month, and I despise that feeling. I need a beach week to regain perspective, but I can't take off.

I hear you. I'm feeling pressure about our first major holiday as a couple, and I need to collect my share of ornaments for our tree. I'm frustrated by our investigation. On top of that, I truly want Auntie O and Frankie to come home.

Let's bake cookies tonight, the four of us. That should help us feel like a family.

You have baking ingredients up there?

Auntie O planned to bake cookies for the masses, and she likes my oven better than her new one, so she laid in baking supplies up here. We're good.

*   *   *

The day passed in a flurry of holiday shoppers. At one point, I went through the stack of mail and saw the phone bill. I thumbed past it, then I decided to pay it right away so it didn't get misplaced during December. One perk of owning this business is that our cell phones came under the umbrella of the business.

Though Sage did nearly all our electronic banking, I knew how to pay the phone bill. Rotely, I tore the envelope open and scrolled through the call records. The calls were listed by phone number: mine, Sage's, and Auntie O's.

A virtual light bulb flashed brightly in my head. When Auntie O left for Florida a few months ago, we'd kept her phone on the shop plan. Most of the November and early December calls for her number were to family numbers, but the day before she left, there were two calls to a number I didn't recognize.

I plugged the number into a search engine. It didn't tell me the name associated with the account, only showed it as linked to an

Orange County, Florida, area code. That's Orlando's county. Did Auntie O and Frankie return to Orlando to hide out?

Only one way to find out. I punched in the number on my phone, and the call rolled straight to voice mail. Nothing to lose by leaving a message. When I heard the prompt, I said, "Hi, this is Tabby Winslow. I'm Oralee Colvin's niece in Savannah. She called this number before she left town, so I'm hoping you know how to reach her. Thank her for the letter. We're fine here, and I'm conducting my own investigation. Please tell my aunt we love her and miss her. Thank you."

Gerard poked his head in the stillroom. "Got a minute?"

"Sure."

He handed me a small paper bag. "MawMaw told me to pick this up for you."

My curiosity rose when I peeked in the bag. "A candle?"

"Weird, huh? Giving a candle to a candlemaker, but this one is special. This should burn completely beside Sage's boyfriend. MawMaw says whatever Alyss did to him will most likely be lifted by this candle. Except the candle can't be blown out. It must burn completely."

I looked in the bag again. Judging by the candle's small size, it would likely take three or four hours to burn. That would work. "Thanks. He's staying with Sage for now. We'll burn it tonight. What's with the two colors of wax?"

"It has to do with the enchantment on Brindle, but I can't explain it. I never learned the ins and outs of people who cast bad juju. Didn't want to know. I saw how tired it made MawMaw to counteract it, and how much time it took from our family. People always wanted something, and with her soft heart, she helped everyone who asked."

I understood his concern. If the energetic community knew I shared energy so freely, I'd be bombarded with requests and run out of juice every day from constant demand. That wouldn't bode well for my longevity. Mom helped a cancer patient by sharing energy daily, and while the constant recharging helped her friend initially, the end came swiftly, for the cancer patient and then for Mom, who'd pushed her limits too often.

I flashed a smile at Gerard. "Don't apologize for being yourself. Everyone walks a different path. Though Sage and I are twins, we are nothing alike. You aren't your grandmother or either of your parents."

"Thank God for that."

"Say, I'm caught up in here. You mind if I step out for the last hour? Got some holiday shopping that needs attention."

"Go for it."

* * *

That evening, Brindle, Sage, Quig, and I baked gingerbread people and chocolate chip cookies. Brindle didn't fuss about burning the black and red candle, and he sat near it as it burned, as requested.

Quig had a certain way of doing things—the right way, he informed us. After that we nominated him the boss of the cookie baking, and everything ran smoothly.

"Where is the she-cat who did this to me?" Brindle asked as he wiped down the countertops.

Sage looked at me with something akin to panic in her eyes. *Tell him*, she urged. *It shouldn't come from me.*

I nodded. "If you mean Alyss Carter, Sage and I saw her a few days ago at her home."

"She didn't weasel her way back into the law firm?"

"Not that we know of." I handed the dried cookie sheet to Sage for her to put away and reached for the big mixing bowl.

"What happened during my hospital stay?"

"Loren Lee died of poisoning. His death was a homicide." Sage said. "I got hauled in for questioning because of my proficiency with plants."

"Did an attorney from my firm represent you?"

"Not this time. I used Quig and Tabby's lawyer, Herbert R. Ellis."

Brindle shook his head. "This health crisis is costing me big-time. Now Ellis is poaching my clients."

"He got me because you were repping Gerard in the last murder case. Not anyone's fault," I added. "No client stealing involved. If you remember. Quig set it up for me. Then I hooked Sage up with Herbert when you were indisposed."

Brindle snorted and leaned against the refrigerator. "Indisposed? What a crock. I would never take pills or lose my marbles like the doctors say happened. Alyss changed me somehow. I improved because I trust Sage and no one else."

"We're not sure how you became *indisposed*, but Sage and I believe you were purposefully afflicted. Whatever the means taken, Alyss had designs on you. That's why my sister sprinkled you with holy water and why we're burning this candle tonight. We're removing whatever spell she used."

"Alyss Carter caught me unaware, but I won't fall for that again. To set the record straight, I am not attracted to her. Not now and not before. Never, in fact."

"We think she acted independently, but she might be a pawn in a larger scheme. Nothing in recent events is as it seems, not even Loren Lee, the murder victim."

"What do you mean?" Brindle asked. "Is my mental health issue pertinent to the homicide case?"

"Possibly. The case isn't straightforward. Loren Lee lied about everything, for starters," Sage said. "Secondly, he acted like a troll to most of his employees. Lastly, he fooled me about his interest in plants. I don't even know why he worked at the nursery."

We finished stowing everything away. "Who killed him?" Brindle asked Sage.

"Don't know yet. My coworker, Mary Nicole, benefits directly from his absence. She became the nursery's interim assistant manager. The police sweep for Loren Lee's killer put me and Frankie through the wringer. Me for my knowledge of herbs and plants, and Frankie for his shared interest in cold case files. There's also a former nursery manager, Chris Kachuba, who got wigged out when Loren Lee fired her. And there's Ms. Chatham, the nursery owner. Maybe she got tired of the man's lies. Lord knows she'd been married to a liar with a wandering eye, and she has zero tolerance for lies now."

"What do you mean, Sage?" I asked. "What did her husband lie about?"

"I didn't know him, but he cheated on her, cheated his employees, and more."

"Not a nice guy."

"Nope. Maybe that's why he hired Loren Lee." Sage shivered. "They were two of a kind."

Brindle turned to me. "Where are Frankie and your aunt?"

"Don't know," I said as Quig dried his hands and stood behind me. He began massaging my neck, and I sighed contentedly. "They bolted at the first sign of trouble and didn't tell us diddly squat."

"I missed a lot. One murder suspect is on the lam, while the rest are sitting tight." Brindle scratched his head. "What poison killed him?"

"Oleander," Sage said.

Quig leaned over my shoulder, pinning my twin with his intent gaze. "How do you know that?"

"Tabby told me."

Quig stared through me.

He didn't intimidate me. I shrugged with upraised palms. "I came by the information fair and square. I overheard bathroom talk at the morgue. Two ladies entered the restroom and didn't realize they weren't alone. They gossiped about your new hire. From that discussion, I surmised oleander killed Loren Lee. You confirmed it."

"We need to institute a no-talking-in-the-bathroom policy at this rate." Quig glared at us. "That information cannot go beyond this room, or there'll be hell to pay. The police are not releasing that information."

Go get 'em tiger, Sage cackled on our twin-link. *Who knew mild-mannered Quig had so much fiery passion. Wondered what you saw in him, but now I see he has plenty of spark.*

Keep your mitts off Quig, Sis. He's mine.

No worries on my account. That man only ever had eyes for you.

"Ready to go home?" Quig asked.

I smiled up at him with adoration. "Let's go."

Chapter
Twenty-Nine

On Saturday morning, Quig and Brindle left early to run holiday errands, Sage walked downtown to work in the tree booth, and I soloed in the shop. People flowed in, busloads of them it seemed. Candles, soaps, wind chimes, and sculptures departed in record numbers.

My Savannah Sunshine candles sold out in the first hour. Three of our regulars came looking for them, and it hurt to tell them they were out of stock. I sold a few perennial favorites to those customers, and two said they'd come back next week for the real deal. I told the disappointed customers that I'd call them as soon as I made more.

I gazed longingly at the peace and serenity of my stillroom, those robin's egg blue walls calling to me. I needed to be in there making more candles right now, but I couldn't spare the time it took, and my troubled thoughts weren't optimal for candlemaking. Creating a bad batch would be worse than having none.

Been there, done that.

If only we had another person in the shop. Someone who could work a weekend day and possibly a few weekly shifts. But who? How would I find that someone? How could I spare the time to train him or her?

Customers came and went in waves. At one point, I had a line of customers waiting to check out. One man set down his full shopping basket and walked out. That did it. Our staffing issue couldn't be ignored any longer.

Soon as I had a break at the register, I stepped into the still-room and phoned Gerard. "I'm drowning in here," I said when he picked up. "Customers are walking out because I can't serve them fast enough. I know you're off on the weekends, but is there any way you could come in for a few hours today?"

"Ooh. Terrible timing. MawMaw and I are in South Carolina this weekend visiting distant cousins. Even if I started driving back right now, by the time I got MawMaw settled, I wouldn't arrive before closing."

Drat. "Do you know anyone who could come in on short notice? We can't continue running on a shoestring like this. I should've thought ahead about adding another hire, but we've never been so short-staffed over the holidays before."

"I might know someone. Let me check and call you back."

The call ended. "Miss? I'm looking for the lip balm you carry," a woman my age said from just inside the doorway. "The cardboard display is empty. Do you have more in here?"

I recognized her in a heartbeat. The way Chris Kachuba eyed my stillroom creeped me out. I moved toward the redhead, herding her back into the public area by virtue of walking her backward. "I'll check. Give me a few minutes."

My herding tactic worked. A man stood at the counter now. He glanced around the other customer. "Do you have any history books in this store?"

"We specialize in books about Savannah. Most of our selection is nonfiction." I walked him over to the shelves. "Is there a particular book you're looking for?"

"Something she doesn't already have," he said glumly.

"Browse a bit, and I'll check on you in a few minutes."

He selected a book, and I hurried to the woman who wanted lip balm. Chris. Should I pretend I didn't know her? Not my forte, but whatever it took to make a sale. "One second. I'm sure we have more lip balm."

I knew we did because Brenda of Brenda's Bees had stopped in last weekend to bring extra inventory of her specialty lip balms. Sure enough, a carton perched on the supply closet shelf. I brought the entire package out to the counter. Chris purchased four on the spot, and other customers nipped in and grabbed items from the box in what reminded me of a shark feeding frenzy.

A soccer mom took six unrepentantly. "These are great for Christmas stockings. I love that they are all natural, too."

"You remember me?" Chris asked as I rang up her purchases.

"I do. My sister and I tried to ask you a few questions about Loren Lee and you said no."

"Small world, isn't it?" Chris smiled weakly. "I didn't want to be rude the other day, but I don't want anything to do with that man or the nursery."

"Where did you work after the nursery?"

Her eyes widened in alarm. "I, um, came into a small inheritance, and I've been helping a relative in recent months."

I couldn't detect lies, but to my untrained ears it sounded like the truth. Odd, though, how she studied me. "Family has to stick together."

She nodded and handed me her credit card. It felt gritty, but the transaction processed without a hitch. I didn't know what else to say to her. Her height looked to be same as mine, though she looked twenty pounds lighter. She didn't seem like a stone-cold killer, but what did I know?

"Yes. My aunt and I have grown close lately." Chris gave a tragic sigh worthy of a stage actor. "The world is a cruel place. People are always trying to beat you down, trying to take what's yours."

I thought of Alyss Carter and her play for Sage's guy. "I hear you." I handed back her card. "Thanks for stopping in."

She left, and I got too busy to think about anything. When I had a slight break in the action, I texted Brenda that I could sell more of her lip balm if she had more ready. She texted back she'd bring another carton before closing today. Whew. That worked out.

Gerard texted me next. *My cousin Eve is on her way to help you. She's in college and looking for part-time work. The last place she worked had a similar software program for the register. She should fit in seamlessly.*

Thanks! I texted back. *Just went through everything we had of Brenda's Bees. It's crazy busy in here. Almost unnatural.*

As in someone's compelling people to buy from our shop? Cool. Let's figure out how to do that year 'round.

I sold five wind chimes today.

Wowsa. I don't remember moving that many of those in one day, ever. One sec.

I checked out another customer before Gerard sent another text. *MawMaw says to look for something that doesn't belong in the shop, something that's been added.*

What on earth?

She thinks magic is at work again. If you want to cancel the effect, remove the item causing the problem. Don't touch it with your bare hands, though.

Now you're worrying me.

You should be worried. Someone spelled your shop. If you can't find it, Eve will.

Because?

It's an interest of hers.

Oh joy. I'd jumped into the fire with hiring and training someone on the same day, but having extra help would relieve my stress. Her unused skill set didn't bother me. We could always reassess later when things weren't so hectic.

My stomach growled. Lunchtime came and went. Still no sign of Gerard's cousin.

I surveyed the shop with pride as people strolled the aisles, checking out customers as they were ready. Nothing I saw on our shelves looked extra or charmed, though Gerard had a good point about leaving the charm alone. We needed the business.

Whenever I had a reprieve at the register, I brought out a box of merchandise from the supply closet. The same feeding-frenzy effect occurred. As I unpacked a box on the counter, customers gathered round and nearly fought over the items, whether they were statues, chimes, lotions, candles, you name it. If I unpacked it, those items sailed out the door as purchases.

Just when I thought the day couldn't get any stranger, in walked the man in black, Frankie's cousin, Vito Morelli.

Chapter Thirty

I created an energy barrier immediately. Vito's energy hit mine full force, slamming into it, trying to bust through. I held strong as he oozed up to the other side of the sales counter. "You're not welcome here," I said. "I didn't invite you in."

"It's not your home, and you're open for business, sexy," he said. "Thus, I am here."

I'd hoped the invitation thing would keep him out. Popular folklore held that vampires had to be invited in, and that should count for energy vamps as well. Hmm. I tried another tactic. "Get over yourself. You can't hypnotize me."

The energy vampire doubled his attack on my aura. A young woman with tattooed arms came up to the counter. "May I use the bathroom?"

I managed to say, "We don't have a public restroom. You might try across the street at Southern Tea."

"You're different," Vito said as the woman left, and he dropped his guard. "Not impulsive like your sister. More strategic."

Flattery would get him nowhere. I wanted him gone. "There's nothing for you here. Go away."

Vito surveyed the room with an assessing smile. "So much energy here. So much compulsion in the air. Oooh, how I love a challenge."

He turned around, and I used the opportunity to help him along toward the door. He didn't resist my energy shove at all. However, my customers gazed at Vito in rapt adoration as if he were the second coming. They moved in lockstep with him. The door opened, and Vito left. Every customer in the shop followed him.

"How did that happen?" I asked the walls. "This is the strangest day of my life." Glad for the temporary reprieve, I locked the door, posted the back-in-ten-minutes sign, and dashed home to make a quick tuna sandwich, which I brought back to the stillroom to eat. What I wouldn't give for a gallon of iced tea.

Next, I heard pounding on the front door. I groaned at the insistent knocking. Probably not Gerard's cousin with such a heavy hand. Quickly brushing the bread crumbs from my hands and mouth, I crossed the shop and unlocked the door. My two least favorite people in the whole world stood there. Detectives Nowry and Belfor.

Nowry shoved a set of papers in my hand. "Tabby Winslow, as Oralee Colvin's next of kin, you are hereby notified of this official warrant to search her premises immediately."

"What?" I sputtered. Had the entire world gone crazy? Not a full moon in sight, and not Halloween either, so why couldn't I wrap my head around this twist of fate?

"We're searching her residence as that is also the home of Frankie Mango, a person of interest in an ongoing homicide investigation."

Belfor sniffed the shop air. "It always smells divine in here, as if you've bottled liquid paradise. I'll select a few Christmas gifts here when we're done with the search warrant."

An all-purpose visit. Oh, goodie.

In the Wick of Time

I watched them leave with dread dwelling in my heart. I hated them snooping in Auntie O and Frankie's home. I needed to observe the process; otherwise, how would I know if they found something incriminating?

A young woman bopped in with a drink carrier with two super-sized beverages. She wore a form-fitted Christmas-colored batik dress and platform flip-flops. A festive scarf held her thick braids back from her face. Her aura felt healthy, and good energy surrounded her. "I'm Eve. Gerard said you needed help and that you needed this iced tea."

"Welcome, Eve." With that kind of service, she had the job already. I took the proffered cup and sipped deeply. "I can't thank you enough for coming in on such short notice."

We discussed pay and hours. Her expression tightened a bit. "Gerard said you needed someone for weekends and occasional shifts during the week. I have to work around my classes at Armstrong, but I need the money. My last boss kept changing my schedule on short notice, and twice he summoned me to work during class time. I hated the crappy uniform there and the erratic hours, so I quit that job."

"No uniforms here. Anything goes so long as your attire covers all the important body parts. What you wore today is fine. I am in a bind and will take whatever hours you can spare. For starters, can you work the rest of today as well as tomorrow afternoon?"

"Yes." She glanced around the empty shop. "Where are your customers? Gerard said they were coming out of the woodwork. Did you toss the anchor item already?"

My brows rose. Gerard had filled her in on everything, it seemed. "I couldn't find it. What happened to the customers will sound very strange."

Interest sparkled in her brown eyes. "Try me."

I froze momentarily, hoping that I wouldn't scare her off. "A powerful man came in and led them all away."

"Like the Pied Piper?" Eve burst out laughing. "This is my kind of shop. No wonder Gerard stayed with this place. The energy's great and the goings-on are interesting."

I drew in a deep breath. Thank goodness she didn't charge out the door when I explained our sudden dearth of customers. "Let's run through how the register operates while we have a few minutes."

Twenty minutes later, we'd covered everything, plus I moved the morning's register take and receipts into the supply closet safe. I'd also drained my jumbo tea, and the caffeine energized me. "Thanks for bringing this tea. On a scale of one to ten, how comfortable are you with holding down the fort alone for ten to twenty minutes?"

"Guess I'm about a seven. Nothing seems too hard. What's up?"

I grimaced because I planned to tell her the truth, and she likely wouldn't take it well Eccentricity in a boss might strike some as strange, but being a murder suspect pushed credence too far. "The cops are up in my aunt's apartment next door right now, searching for a murder weapon. Someone poisoned my sister's boss, and the cops think my aunt's boyfriend killed him."

"Wow. For real?"

"The search warrant is real, but Frankie isn't the killer. I don't know who committed the murder. My aunt and Frankie are hiding out, and I'm worried about them." I paused to gauge her reaction. Eve didn't seem horrified. "If this is more than you bargained for, I understand. Normally there's not so much high drama around here, but with the holidays and the murder, we've hit a new high of unusual events."

Eve grinned. "I love drama. I'll find your trickster piece if you like, but if it's boosting sales, maybe you should let it be."

"Whatever you decide." The door chimed and our regular group of SCAD students flooded in. Blue Hair waved at Eve. "You know her?" I whispered to Eve.

"Sure. That's Fawn Meldrim. We attended the same youth camp for a coupla summers. Gerard says she's got the hots for him."

"Gerard's right. Her group stops in every weekday and some weekends. They hang out in the book nook, and I'm fine with that. I know what it's like to be different."

"Got it."

"Also, one of my consigners, Brenda Wartina, who makes our Brenda's Bees products, is stopping by this afternoon with more inventory. Sign off on her inventory sheet after checking off what she brought." I pulled out a white binder. "We keep this notebook of printed product codes under the register. Vendors have tabs. Place bar code stickers on the matching items before you set them on the shelves."

"Ooh. I need some of her lip balm. What kind of employee discount do I get?"

"Fifteen percent for new sales associates on regularly priced items. If you are here in two months, we'll bump you up to twenty percent."

Eve stuffed the binder under the counter and pointed to our music system. "What about music?"

"Gerard likes pop. I prefer instrumental. Keep it light and upbeat and dial the music volume to background levels. Customers should be able to converse over the music or hum along if that suits them. I need to check on my aunt's place. My cell number is taped to the register if you need me."

"I got this."

I believed her. I hurried out the back door and stumbled into a hornet's nest of police officers. Detective Nowry stood in the alley holding court to a bunch of uniforms. I couldn't tell if that boded well or not. Mostly I wanted them to go away empty handed.

I mounted the stairs hoping to go unnoticed. A patrol officer guarded Auntie O's door. "You can't enter right now," he said.

With my five foot four height I had to gaze around him from where I stood on the landing. Fingerprint dust coated every surface. Items looked out of place. I groaned aloud. "They just moved in here. My aunt will be steaming mad at what you've done to her brand new home."

The officer shrugged. "Nature of the beast."

"Who cleans this up?"

"Not us," the cop said.

Where was Mary Poppins when you needed her? "This is bull. You can't treat people like this."

"This is how it's done."

I growled, but the officer didn't react. Then Detective Belfor padded to the door and motioned to her colleague below. "Nowry. Up here."

Detective Nowry breathed heavily as he passed me. If he said anything or tried to force me to leave, I'd do more than growl. A few minutes later he walked out with Auntie O's shoebox of photos from her brief stint in Orlando, the city where she met Frankie.

"You can't keep those," I said. "Those belong to my aunt. You found those in her bedroom. She is not a suspect."

"Our warrant covers the entire premises, ma'am," the officer said.

Dark thoughts clouded my mind at this intrusion. My fingertips tingled with current, but I managed to avoid blasting cops with energy spears. Instead, I scrubbed my temples with those hands. It upset me that they could take my aunt's personal possessions. The warrant may give them the right to search, but there's no way those photos had anything to do with oleander extract. How much would it cost if I sicced my attorney Herbert R. Ellis on them just on general principles?

Brindle sauntered out to the alley landing atop Sage's stairs. "What's going on?"

"Search warrant," I said.

"Good grief."

Brindle knew the law. In all the commotion, I'd forgotten he spent the day in Sage's apartment. "Hold up. I'm coming over." I charged down Auntie O's steps and dashed up Sage's. "Can they take stuff from Auntie O's room if Frankie is the person they're after?"

"They can, though they should hand you an inventory list of what they removed before they leave. Unless the item proves relevant to the prosecution of the killer, you'll get the items back in due time."

I didn't like that answer. My nose tingled as if I were about to sneeze. "They created a mess inside that apartment. Everything is coated in fingerprint dust."

"Works best to hire a pro to clean up."

"Don't know any pros."

"I do," Brindle said. "I'll make a call, though this service is pricey."

"We'll pay whatever it costs. I don't want Auntie O to come home to that supersonic mess in there." I hiccupped and panicked. Did not want to look down and be invisible. I cupped my hands and breathed into them. *Not now.*

"Tabby, are you all right?"

I couldn't get home from here without discovery, not with the cops milling in the alley and on Auntie O's stairs. The new shop clerk would freak if I trotted my invisible self in there. I couldn't stay here either. Someone would notice my condition. I had to hide.

"Need to use the bathroom. Excuse me." I twisted past him and darted into Sage's bathroom. Hiccups came fast and furious as I strobed in and out of sight.

Chapter
Thirty-One

B rindle banged on the bathroom door a while later. "You all right in there?"

I hiccupped again, faded again as I waited on the floor for a miracle. My fingers curled into the fluffy bathmat in frustration. "Just a few more minutes. Some bathroom visits can't be rushed."

He snorted. "Just so long as you're alive in there. You got pale as a sheet out there."

Yikes! He must've seen the start or end of a fade. "Low blood sugar and the hiccups, that's all."

"You're on your own for the hiccups, but I know what to do for low blood sugar. I'll pour you some orange juice and leave it on the counter."

His words alarmed me. "You're leaving?" Another hiccup racked my body. I leaned against the tub, knees close to my tummy.

"No such luck. Just grabbing clean clothes and changing in your old room."

I took a few more minutes to focus my energy and finally banished the hiccups. When I emerged from the bathroom as a visible human being, a super-sized tumbler of orange juice awaited me. Sage would be upset if I drank all her juice. I poured most of it back in the carton and then chugged the last third.

"You look better," Brindle said when he emerged in black jeans and a loose-fitting white dress shirt. He'd even combed his hair and put on shoes. I'd always thought he looked like a Renaissance warrior or something, and his clothes enhanced that image.

I grinned. "So do you. What about the inside of your head?"

"Far as I know it's brighter in there too. I can't thank you and Sage enough for letting me stay here. I'm feeling like myself again."

"And your vision? Every woman still look like Sage?"

"The effect varies. Feels like something between a brain short circuit and a hallucination," he said. "Got to the point where I learned not to mention any visual disturbance at the hospital. That's how I got out of there. I lied about still having issues."

"Sage and I think you got spelled by someone who bends magic for self-serving purposes. The holy water spritzer of a few days ago and the candle burning from last night must have dialed back the effect, but I bet you'd love to permanently get rid of the spell."

"You know how?"

I hoped he didn't freak out. "I don't, but a friend of the family is helping us figure it out. Lest I forget, let me introduce you to our new shop clerk, Eve. And before you ask, she looks nothing like Sage."

He grinned. "Good to know."

* * *

Eve took a long look at Brindle after the introduction and clucked derisively. "Who'd *you* cross?"

He shrugged. "Could be anyone. I just want my problem gone."

A crowd of customers milled about in The Book and Candle Shop, and the shop buzzed with conversation. While I loved having shop income, the glut of customers felt surreal. Why weren't all these people getting ready for the Festival of Lights in a few hours?

Eve waved Brindle to the back counter. "Let me see if I can help. Please, join me over here. Empty your pockets."

Amazed that he complied, I stepped in her place at the register to start checking out our next customer. I greeted the woman and said all the right things as I worked, but I also kept my senses tuned to what happened behind me.

Eve picked up each of Brindle's items in turn, muttered under her breath as she made a few hand gestures, and then handed everything back to him. "These are good now."

I glanced over in time to see Brindle stiffen. "Just like that?" he said. "I've lost days of my life, the respect of my peers, and with merely a few words you made my issue vanish?"

"It's not rocket science. You should feel like yourself now."

Brindle's hand went to his temple, as if it hurt his head to process what she said. When I looked closely, his aura pulsed normally. Eve had done what the rest of us could not do.

"Trust her," I said before turning around to finish the transaction.

The customer left, and Brindle whooped with joy. I heard Eve's startled gasp, then Brindle mugged me, though I couldn't respond to the backward embrace.

"Wait, before you go charging out of here," Eve said. "I cleared the murkiness around you. Whoever spelled you might have a bag of tricks lying in wait at your home or office. If you want me to work protection for you, that'll cost you. What I've done is a temporary fix."

"If I were footloose, I'd never let you out of my sight, Ms. Eve. Definitely, you're hired to cleanse my home and office. This is the best news I've had all year, perhaps my entire life. Because now I know to hold onto the things that matter. Success is fleeting. I gotta show Sage I'm me again."

With that, he zoomed out the front door. Eve moved close to me, and I hugged her. "He looks so much better. Thanks. Didn't know you were so multitalented."

Her eyes sparkled. "We all have hidden facets. Glad I could help your friend."

I gestured toward the back counter. "Is that something you do regularly?"

"There's no such thing as regular, and that kinda work doesn't pay as well as you'd think."

"Where'd you learn?" I asked quietly, aware of other people milling around in the shop.

She grinned. "Runs in our family. MawMaw earned quite a reputation in her day. In recent years her knowledge comes and goes, so she gave it up. She taught me the old ways, and I'm glad I caught the gist of it several years ago. I don't know much, but I'm confident in certain areas. Plenty more out there for me to learn about the craft, but I have a strong foundation of the basics."

"There's always more to learn in every field."

"I see it, you know."

My brows shot up. I thought I'd been paying close attention to the conversation, but I'd been daydreaming. "What are you talking about?"

"Your very fine, golden energy. It's splashed all over this room, singing to me. It's in the candles and the soaps, especially the ones that smell amazing."

"You see energy?"

"Don't know how to describe it any better than that. Just know what I see. You got some power, lady."

"Thanks, I think." My phone rang. Sage. "I need to take this call. You okay out here for a few more minutes?"

"Sure, but I'm going to need a big old chocolate bar real soon."

"I'll get you one." I hurried into the stillroom to take the call. "Sage? What's going on?"

"What's going on?" she asked. "I received a cryptic text from Brindle. Says he's on the way here. How could you let him go out in his fragile condition?"

"He's fine, or at least fine for now. We now have someone here who can help us with these kinds of cases. The last two hours have been nuts on Bristol Street. The cops brought a search warrant, and they combed through Auntie O and Frankie's place. Made a huge mess over there, and Brindle recommended a cleaning service to get up all the fingerprint dust. Anyway, I got slammed with customers galore in the shop, so I called Gerard to help, only he and MawMaw are out of town. To make a long story short, I hired his cousin Eve to help on the weekends and a few afternoons, depending on her class schedule. Best of all, she could start immediately so she's here already. Eve took one look at Brindle and fixed him. What's more, she made it look easy."

"What?" Sage screeched. "All this happened today?"

I held the phone away from my ear. "You nearly broke my eardrum."

"Why didn't you call me?"

"You're working. I solved two of our problems. Oh, and Vito Morelli visited today as well. Get this, he marched every customer out of the shop."

"What the hay? This is happening too fast. I can't take it in, and I hate that I'm not there with you. Brindle is suddenly okay. You hired a new employee. The cops searched Auntie O's place. Vito came to the shop. Did he try anything with you?"

"He did. I blocked him." Pride laced my voice. "He didn't like that, but I told him to leave so he left."

"What's happening right now?"

"Pretty sure Brindle is on his way to profess his undying love to you for saving his bacon."

"Ohmigod. I'm not prepared for drama."

I stifled a chuckle. Drama and Sage went together like fish and chips. "Brace yourself. Today is racing along at warp speed. My advice is to cut your guy some slack. He genuinely cares for you."

"Where's Quig?"

"Not sure, but he isn't here. He and Brindle went shopping earlier, and he and I plan to meet after the shop closes. We're coming down to the waterfront to watch the Festival of Lights with you, remember?"

"We're nearly sold out of trees again."

"So? Order another batch."

"I can't get ahold of Ms. Chatham. I refuse to go through Mary Nicole for anything, regardless of her blistering my ears last time I did it my way."

At the sound of voices, I glanced in the shop. Recognition flared, followed by a rip current of suspicion. "How bizarre. Ms. Chatham is in The Book and Candle Shop. Let me see what she wants."

Chapter
Thirty-Two

Sage squawked in my ear, but I cut the connection and peeked through the open doorway. Ms. Chatham stood opposite Eve, with several items clustered on the counter. "That's the sweetest cat," Ms. Chatham said. "Have any kitty treats I can give him?"

"No, ma'am, I don't," Eve said as she rang up the items.

"You're new. I didn't know the Winslows had employees other than the young man who's been here a few years."

Why would she keep up with my staff? I stepped out, automatically shielding myself from her energy. Until I found the killer, it paid to be cautious around anyone who had worked with Loren Lee. "Good afternoon, Ms. Chatham. I'm Tabby Winslow, Sage's sister. We've met before at your nursery. Is there something else I can help you with?"

"No, no, everything is fine. I'm headed to the waterfront for the festivities, but I stopped here first because I needed a few gift items. Quite the place you all have."

"Thank you." My cat darted under the tablecloth on our round table display. Harley didn't hide in the shop, another oddity in a strange day. In fact, he stayed under my feet or up on the shelves people-watching most of the time. Something was up with him.

"Love the shop cats," she said as if she knew where my thoughts had drifted. "The big one is so soft and cuddly. I should get a cat for the nursery. Pets make everything seem comfier."

Eve finished Ms. Chatham's transaction, and the woman collected her purchases and caught my eye. "Will you be joining your sister at the festival tonight?"

"That's the plan."

"Good. She's sold quite a few potted trees through that waterfront booth. It is quite an untapped market for us. Kudos to her for knocking it out of the park."

"As it happens, I just spoke to her. She's trying to reach you about ordering more trees. She's nearly out again."

Ms. Chatham's brow furrowed. "Oh. I'll check my messages."

She left, and Eve turned to me. "Is she a friend of yours?"

I glanced at Ms. Chatham walking down Bristol Street. "No. I only know her because Sage works for her. Why?"

"Something hinky about her."

In this context she meant odd, I hoped. "My information on her is secondhand. Here's what I've heard. She's a bit all over the place emotionally. She inherited the nursery from her late husband, and she only got involved in daily operations recently. After her husband passed, she relied on the nursery manager to do everything but the administration, which she handled. He died recently, so she needs to hire a good manager."

"Hmm."

When Eve looked puzzled, she did it with her whole body. My curiosity ignited. "Whatcha thinking?"

"There's trouble at her nursery."

In the Wick of Time

"New trouble?"

She barred her arms across her chest. "You tell me."

"The police investigation into her manager's death stalled, though they suspect my aunt's companion now, which is why the cops are searching their place today. I know nothing of the nursery's financial status."

Eve got busy checking out another customer, so we'd pick our conversation up later. I glanced around the shop, noting we had more than a Saturday crowd in here, but the number of shoppers felt right for a holiday weekend. With time on my hands, I wandered back to the stillroom, noting I still had a few hours before closing.

Time to make soap or candles.

Soap first, because we needed it the most. As I prepped and made the soap bars, I heard Eve engaging the customers and their happy replies. Eve didn't have a single question about checking customers out. We were fortunate to have her.

I dashed off a quick text to Sage. *All good here. Let's talk tonight.*

Soon my hiccups started again. Crap. I glanced down and saw I flashed between visible and invisible with every hiccup. I closed the shop door for privacy. Then I tried breathing into cupped hands. I tried breathing into a bag. I even tried pulling on my tongue, something the internet touted as a proven hiccup cure. Nothing helped. I slid down the island, out of sight in case Eve opened the shop door. Minutes passed. I tried holding my breath. I pinched my nose while exhaling with my mouth mostly closed.

Oh man. I needed to pull it together, fast. It had to be stress that linked my breathing and hiccups. My murder investigation felt stagnant. Sage's work and boyfriend had troubles. My aunt and Frankie felt unsafe at home, so they were hiding elsewhere. I still needed to find a Quig gift for Christmas.

Still stressed, I reached for thoughts that made me happy. Eve would return tomorrow afternoon, which suited me fine. Her presence offered me respite from working every shift. She'd fixed Brindle too, even if his improvement might only be short-term.

The door opened. "Tabby?" Eve asked. "You okay?"

"Taking a break," I said. "You need me?"

"Are there more wind chimes? I sold the last set on the shop floor."

I hiccupped and faded out. "We're out of stock, then. I'll call our supplier."

"Want me to do it? Things have slowed down out here."

Footsteps approached. Like a prey animal, I searched mentally for a hiding place, but I couldn't fit in any cabinet nearby. If Eve saw me in strobe mode, she'd quit for sure. "I can do it."

"Goody, I have chocolate for you." Eve's footsteps stopped by the bar I'd placed on the counter. "Sounds like you got a bad case of the hiccups."

I closed my eyes, albeit I wanted answers. She stood a few feet away. I cringed, expecting Eve to scream any moment. Another hiccup rolled out. Energy cycled through my body, flashing my physical self into from visible to invisible.

"This shop is full of foolishness today," Eve said. "Why does your body fade out of sight?"

"You're not weirded out by my issue?" I asked, daring to hope she wouldn't quit.

"Takes a lot to weird out someone in my family."

I hiccupped again. "This is something new over the last few days. I don't know what caused it or how to stop it. Seems to run its course after a while, then I stay visible."

"Hmm."

Hearing her thinking sound encouraged hope. "Wait," I said. "Is my new problem from your world?"

She hummed for a few more moments. "Could be."

I opened my eyes, hungry for answers. Eve stood a few feet away. "Can you help me? I never know when this malady will strike."

"What have you tried?"

I ran through a long list of home remedies. "Try this," she said. "When you feel a hiccup coming on, inhale and hug your knees. Stay like that for a few breaths."

The next hiccup came, and I tried her suggestion. I only faded partially instead of all the way. "Almost worked."

"Stay down," she said. "Keep those knees tucked to your belly."

The next hiccup came, and I remained visible. Joy spread through my body like sunrise on the marsh. "It worked."

"Wait a few more breaths before you unfold," she said.

I waited three more breaths. I uncurled and stood beside her, wanting to hug her again, but I'd already hugged her for fixing Brindle and may have exceeded my hug quota for the day. Instead, I clasped my hands to my chest. "You're amazing. How'd you know what to try?"

"Got lucky. But at least we know what works for you. That should help when the attacks come."

Attacks raised a red flag. "Someone did this to me?"

"Yep."

"How do I get rid of this problem?"

"Hmm." Silence prickled in the room. "When did it start?"

"Last week sometime."

"It's important to pin it down exactly. Think harder."

"All right. Sage and I were talking after the cops took Frankie in for questioning about Loren Lee's murder. He's Auntie O's companion. Sage's nursery boss got poisoned, and because Frankie met Loren Lee at the nursery and then the cops found his finger-prints in Loren Lee's house, the cops felt their relationship had a bearing on the case."

"Your hiccups are related to the case. That feels right to me. Someone wants you sidelined from the investigation."

Her response stunned me. "Who?"

"Isn't it obvious? The killer."

Chapter
Thirty-Three

Eve's comment knifed through my thoughts for the rest of the day. The killer wanted me out of commission. That meant I'd met the killer. But who? I couldn't begin to list the one hundred plus people who'd passed through the shop today. Nor could I connect any one person to my hiccupping incidents over the past few days.

I worked on soaps and swung out into the shop to lend Eve a hand when a checkout line formed. At first, I scanned each customer's aura, not trusting anyone. Many energy fields were flaring and raging, and so I siphoned off their negative energy to help them feel better. Stopped that right away because the process tired me, and I didn't know if my actions helped my customers.

As I cleaned my stillroom, I rewound my thoughts on the case. The cops had Frankie and Sage on their suspect list. Neither of them would've killed Loren Lee, nor would they inflict disruption on me.

That left three original suspects I hadn't cleared yet. First, the nursery owner, Ms. Chatham, could be the killer, though it made no sense to me why she'd kill her employee when she could just fire him. Next, the redheaded former assistant manager for the nursery,

Chris Kachuba, threatened to kill Loren Lee when she got the axe two years ago. And last, I couldn't overlook Mary Nicole, the current interim assistant manager at the nursery, who truly disliked Loren Lee and wanted to keep Sage firmly under her boot heel.

Since then, I'd met another nursery employee, Larry Rau, who worked closely with Sage, but Larry's agenda seemed clear. He wanted to spend time with Sage. So far, Larry seemed utterly transparent. Also, Frankie's Chicago relative. Vito Morelli, radiated trouble any way I cut it, but he didn't know his cousin lived in Savannah until Frankie's old identity hit the national news after the murder. Therefore, neither Larry nor Vito graced my suspect list.

Something wiggled in the corner of my mind. Something I knew about Chris. She'd threatened to kill Loren Lee. She had a hot temper.

Eve left as soon as the clock ticked five o'clock. I closed the shop and realized I hadn't seen my cat all afternoon. I called him with increasing urgency. Harley enjoyed being under my feet. He adored cuddles, lofty heights, and sunny windows.

When I shook the treat container as a last but surefire method of cat wrangling, Harley stumbled from underneath the round table on the shop floor. He seemed dazed.

At the same time, Quig strode in through the back door. "Tabby, you in here? I thought we were meeting in our place."

"Yeah. I'm here. Something is wrong with Harley. He isn't acting right." I tried to scoop him up, but he dashed over to Quig and rubbed against his legs.

Quig studied the frenzied cat. "I see what you mean. This is odd. He's never done this before. In fact, he always gives me stink eye."

A sob caught in my throat as I gathered Harley in my arms. At the same time, Quig moved in for a hello kiss. The cat thrashed and squirmed, then leaped onto Quig's shoulder like a circus acrobat, purring loudly from his new perch.

"What the heck?" Quig said as the cat rubbed faces with him. "Take him, Tabby. I'm uncomfortable being a kitty pillow."

"Harley believes he's your best friend."

"You're my best friend." Quig's eyes heated.

I removed my cat and cuddled him close. To my dismay, he clawed my belly and yowled as if I were an encroaching tomcat. I set him on the floor, and he immediately raced to Quig.

My cat's rejection stung, but the puzzle of it intrigued me. "Okay. This is officially weird. I've been number one in this cat's life since his kitten days. Right now he wants nothing to do with me."

"Maybe he knows a good thing when he sees it." Quig ignored the cat rubbing against his legs and pawing him.

Harley had never acted like this before. His behavior looked and felt off, and he seemed disoriented. My heart went out to my confused kitty. "He wants you to pick him up."

"That may be, except I don't want to pick him up. I have nothing against cats, I've just never spent much time around them. He's so small, I don't want to accidentally hurt him. Or step on him."

As if I'd been spinning the dial of a combination lock and just aligned the last number, I had a blinding revelation. Someone else in our circle of friends recently behaved oddly. He'd fixated on entirely different objects of affection. "We have a problem."

Quig looked my way, gesturing open-handedly at me. "The cat has a problem. I did nothing to encourage him. This is all Harley."

"Exactly, except that isn't how he acts, ever."

He frowned. "I don't get it."

"The cat's problem is suspiciously like Brindle's problem, wherein the person of his affections is now a different person. When Sage called Brindle on his betrayal, he became unstable and overdosed with meds, or so the story goes. I'm worried for my cat's health and safety."

"Did he eat anything unusual today? Some spicy chili from the Southern Tea café across the street perhaps?"

"Nothing like that. This is more personal. I believe someone spelled him. That's the only thing other than a terrible illness that might cause his odd behavior, and he doesn't appear sick. His coat is thick and shiny, his eyes are bright. He ate a good breakfast this morning, and he's not underweight. His overall physical condition is excellent. Something or someone rewired him, that's my theory."

Thinking aloud, I reviewed the course of the day. "Harley shadowed me all day until late afternoon. After that I didn't see him. Further, only Ms. Chatham from All Good Things Nursery paid him any attention. She shopped here this afternoon."

Quig moved closer, sliding his feet along the floor so as not to inadvertently injure the cat. "Your sister's big boss? Why would she, or anyone for that matter, meddle with your cat's head? I'm not following you."

"She must know how much I love this cat." I had another realization, one that connected some stray dots in this case. The sentences flowed like a geometry theorem. "A concerned pet owner would stay with the pet or take him to the emergency vet. I would prefer not to leave Harley in this condition. Under most circumstances, I wouldn't go to the waterfront this evening. Ms. Chatham specifically asked me if I planned to attend the festival, and I said yes. Since she commented on Harley's friendly personality today, something customers never mention because Harley's normal behavior is aloof, it seems obvious. Ms. Chatham wants me otherwise occupied."

"I'm not following your logic. Why would she prevent you from viewing the luminaries and lighted boat parade? That's bizarre."

The final piece of the puzzle slid into place. A rising tide of dread surged through me. "Not if she's going after my sister tonight. Sage and Brindle are at the tree booth right now. I need to warn them." My phone calls and texts to them went unanswered, as did my mental ping to Sage on our twin-link. My insides trembled. Something felt very wrong. The dissonance resonated deep in my bones.

I had to act. My sister and my cat were likely in danger. I gazed at Quig, fire in my eyes. "I have to find Sage. Please drive Harley to the emergency vet for me."

"The cat may be acting strange, but he will be fine here. If there's a problem at the waterfront, we should go together, or I should go. There's a killer running around this town, in case you forgot. I don't want you in harm's way."

"My cat and my sister are in jeopardy. I can't reach my twin. That's beyond unusual. Sage is expecting us down there any minute, so she'd answer my call, or return it right away. I'm sure Sage is in trouble. Because we're twins, we have close ties." I knew that sounded presumptuous, but I didn't have time to explain. "I can spot her in a crowd, so it makes sense for me to go. I'm concerned Ms. Chatham has already hurt my sister."

"I don't like splitting up, but I understand now. I'll drop the cat at the vet and meet you at the tree booth as soon as I can. But first, should I call the police?"

"No. I have no real proof anything bad has happened. Detectives Nowry and Belfor already think my entire family is crazy, yet everything in me is shouting at me to hurry and help Sage. I feel like I stepped in a fire ant nest and I need to run. It's bound to be gridlock on the streets. My best chance to reach her is on foot. Time is of the essence, and the element of surprise is in my favor. I must find my sister right now. Please believe me."

"I believe you."

Quig and Harley left. I grabbed a big sun hat, donned a long-sleeved shirt as a disguise, and dashed to the waterfront.

The sun skimmed the horizon as five thirty approached on this chilly December eve. I didn't need sunlight to find my way, but I could move faster if the sidewalks and streets were less crowded.

Halfway there, my hiccups struck in full force, I kept my head down until I reached the nearest square. *Not now!* I shouldn't stop, but I couldn't risk discovery either. So I jammed my hands in my pockets and kept my head tucked down until I could sit for a few moments on a fountain ledge. Then I hugged my knees, remembering to inhale during a hiccup as Eve suggested. After a few breaths, I pulled my act together and resumed my dash to the river. I tried Sage again on our twin-link. No answer.

Dark forces mushroomed from my fear and radiated through my aura. People on the thronged sidewalks moved out of my way as if I were a fierce predator. I'd never had that happen before, but I accepted the gift of personal space and pressed forward, calling for Sage on the twin-link and getting dead silence in return.

It had to be Ms. Chatham behind all this.

Nothing else fit the circumstances.

Neither Larry nor Sage were at the booth when I arrived, my chest heaving for breath. The luminary bags were placed around the booth and waterfront, but the ones here were unlit. I scanned the throngs on River Street, searching faces for Sage and Ms. Chatham. Too many faces, too much excited energy to sift through.

I reached out mentally through our twin-link again. Nothing. A big fat zero. In the distance city workers lit the luminary candles, each flame a tiny spark in the thick curtain of approaching night.

Think. If I couldn't track her energy, connect through our phones, or find her through the twin-link, how could I locate my sister? I never should've bragged to Quig that I could find her. With fumbling fingers, I rifled through the under-counter stuff at the booth, hoping to find something to indicate her location.

Anything.

Nothing leaped out at me.

I sank to the ground. Despair narrowed my vision, constricted my lungs. I gave myself a stern talking to. *Don't give in to fear. You can't help her if you freeze now. Think. You can find her. If there's nothing extra here, what's missing? Use your brain and your senses.*

Breath huffing, I gathered my frenzied thoughts. *I must be missing something. What is it? Her phone.* I glanced high and low around the booth. Sage's phone was missing. I called it and listened for her ring tone. Nothing but hundreds of people walking and talking.

My teeth chattered like a nor'easter blew despite the mild weather. If only I could track my sister.

Track her. Aha. I could track her phone. If this worked, I'd never fuss about technology ever again. I clicked over to the Find My Phone icon on my phone and opened the application. With Auntie O's phone out of commission, only Sage's phone location blinked on the screen. I closed my eyes as a swell of relief flooded my veins.

I hoped Sage and her phone occupied the same geography. What if they didn't? How would I find her? Quickly I banished the pulse of doubt. She had to be there.

I followed the signal. She couldn't be far. I darted out of the booth into the crowd using the phone display as a divining rod. I couldn't be too late to save her. I wouldn't be too late. I dodged happy people, laughing people, my intensity focused entirely on my twin. At the corner of a building I paused. The indicator blinked in the alley to my left.

The dark, empty-looking alley.

People flowed around me on all sides as if I were an island in a rip current. So much background noise here. No one would hear anything that happened in this alley. I trembled with fear and wished Quig were beside me, but all I had to call upon in the name of help were this phone app and my energy talent.

That had to be enough.

I wouldn't let Sage become a casualty of this day, of this case. I couldn't.

She didn't deserve to die.

With that, I crept into the thick shadows, silencing my footfalls and moving slow as a box turtle. I dared not use the flashlight app on the phone. I needed the shadows to conceal my presence. Using my aura vision, I searched the alley for life signs. No one standing.

That meant no one would jump out and surprise me. It also meant only her phone was here. I trudged forward, searching and daring to dream of a positive outcome. Even so, all my senses pegged in high alert mode.

I felt a low-grade energy field near the dumpster. The phone had been tossed there. As fear for my sister's safety resurfaced, I clung to the truth that an energy field indicated life. That person or those people were alive.

Now that I'd traveled halfway down the alley, I took note of its length and breadth. A panel van with the mirrors folded in might fit in this narrow lane. The crowd noise faded behind me, and I focused entirely on what lay ahead of me. I squinted in the deep twilight. Listened. Checked for additional energy sources with my other vision. Finding none, I switched back to my regular vision.

I wanted to shout my sister's name, but prudence and caution kept me mute. I would be of no use to her if I fell into the same trap that had snared her. I pinged her on the twin-link again. Nothing.

Was Sage's life hanging by a thread? *If she'd lost her phone . . . don't go there. She had to be here. Energy meant life.* I repeated that phrase until it became as natural as the air I breathed.

More questions rolled in as relentless as flood tide. Why couldn't I sense her unique energy? She might be unconscious. Fear slashed at me with hurricane strength. *Come on. You've come this far. You must be close. You have to believe you can save her.*

The cloying stench of garbage filled the narrow, dark space. My heart raced as I reached the dumpster, and I braced for whatever I might find. Because I moved so slowly, I didn't fall when my toe snagged on something solid. Something warm. *The energy source!* I ducked down and felt a leg-shaped obstacle, realizing I'd found a nonresponsive male. Larry. Next to him lay Sage and then Brindle.

I'd found my sister. I shook each of them in turn, loudly whispering for them to wake up.

They didn't respond.

The distinct scent of booze hit me next.

I held my hand above Sage's nose and mouth, physically feeling her shallow breaths. She lived! Thank goodness. I checked the men. They were alive too. I also checked their breath. The alcohol scent didn't emit from their mouths. Their damp clothes reeked of alcohol.

No matter what I did, I couldn't rouse them. Someone had incapacitated three adults and poured booze all over them.

I had to save them, but how? I couldn't carry a single adult, and odds were this triple state of unconsciousness would flummox EMTs if they were called. I had to handle this solo.

Sage's energy field registered too low to have dropped naturally. I pushed energy her way, but it would take too long to top her off at this slow rate, and I didn't know how long I had until her kidnapper returned. I lightly tapped all three faces. If even one of the men awakened, we could drag the others to safety.

No such luck.

The hair on the nape of my neck electrified at a faint sound. Footsteps echoed in the alley. More than one person, likely two. Why didn't I bring a weapon? Self-preservation made me dart behind the dumpster. I quickly texted Quig. *Call the cops. Am in alley with unconscious Sage, Larry, and Brindle. I hear footsteps. Trouble is coming.*

I silenced my phone, knowing Quig would respond. I couldn't ease his fears because I couldn't stop worrying. Maybe my suspects of Ms. Chatham, Chris, and Mary Nicole didn't do this. Maybe the killer forced their compliance.

I wouldn't know until they arrived. If none of us survived this encounter, I wanted to create a recording of this confrontation. Surely cops would notice my phone and use the recording to catch the killer.

If I had spider legs, I'd climb this brick wall and skitter out of here. But I couldn't leave without my sister or the others. I set my phone to record any conversation and placed it on the cobblestone lane.

The newcomers murmured softly. Two women, I surmised from the pitch of the voices. One carried a flashlight. I tried not to breathe, not to move as I recognized Ms. Chatham walking up with Chris Kachuba.

"Do it," Chris said. "Burn 'em."

What? That's why Sage and friends reeked of booze? This pair planned to set them on fire. To roast them alive. Omigod. Chris and Ms. Chatham were monsters!

Ms. Chatham stilled and made a mewing sound.

I couldn't breathe. I couldn't think. I couldn't not think.

"Do it, or you'll go up in flames with them," Chris said. "They interfered with our plan and must be punished. Light a match and set all three on fire."

No way would I allow that to happen. I rose and gathered shadow energy to make myself invisible, also using shadow energy as a barrier between me, my twin, and our enemies. I shoved Ms. Chatham's hand away with an energy burst, knocking the matches she held way down the alley and far away from her. She struck her head as she fell.

Chris shrieked like a banshee and came at me, though I didn't know how she pinpointed me in the dark alley. To stop her, I wrapped her body in coils of energy, trapping her arms at her sides. Chris let out another screech as she fought her invisible bonds. When it looked like she might break free, I directed an energy spear at her heart, using just enough current to disrupt her natural heart rhythm.

Her eyes rounded at the unexpected attack. "No!" She folded in on herself and collapsed. I released the energy coils. Chris lay still on the uneven cobblestones. One down, one to go.

Ms. Chatham crawled over to the fallen woman and smacked her face. "Chris, wake up. We can't let them walk away."

I didn't understand her behavior, but Chris was calling the shots. Did Ms. Chatham have Stockholm syndrome, the behavior where captives developed positive feelings for their captors? Or did she act this way to fool me?

I dropped my shield, became visible, and knelt protectively beside Sage. "Move away from that woman, Ms. Chatham."

"She's family, my niece."

"I stopped both of you from making a mistake." Family ties explained their unlikely association. Seeing as how Chris gave orders

225

and Ms. Chatham followed them, Chris seemed the bigger threat. "She had you do her dirty work, didn't she?" I asked Ms. Chatham. "What's wrong with Sage, Brindle, and Larry?"

"I don't know. She made them walk here. Then she muttered something else." Ms. Chatham's voice sounded tinny. "They fell down, and we dragged them out of the lane so they wouldn't be in the way."

"Hid them here, more like." Did Chris study the dark arts? She didn't have a mystical or magical vibe. Whatever she was, I had to protect my family and friends.

I reached for my phone, leaving the recorder on, and dialed Quig. "Sorry for the brief text message earlier. I can talk now. We're in an alley about three blocks down the street from the tree booth. Did you notify the police?"

"Called Detective Nowry. They're on the way. Are you all right?"

"I'm shaky but coming around. Glad the cops are en route. I need their help and an ambulance to boot."

"I'm parking my car now. How is everyone?"

"Everyone but me and Ms. Chatham is unconscious. I'm trying to revive Sage now."

"I'm coming."

I ended the call. Sage's energy now responded faintly to mine. Odd, because not enough time had passed for her to recover. Did Chris dampen her energy field separately from the harmful spell? If so, with Chris out of commission, would Sage awaken naturally? Not taking any chances with her health and well-being, I lay on top of her to maximize points of contact and accelerate her healing process. Energy flooded into my twin.

"What kind of pervert are you?" Ms. Chatham shrieked. "Get off my employee. You're squishing her."

226

"I'm not hurting her." I glanced over at Ms. Chatham. "What happened here?"

"Chris did this. She learned mischief-making from her swamp friend."

"Did she now?" Beneath me, I felt my sister's heart steadying. Whatever Chris had done to her body receded. "Why'd she come after Sage?"

"Because Sage kept turning a profit at the shop and the tree booth, and you wouldn't stop looking for Loren Lee's killer, that's why."

"My sister and a family friend were questioned about his murder. I couldn't let that slide. What did you expect to happen when they were falsely accused of the crime?"

"I expected a scandal would rock your family, and Bob's nursery would fail catastrophically. That's what. No one was supposed to die. Chris went too far."

"Keep going," I prompted when she fell silent.

"I wanted the nursery to fail miserably, only Loren Lee and your sister messed that up, time after time. They kept improving everything. Customers raved about the healthy stock at All Good Things. That lousy business started making money!" She shuddered. "Every time I thought Loren Lee's brusque personality would drive the good workers away, your sister and a few others picked up the slack, and we had another stellar week. Sage ruined everything."

You could've knocked me over with a sea fan. "You wanted the nursery to fail?"

"Yes. I thought this tree booth at the Festival of Lights would sound the nursery's death knell. Instead, your sister restocked several times over. She wrecked my plans to destroy the business."

Why wouldn't a business owner want to be successful? "If you didn't want the nursery, you should've sold it. Why not pocket the money and walk away?"

"Because my late husband bragged about his fantastic nursery and at the same time he squashed me like a bug. Said I was no good. That nobody wanted me. That I was a waste of fresh air. I hated Bob and the nursery. He hurt me over and over again, and I couldn't stop him."

Her gut-wrenching sob got to me. Her husband broke her with mental abuse. I didn't want to feel sorry for her, but nobody deserved to live like that. "I'm sorry this happened to you, and I hope you get help. Setting my sister and her friends on fire won't fix your problems."

"You're wrong. It'll headline the news. My husband's abusive nature and lechery must come out. People must know he was a sexual predator and a master of domestic violence."

"You don't need to hurt anyone to share that story."

"I must destroy Bob's legacy to stamp out all traces of him, don't you see?"

Ms. Chatham was lost in her delusions. I didn't doubt Bob had been a dirty, rotten scoundrel. Sage had never liked him, and that was all the proof of his character I needed.

"Don't you see?" Ms. Chatham continued. "All Good Things became his golden goose despite his tyranny. Worse, he had constant access to young women. He took racy pictures of them with him and left them on our bed for me to see. Said he thought they'd inspire my performance. Instead, that was the last straw. I no longer cared about his threats to have me institutionalized or that he'd divorce me and keep all my money. I wanted him gone."

Her logic still didn't track for me, but it was apparent he'd broken her. Bent her until she snapped in two. A terrible possibility occurred to me. "You and Chris helped him into an early grave?"

"He's gone," Ms. Chatham said coolly. "That's all that matters."

If they'd poisoned him, the toxin or its metabolites might be detectable. I saved that thought for Quig. This chance to record her confession about Loren Lee's murder wouldn't come around again. "You intended to set my sister and her friends on fire tonight. Why?"

"I'm headed straight to hell, that's why. Nobody should've gotten hurt, but Chris changed my plan because she had her own axe to grind against Bob. I hired her to work at the nursery when Bob passed two years ago, and she ruthlessly killed plants and upset customers upon my request. She loved being my secret agent until Loren Lee caught on and fired her on the spot. His action made her livid. She expected to run the whole shooting match, but I grew increasingly nervous about Chris when Loren Lee became ill. After his death, I put Mary Nicole in charge of the place, sure that sourpuss would run it straight into the ground. Imagine my surprise when nobody quit the first week. Apparently, even a terrible manager can keep a sinking nursery afloat."

My sister groaned in my head for the first time since I found her unconscious.

Her thoughts blazed through our twin-link like Halley's Comet. *What the heck happened?* Sage mumbled. *Where am I?*

Chapter
Thirty-Four

I silently gave Sage an abbreviated version of recent events as she struggled to sit up. I moved so she could prop her back against the brick wall. She couldn't stand yet, but she would soon be mobile. I hadn't been too late. I clung to that fact so I wouldn't snuff the lights out of these interfering women.

Chris did this to me?

She did. Ms. Chatham played a role too. Ms. Chatham had the idea initially, and Chris riffed on her plan, killing your late boss. Can you smell booze on your clothes? If I'd arrived five minutes later, these women would've barbecued you.

Without hesitation, Sage raised her hands and blasted Chris and Ms. Chatham with a barrage of lightning spears. Ms. Chatham cried out and collapsed beside Chris.

My twin's knee-jerk reaction ensued from her kidnapping and incapacitation, but since our lifelong mission involved keeping a low profile, her over-the-top behavior would draw notice.

Stop! You have no energy to spare and neither do I. We still need to rouse Brindle and Larry, or they'll be sent to the hospital. Last time that happened Brindle ended up in the psych ward. *He can't go through that again.*

You fix 'em. I'll destroy both women for daring to harm me and my friends.

Get a grip, Sage. I already spent most of my energy on you. Forget vengeance and think about Larry and Brindle. They need our help.

She huffed for a few minutes before saying, *You sure squeeze the fun out of everything.*

Hoping she had her vengeance under control, I infused Brindle with energy. In several places his aura looked bad, so I tweaked those bands as I revived him. His color brightened right away, and his pulse quickened too. Next I turned my attention to Larry, silently urging Sage to hold Brindle's hand and bring him back the rest of the way.

I remember what happened. Chris tried to kill me, Sage said on our twin-link. *She needs to die. I don't trust our justice system.*

Not so fast. Given her dark arts skill set, she has a good chance of getting away with murder. We need a taped confession from her to hand Nowry and Belfor. We didn't come this far to let Chris slip through the cracks of law enforcement.

I want to set her on fire.

No one's setting anyone on fire tonight. Get a grip. Beneath my hands, Larry's aura stabilized. My energy boost to him worked. He'd heal the rest of the way on his own if he wasn't peppered with drugs by well-intentioned medics. Besides, he didn't need to witness Sage lash out with energy. Until she calmed down, anything could happen.

On the twin-link I shared, *My phone is on audio record mode. Let's secure Chris and rouse her. Without a taped confession, the cops may still draw a bead on you and Frankie for Loren Lee's murder. Work with me on this. How can we tie her up?*

Larry's got a pocketknife in his right front pocket. Cut your purse strap or rip fabric off the bottom of someone's shirt, preferably Chris's. Let's smear garbage on her face first.

Sage.

I need revenge for all she's done to us.

Revenge will make her target us again. It becomes a lethal circle of hatred. Leave well enough alone.

It must be a terrible burden to be the levelheaded one.

You have no idea how hard it is. You think I don't get dark urges? I do.

In minutes, we secured Chris and Ms. Chatham's hands and feet. Casually, I placed my phone in the dark shadows between the two conspirators. Ms. Chatham wept silently into her bound hands. Chris lay quietly until she flopped over on her back and began talking a mile a minute.

"You can't do this to me," Chris wailed. "You can't bind my limbs like I'm some farm animal. My aunt forced me to help her get revenge. She's behind everything that happened."

"Cut the crap, Chris," Sage said, jabbing her finger at the belligerent redhead. "We know what you did. We even know about your boyfriend. Your auntie said you changed her plan. That you killed my boss."

"Her plan sucked," Chris said. "Loren Lee deserved to die. He fired me when I acted on my aunt's request to destroy the nursery. So I went after Loren Lee and the nursery with a vengeance."

"Why destroy either one? Most people would sell a profitable business and enjoy the proceeds. That's the smart move."

"Ha! This isn't about smart. It's about revenge. Anyone aligned with good old Uncle Bob is fair game. Loren Lee was Bob's toady through and through. Uncle Bob hated women, but he got his comeuppance, same as Loren Lee. Both men are gone now, and it's just me and my aunt."

Chris and Ms. Chatham operated in a different reality from the rest of the world. Even so, the cops needed hard evidence to prosecute and convict them. Finding hard evidence was essential.

"Why'd you use oleander to poison Loren Lee?" I asked.

"Thought his death would slide under the radar. Everyone knows the county can barely make ends meet. Running those expensive tests on Loren Lee cost the county a passel of money. That new ME nearly screwed me when he figured it out. He's next on my to-do list. Good thing your sister made such a fine patsy."

Behind me one of the men moved. Good. We might need their strength before this was over. I shuddered to think of this unstable woman having a kill list. "What is it with you and murdering people? Who made you God?"

"Watch it, girlie," Chris snapped. "Just because my hands and feet are bound doesn't mean I can't spell you. I'm that good."

"Leave Tabby alone. She's a good person," Sage said loyally. "You're headed to jail for kidnapping and attempted murder."

"You're wrong. I won't serve time, and it'll look like you're to blame. Two men and one woman, that's fuzzy math right there. You and your two beaus are a romantic triangle if I ever saw one. Besides, my aunt conceived this scheme. I'm merely a gullible kid following her lead."

"Think again. You're an adult," I said. "You're responsible for your own actions. You gave the command for Ms. Chatham to light Sage, Brindle, and Larry on fire. I heard you order her around."

"I hate you," Chris screamed. "I hate all of you. Uncle Bob promised the nursery to me. He owes me for stealing my innocence."

I got a very bad feeling in my gut. "What do you mean?"

"I mean I paid for that business on my back for years, that's what."

If I could get my hands on Bob, I'd strangle him myself. "That's unfortunate. I'm sorry that happened to you."

Chris shook her finger at her aunt. "She should've done something. She knew."

"Oh, Chris, I didn't know," Ms. Chatham said. "I couldn't protect you because I couldn't protect myself from his abuse. He broke me in every way possible. Bob was a monster. It took everything I had to survive each day."

"Bull. You came up with the poison idea. You brewed it. You killed Bob."

"That's a lie," Ms. Chatham said. "I defended myself. I didn't murder anyone."

"I won't go to prison for your crime," Chris said. "There's a bottle of her home-brewed oleander extract in her kitchen spice cabinet. She murdered Loren Lee and Bob."

I didn't believe a single word Chris said. Her story changed every time she opened her mouth. Her midnight-flecked aura backed up my suspicions that she lied. "The cops will sort out the evidence. Meanwhile, you're staying put."

Chris thrashed against her bonds and groaned out her frustration. "This alley smells like pee and garbage. I'm truly in hell on earth."

"You picked this location," I said. "How'd Loren Lee ingest the poison?"

"Easy. He drank a liquid health supplement daily and that got spiked. His toxin dose depended on how much of a swig he took from the bottle or if he forgot the holistic brew. The longer duration of poisoning worked out in our favor, lending credence to a lingering illness like undiagnosed cancer. He deserved that agony for being Uncle Bob's stoolie and for firing me."

I heard her mumble softly and scramble to her feet, her bindings falling uselessly on the cobblestones.

Fear arced through my body like electrical current. "Don't come any closer," I warned.

Chapter Thirty-Five

E ven as I spoke, Chris withdrew white powder from her pocket and blew it at me. I turned away, but the stuff peppered my face. I scrubbed at it furiously and tried not to inhale. Why didn't I keep my energy barrier up? No telling what she sent my way. I never should've relaxed my guard. The powder had no scent, but that didn't guarantee safety. It could be anthrax or ground oleander for all I knew.

My next breath hiccupped out. I flashed from visible to invisible as my body flickered in and out of view with every hiccup. Horrified, I could only watch myself cycle from visible to invisible in the thick twilight. Realization dawned. *I got the vanishing hiccups after Chris blew powder. She did this to me.* "You're the one."

"I sure am," Chris bragged. "I didn't sell my soul to that devil man for nothing. I learned how to blend this hiccup powder, among many other potions. I spelled it specifically for you. Came by your shop several times and threw it in your air return. Gotcha good, didn't I?"

My fists balled, and oh, did I want to punch her. Instead, I hid my cycling body in the shadows behind the dumpster so Brindle, Larry, and Ms. Chatham wouldn't see my vanishing act.

Sage jumped on Chris and wrestled with her. I had no doubt that Sage stabbed her with energy spears. If only I could get a handle on my hiccups, but they freight-trained through me.

A flashlight beam illuminated the alley and approached swiftly, accompanied by pounding footsteps. "Stop right there," Quig said with authority. "The cops are behind me."

Relief danced with horror. I wanted to run to my boyfriend, but I couldn't reveal my malady and still stay under the "normal" radar in front of all these witnesses. Even so, I peeked from my hidden position and saw Chris face Quig and her palms extend toward him. She trapped him in stasis. He stood there, unmoving and mute, his flashlight beam never wavering. Sage lay crumpled on the ground atop Larry and Brindle. All three men and Sage, sidelined.

Bad news for the home team. I cringed inwardly, knowing Quig faced terrible danger, and I had to do something. Panic bit me. My thoughts circled. *This can't be happening. Chris is loose and attacking us again. I can't let her hurt Quig, but how can I help him?*

Sage roused and tried to help Quig, but she didn't have enough juice to reverse whatever Chris had done. She sagged to the ground. Quig didn't collapse, so I hoped he'd hold fast a few more seconds. I breathed through the next hiccup nice and slow and stayed visible.

Close enough for dark alley work.

I scurried out from behind the other end of the dumpster, emerging near Quig. I stepped beside him with my energy shield raised and protected him. Chris howled like a banshee at my intrusion.

Quig's body twitched, and then he spoke. "How'd you free me? She froze me in my tracks. Didn't know anyone could do that."

I leaned close to his ear and spoke softly. "My energy barrier keeps her from harming you now." I didn't add that Sage helped with my energy supply, and so did he. I'd automatically reached out to tap nearby energy fields to strengthen our combined defense.

When Chris attacked again, her energy struck my barrier and reflected perfectly. "Don't move. She's trying to hurt us again," I murmured in his ears.

"Don't understand what's happening, but I'm glad you're safe."

"I won't let her hurt you again. Thanks for getting here so quickly. You turned the tide in our favor." His fresh energy helped me stop Chris, though I didn't know how long I could hold her off if I fought alone.

"I didn't do much besides show up. You Winslow gals are tough."

His words infused me with courage. "Showing up means a great deal."

Suddenly Chris collapsed in a puff of hiccup powder and ugly words, but given her secrets, I couldn't chance she wasn't faking to lure me in. I scanned her energy field from where I stood with Quig, and her power registered at a fraction of what it'd been. The troubling emanations previously lacing her aura flickered out. What remained looked sickly, like someone with terminal illness.

If her spark of life had been reduced, her time on earth shortened. That was what happened to Mom after she tried too hard to help her cancer-riddled friend.

Ms. Chatham rose slowly and crawled toward my sister, as if nothing had happened. "Are you okay, Sage? I'm sorry about this. My niece is crazy. I couldn't stop her."

Sage edged away from her boss, and I didn't blame her one bit. Who knew what that woman would try next? I certainly didn't believe anything she said either. As a precaution, I kept the energy barrier intact around Quig and myself.

"Don't try to hoodwink me," Sage said. "There's no way you're innocent. I believed you earlier when you said you wanted to sink the nursery. That's why you gave the job to Mary Nicole instead of me, isn't it?"

"You're partially right. I hate that place. My husband verbally abused me at every opportunity. He told me what a waste of space I am and that the nursery shone beacon-bright as his true legacy. His legacy? When Bob died, I had to destroy the nursery to destroy him. Erasing him is the only way I can survive. I'd rather starve than have any remnant of him left in this world."

"Many people work for you," Sage said. "Some of us literally worked our fingers to the bone to keep that place afloat. You say Bob was a monster. You're a monster too."

Ms. Chatham made a dismissive gesture with her hand, briefly illuminated in Quig's fallen flashlight beam. "Collateral damage. You and your interfering sister had to be stopped. You ruined my revenge, and I won't forget your meddling. I'll get you yet."

"I'm underwhelmed by your threat," Sage said, energy buzzing in her words. "You charged after us with a vengeance, but we're the victors. The cops will hear the truth in our words."

Ms. Chatham cackled. "That's the best part. Who will they believe? An upstanding member of the business community? Or the hippie spawn from the candle shop? You have a track record of bouncing in and out of the Law Enforcement Center. That criminal taint will haunt you for the rest of your days. The cops will hound you forever. You think you caught me? Well, I got you good. I have witnesses who will swear Chris took advantage of her elderly relative, so she'll go down for this fail. I'm still standing too. Better yet, I can get the ME fired with a rumor campaign, same as I ruined Sage's boyfriend's law career because I could. How you like them apples?"

Though I didn't know for sure if Chris or Ms. Chatham masterminded the scheme, in my mind they were both complicit. I boiled with anger. "Bull. You and Chris were in this together. Why did you hurt my cat?" I asked. "It is unforgivable to hurt animals. Harley never did anything to you."

"Divide and conquer. I thought for sure you'd focus on your cat, while I literally roasted the competition. Who knew you'd send a proxy to deal with your precious feline?"

Sage planted her hands on her hips. "My sister outsmarted you. She did what any good manager does, she delegated responsibility. Not only that, but Tabby also saved me, Larry, and Brindle from fiery deaths."

Cop cars blocked both ends of the alley, and officers advanced our way on foot with riot shields. Their headlights barely pierced the thick gloom.

"Hands up," Detective Nowry shouted. "Everyone, hands in the air."

My hands rose, as did Quig's and Sage's. Larry and Brindle's hands lifted partway from where they lay on the cobblestones. Chris did not respond, while Ms. Chatham raised her hands shoulder high. "Can't move my arms higher," she said. "Bursitis in my shoulders."

"Don't believe a word she says," Sage called out in ringing tones. "She and Chris tried to kill us."

"Liar," Chris said. "These freaks tied me up and would've killed me."

"Pause the chitchat," Nowry said. "I want everyone's stories, but no talking to each other unless you want to spend the night in jail. The sooner you cooperate, the sooner we can all get out of here."

Quickly he directed everyone to different officers. Belfor stood at my side, and I offered her the audio recording on my phone as proof of what went down. "Thanks." She examined my phone and copied the audio file. "This will come in handy in sorting out what happened."

"What? Where'd that audio recording come from?" Ms. Chatham yelped. "I didn't authorize her to tape me. She can't invade my privacy this way. I have rights. I demand you erase that recording."

Belfor shot her a stern look worthy of a school principal facing locker vandals. "This is evidence, ma'am. Do you have your own recording to use for comparison's sake?"

"I do not. These women are dangerous. They're crazy. They hurt people."

"We'll see," Belfor said.

Since Quig arrived last, Nowry cleared him first, though Quig didn't leave. He stood beside me, and I got teary-eyed at his steadfast support.

Ambulances came for Ms. Chatham and Chris Kachuba and took them to the hospital. Larry and Brindle were diagnosed with exhaustion by the EMTs and offered a stimulant, but they refused that and transport.

"Your turn, Winslows. Tell me what happened," Nowry said, looking at Sage. "Go."

"Chris attacked the three of us," Sage said, loud and clear as she gestured to herself, Brindle, and Larry. "She is a practitioner of magic, and she previously used an enchantment on Brindle Platt and put him in the hospital. She and Ms. Chatham are hell-bent on destroying All Good Things Nursery and thus destroying the late Bob Chatham, but they had separate agendas. I don't know which woman is the guiltiest, though Chris called the shots tonight."

"Nice of you to leave some of the case for us to solve," Belfor said wryly. "Though you can keep the weird part to yourself."

I cleared my throat. "I believe Chris poisoned Loren Lee Suffield. She did it because he got in her way. Chris claimed Ms. Chatham has the oleander extract at her house, and that her aunt is the killer. I don't trust either woman. It would certainly be prudent to dust that bottle for prints."

"I see." Nowry gazed at Sage. "How did everyone end up in this service alley?"

"Can't explain it. One minute Larry and I staffed the potted Christmas tree booth, and Brindle joined us. Then I woke up in this alley. Chris must've used hypnosis or an enchantment to make us walk here under our own power. Otherwise people would've noticed her dragging three people through the crowded street."

The police officers exchanged looks. "Enchantment? Hypnosis?" Belfor asked.

Nowry scowled and turned to me. "Moving along . . . you found them?"

"I did. My sister and I planned to meet at the booth after work to watch the boat parade together. When I arrived, she wasn't in the booth. I called Sage's phone. When she didn't answer, I used the Find My Phone app on my cell. It led me to this alley, at which time I notified Quig of my whereabouts. I found Sage, Brindle, and Larry unconscious on the cobblestones, with their clothes soaked in alcohol. I tried to rouse them, but then Chris and Ms. Chatham returned. I hid behind the dumpster trying to figure out what to do next. Next Chris told Ms. Chatham to light Sage, Larry, and Brindle on fire. I couldn't allow that so I confronted the women. Then Quig arrived. He announced he'd called the cops on the way here. That's pretty much the whole story."

In the Wick of Time

"Not quite," Nowry said. "We need statements from everyone. Come to the station tomorrow to make individual written statements. You're excused for tonight."

Feeling like a kid let out for recess, I clung to Quig's hand and Sage's and hurried from the alley. A boisterous crowd thronged the waterfront. Boats motored by on the river decked out in twinkling lights, and the luminary candles gleamed in the darkness. The noise and activity felt surreal.

We almost died tonight.

My steps slowed as we merged in the crowd. I had no idea how to decompress from this awful night. Chris and Ms. Chatham showed no remorse for their criminal actions, but they'd been no match for the Winslow twins. Surely, with my audio tape evidence, the cops had enough on Ms. Chatham and Chris to keep them behind bars for a very long time.

Chapter
Thirty-Six

After three months of dating Quig, I now realized he had depth. However, for twenty years, I'd taken him at surface value and only enjoyed his steadfast friendship. Given his help in taking down Loren Lee's killers, I needed to pivot my thinking to that of him being a man of mystery and of power. I mean, I knew he had some power or he wouldn't have known I was in trouble a few months ago when that developer came after our street.

How did I forget that for a second? Seems like there should be power in his aura. Unless . . . he knew how to cloak his aura. Impossible as that sounded, my brain couldn't handle another strange concept tonight.

Walking out of that alleyway where we'd nearly died seemed surreal, and yet here we were. The festivities on River Street continued despite our close brush with death.

We had survived. My feet still touched solid ground, Quig held my hand, and the night sky twinkled overhead. People laughed and talked with friends like any other night. Except we'd knocked on death's door. Every time I hit this point in trying to make sense of the evening, panic welled in my gut, choking me. Just as quickly, I squashed it down. I couldn't fall apart here, not now. Soon, though, I had to deal with the toxic negative emotions simmering in my body.

Before I could summon a normal conversation topic, Quig said, "Didn't get a chance to mention this yet. Harley is getting fluids and supportive care at the emergency vet. We can pick him up tomorrow after two, unless his condition changes."

"Thank you." I let out a shaky breath, feeling relieved my cat appeared fine. Not my best day, not by a long shot. However, I couldn't beat myself up too badly. I'd delegated my cat's care to save my twin. Quig's help allowed me to focus entirely on the true life and death threat. "I couldn't have done this without you."

"We're a team," he said. "I took the cat to get medical attention, but you saved people's lives tonight, mine included. You're amazing, Tabby Winslow. A woman of diverse talents."

I hoped he spoke literally because exhaustion ruled my thoughts, and I had nothing left to read between the lines. Now that my adrenaline rush faded, walking and talking at the same time seemed an extreme feat.

"Yes, you are amazing, Sis. I wouldn't be alive without your courage and bravery." Sage glanced back at Larry and Brindle, who followed us closely on the crowded street. "None of us would. I feel like I got a do-over."

"Me too," Brindle said as he caught up and gripped Sage's hand. "And I desperately need a do-over."

"I'm glad to be alive," Larry muttered.

By silent accord, we turned in at the dimly lighted nursery booth. "Anything need to be done here before we go home?" I asked my twin.

Sage glanced around at the bare counters and the scant trees. "Not much. Ms. Chatham took the cash box earlier. Let's lock the booth door, and we're done."

"What's the plan?" Larry asked Sage, speaking loud enough to catch her attention.

I had a feeling he asked about more than the booth.

Quig started to respond with our unspoken plan of heading home, so I squeezed his hand in warning.

Sage's chin went up. "I'm done for the night, that's what. I'll see you tomorrow since we have a few more trees to sell, then I don't know what happens next."

Larry nodded, looked like he wanted to say something else, then he melted into the crowd.

"A man of few words," I muttered to myself as I watched Sage lock the booth. Neither the colorful boats on the water nor the glare of luminaries along the bank seemed festive now. The weight of tonight's events lay heavy on me, and I desperately needed rest.

"My car is two blocks away," Quig said. "Anyone who wants a ride, follow me."

"We're in," Sage and Brindle said.

My smile felt bittersweet. "Don't have to ask me twice."

*   *   *

Sunday morning arrived long before I wanted to move a muscle. More than anything, I preferred to stay in bed all day, but I had to work at the shop, so I practiced adulthood by rising, dressing, and breakfasting. Two positives fueled me on this cloudy day. Eve would be helping me. Harley would come home after two PM.

"You could stay here with me," Quig said as I handed him the Sunday paper with a kiss.

The case headlined the paper, but he didn't glance at it. He tugged me until I sat in his lap. My body sizzled as his energy got personal with mine.

He wanted me to stay home with him. Truth be told, I wanted that too, except I couldn't. I hastened to explain. "Wish I could, but I can't play hooky on one of the last big holiday shopping days, and Eve doesn't have a key to open the shop. I'm hoping for calm but steady sales. Yesterday had too much excitement. Besides, you'll see me this afternoon when we give our statements to the police and pick up the cat."

"I'm afraid to let you out of my sight." His fingers threaded through mine. "I feared for your life last night."

"I feared Chris and Ms. Chatham would kill all of us."

"They tried to take us out," he said. "When I realized how dangerous they were, I wanted to scoop you up and run far away, but I couldn't move."

"How'd you keep standing during her energy attack?" I asked, needing to know.

"Never felt anything like it before." He shook his head. "Not sure how I managed. I couldn't move my arms or legs. My brain worked, but my body didn't. I shouted in my head for you to run, but you stood with me, facing our enemy."

"Pretty sure she tried the same takeout maneuver on you that she used on Sage, Brindle, and Larry earlier in the evening. They went down hard. You didn't go down."

The morning sun reflected off his glasses, fire-bright. "Neither did you."

Beware the tiger. My free hand strayed to the white gold locket at my neck. His locket. "This may sound boastful, but I didn't expect to succumb. I brazenly assumed I could handle anything she dished out."

"You are many things, but invincible isn't one of them. I was frightened for you."

"I was frightened for all of us, believe me. I couldn't have handled Chris's undivided attention alone for long. Our united front gave me courage and strength. Failure meant death, and we had to stop her."

"You did good, though I don't follow the logic of what happened."

Logic had nothing to do with that attack on us, and I wasn't above using that as an excuse. "Me neither. I can't explain what happened with any amount of logic or reason, but I'm delighted with the outcome. We're safe at home, while Chris and Ms. Chatham are in police custody."

"I gather that Chris attacked us with the dark arts, and she hypnotized us. What happened is very foreign to my way of thinking."

"Chris is different. From what I've observed, magic isn't good or bad per se, but Chris is a dark person. She embraced the darker side of her craft."

"When I hear her name, I remember with crystal clarity how I nearly lost you."

"I'm right here, and I'm not going anywhere, except to work."

Quig held me close. "After last night, I may need to accompany you. You are my everything. I nearly lost you. My heart can't take that level of fear."

"Mine either, but here's the thing. When you break this down to the core elements, our attackers are schoolyard bullies. We stood up to them, so they'll leave us alone now."

"I hear what you're saying, but I'm irrational about your safety, Tabby-mine."

"You're always welcome in the shop, but I can't have you glowering at every customer out of fear. That negativity will kill our sales."

He swore inventively, so I stroked his stubble-roughened cheek, soothing his warrior nature. "If you keep doing that, you'll be very late for work," he warned.

"Can't disappoint my shoppers," I said. "Feeling better?"

"Yes, and thanks. I'm new to this serious relationship business, and I'm concerned I'll mess it up somehow."

"You're doing fine, and I share your concern about myself. We're figuring it out as we go." I sighed out a deep breath. "Everything would be perfect if Auntie O and Frankie came home for Christmas."

"That's out of our control," Quig said. "However, speaking of Christmas, Mom invited all of us for dinner that day," Quig said. "Will you join us for the meal?"

I believed his mother disliked me. His dad had welcomed me, so that felt positive. "I would love to, but first, please clarify. All of us being us two plus Sage? Or a few more?"

"Everyone who's here, but Mom is a planner and expects a head count now. Brindle is welcome if he's Sage's plus-one. Your aunt and Frankie are welcome if they return. Anyone else I should invite?"

"That's all the Winslow family, and yes, I'll be there. I'll ask Sage if they will come. FYI, we always close the shop for Christmas day and the day after."

"Speaking of being off from work, I would love for us to take a trip together after things calm down. The Christmas rush will be over, no shop emergencies to contend with, no county admin meetings to attend. Just the two of us. Alone."

Oh. Not good. I couldn't travel. What could I say? What could I do? My mind quieted, so I stalled for time. "Can you get away from the morgue?"

"Sure. My new assistant will be fully versed in our standard procedures by February, which means I could take off that entire month. Would that work for you?"

It felt as if the walls pressed in on me. I hated to disappoint Quig, but I couldn't leave for a month. How could I explain without spilling family secrets? He watched me expectantly, probably thinking he'd dangled a big enticement before me when the reverse appeared true. I had to say something.

"You want me to take all of February off?" I winced at the squeakiness of my voice.

"Block off at least one week in February for us. Two if you can swing it."

My tummy knotted at the thought of even a two-week trip. What could I say without hurting his feelings? I blurted out the first thing that came to me. "I don't have a passport, so we can't go too far."

"You should get one. Not for our first trip, but another one. I'd love to show you the world."

Reality often felt harsh, and my reality right now insisted I couldn't sugarcoat my deficiency. Best to rip off the bandage and expose my shortcoming to him. "Here's a fun fact or two about me that you don't know. I'm stalling on my answer because I don't travel well, so I don't do it at all. For instance, I hate being cold for any reason. My preference is to stay home. On Bristol Street."

A dangerous heat flared in his eyes, a heat those dark-framed glasses couldn't hide. "What are you saying, Tabby? Are you ashamed to be seen with me?"

"My gosh, no. I want everyone to know we're together." My energy spiked in response to his sharp tone, putting me on the defensive. I had a right to my energetic secrets. They went to the core of my being and my actions. "You picked the wrong Winslow sister for a traveling companion. Sage flew to Europe a few summers ago. I'm the sister who wound up coming home to finish college in Savannah. I don't do well if I venture far from home. I am my best self here. I am a homebody in all senses of the word. This reluctance to travel has nothing to do with my feelings for you, and you know there's no one else."

He stared at me, slack-jawed. "I didn't realize that's why you came home. I thought your family needed you, so you came home to help them." He paused for a moment. "Is it an anxiety thing?"

"More like an energy thing. I get too tired if I don't sleep in my own bed."

"Our bed. You sleep in our bed."

"I feel comfortable in our home too. I just can't be your traveling companion, and I hope that's not a deal breaker."

When he didn't answer right away, my heart broke. I tried to rise.

"We don't have to travel." He clung to me. "I didn't realize you had health concerns. You always seem the picture of health."

I risked a glance his way, but I couldn't see much more than a blur with so many tears in my eyes. "I'm weak in nontraditional ways. Why'd you pick me out of all the women in the world?"

"You aren't weak. You're the strongest person I've ever met. You saved my life last night." Quig caught my chin and lifted it until our gazes met. "I've always wanted you, love. The men in my family are that way. We recognize our mates on first sight." He tenderly wiped tears from my cheeks. "I thank my lucky stars I found you when we were children. It isn't usually that way for my kinfolk."

Mate was a primal word. It made me feel uneasy. Targeted even. I took a step back mentally. Maybe I should do that in the flesh too. "You're crowding me."

He pressed his forehead to mine. "You noticed."

"I did, and not in a good way. Are you fixing to go all caveman on me?"

A slow smile filled his face. "Are you into that?"

"I'm into you."

"Right answer."

Chapter Thirty-Seven

Six days remained until Christmas. Six more days until this frenzy of shopping, gifting, and socializing simmered down. Usually this holiday season exhausted me. This year exhaustion preceded the main event. Despite my need to stay on Bristol Street, I longed for a break from the constant demands of the shop.

After I finished a batch of soaps and began cleaning my stillroom under the watchful eyes of both cats, Eve called out from the shop, "Tabby, come out front right now. I don't do cops."

I hurried to her without removing my apron or purple cleaning gloves. Knowing the detectives were here for me, I nodded to Eve as I joined her. "Take a break if you like. They want to speak with me."

"Right. I'll take that break out back. Could stand some warm sunshine on my shoulders."

As she left, I moved behind the sales counter and tugged my gloves off. There were five browsers in the shop, and all our carry baskets for shoppers' purchases were in use. Perversely, I hoped everyone checked out while the Inquisition grilled me.

The door chime rang, and Nowry stalked in like an alpha lion. Detective Belfor's steps slowed as she inhaled deeply. An expression of bliss crossed her face before she reached me.

"Good afternoon, Detectives," I said easily from behind the counter. "What can I do for you today?"

"We have more questions after speaking with everyone in the alley last night." Nowry tapped his slender notebook in his palm. "May we speak in private?"

"I'm working alone and have customers to serve. This is the best I can do for now."

"We can invite you downtown with us, if you prefer."

I clung to the word invite. They wouldn't forcibly escort me downtown, which mattered because my lawyer hated weekend work, and I hated interrogations. I put on a good face. "Gerard can cover the shop alone tomorrow if you wish to speak with me downtown. Right now isn't good for me." I gestured widely with my arms. "The holidays are important to small business owners."

"Bah humbug," Nowry said. "Robbery and larceny are king in December, what with all the extra money people carry around and gifts left in parked cars. However, our boss is pressuring us to wrap up this nursery manager homicide. We're darn close except for a few loose ends."

They were darn close because I'd caught the killer. Not a good idea to mention that I'd done their job. Again. "Sage is at the heart of this case. Why aren't you talking to her instead of me?"

"Tried that. She and her coworker Larry Rau are giving a seminar on care for live potted trees. Your sister has thirty people hanging on her every word."

"Glad I got my tree from them already," Belfor said. "That booth on River Street is a hot spot of activity. It really filled a need this year."

"I bought a tree from them too," I added. "And I don't have a green thumb. Just seemed the way to go."

"Enough about trees. Next thing you gals will be swapping recipes," Nowry growled. "Back to the case at hand, although we have an audio recording of the alley showdown, it isn't clear why these women did what they did. We need a clear motive for their actions."

"If you're asking my personal opinion, I thought this case centered on the nursery, about what it meant to the parties involved. Both women hated Bob Chatham, a man who was no prize. He heaped verbal abuse on his wife and physical abuse on his niece. Good chance he was poisoned, same as Loren Lee."

"What'd they have against the manager?"

"He'd been handpicked by Bob, and he kept the nursery afloat when both women wanted to wipe it off the face of the earth. Bob called it his legacy. The women took great offense at that."

"We heard that version of events. But this homicide has been so convoluted all along it feels wrong that the ending is straightforward. We're not satisfied and neither is the chief."

Darn it. Nowry had articulated the worries lurking in my mind. "You have my attention," I said. "How can I help you?"

"Chatham and Kachuba were on our radar all along," Nowry said. "However, one suspect came through this unscathed and is in a winner-take-all position."

He couldn't be talking about Sage. I drew in a deep breath and tried misdirection. "You're talking about Mary Nicole?"

Nowry gave a nod. "While the future of All Good Things Nursery is unclear, Ms. Frazier came out smelling like a rose."

It took me a sec to remember Frazier was the woman's last name. "Seems like Ms. Chatham has to close her business if she's incarcerated," I said. "How does Mary Nicole benefit from that?"

"It isn't unheard of for a prisoner's business to stay open," Belfor said. "There are ways to keep businesses going, even if someone is convicted."

"I see." I drummed my fingers on the countertop. "Well, in that case, Mary Nicole is who you should question today. Not me."

Nowry huffed.

"The thing is, twice now you've zeroed in on a killer while we focused elsewhere, as our captain pointed out." Belfor shot me a fleeting smile. "We need to pick your brain."

"That sounds gross. No thanks."

"Not literally. We're concerned something else will blindside us. That would look bad for the department, so we need to cover every contingency. What's your crime-solving secret?"

Oh dear. The less I said the better, but I had to say something. "I felt the same frustrations you did, but then Chris and Ms. Chatham came after me. I never saw the partnership of Ms. Chatham and Chris Kachuba coming. This was my first brush with the dark arts. I would think you two would've had more experience with it in the Low Country."

Belfor smirked. "Management frowns on using words like magic and hypnosis in incident reports. We need different answers, the kind that will satisfy a court of law."

I glanced from one detective to another. "But you've run across cases like this before?"

"No comment," both cops said in unison.

That solidarity got my attention. "I assume the party line is excluding anything other than normal motives and means of death. Nothing paranormal allowed."

"We require normal motives and means of death, yes," Belfor stated woodenly. "Those are necessary for successful prosecutions."

My brain tiptoed through this minefield. "Is the problem that you can't prove which woman killed Loren Lee?"

"Ongoing investigation," Nowry growled. "Besides, we ask the questions. Assuming the legalities are satisfied and the nursery stays open, would your sister work there?"

I shrugged. "Ask her."

He ignored my answer and added, "Larry Rau. What do you know about him?"

"He likes working with Sage. He likes plants. I don't know much more about him. Why?" Oops. I asked another question.

"In the course of our investigation, he and all the other employees at All Good Things were investigated. His background is thin and that looks suspicious."

I knew exactly what Larry was. He was the human equivalent of a golden retriever for Sage. He always looked happy to see her and to be with her. If they couldn't be together, he vanished until she had time for him. Other than that, Larry Rau was a big old mystery.

Of course, I couldn't mention any of that to the cops. "He's with Sage today at the waterfront, so there's your chance to talk with both of them."

Nowry and Belfor exchanged a shuttered look. Nowry shook his head and turned. Sharmila Belfor raised her eyebrows before warning, "We'll be in touch."

Chapter
Thirty-Eight

Once the cops left, customers checked out in a flurry. Eve returned, and she helped process everyone. I loved being busy, but this year's holiday rush felt beyond ridiculous. I felt like a machine cog on an assembly line, and I didn't dare slow down. Eve made everything better. She kept up the customer chitchat, so I smiled as she engaged them and bagged the purchases. Meanwhile, I scanned items, totaled purchases, and accepted payments.

"How'd it go earlier?" Eve asked when the shop cleared.

I sank onto the stool to get sensation back into my feet. "Everything felt fine until the cops barged in with their negative energy. Pretty sure the Loren Lee Suffield case is closed, but they have questions. They said they can't use paranormal explanations in their reports, so I took that to mean their information didn't hang together as tightly as needed."

"That's their own fault. They don't deny electricity or miracles happening, and I'm certain they can't explain either occurrence. Ignorance." She tsked. "Can't fix that."

I silently agreed, but the dark arts had the same stigma as anything outside the realm of normal. People feared it. Until acceptance occurred, our family's energy abilities would remain shrouded in shadows. Much better that way. Humanity had been cruel to witches for centuries, and I'd rather not look for trouble over my shoulder all my life, even though I didn't count as a witch in any sense.

Since everything paranormal and occult had been tarred with the same brush, we were forever bound as one great big fat scary unknown. People shouldn't be afraid of those who worked energy, or even of those who practiced magic. On the other hand, they should be very afraid of people like Frankie's Chicago cousins.

Therein lay the rub.

Eve hummed along with the soft Christmas music that piped through the shop. I studied her until she caught me at it. "What?" she asked.

While I composed my thoughts, I pulled out my tube of Brenda's Bees lip balm and applied a thin coat. It tasted like honey and coconut. "You belong here."

"So?"

"I dreaded finding someone who would work part-time. You understood our software from the jump. You're okay with our customers and with my strange ways. You'll have a job here long as you want it."

"Thanks. And there's nothing wrong with you. Nothing wrong with me either. I like it here, and I'm happy to help, for now. At some point, I'll open my own store featuring batik fabrics and more, but I gotta learn the business side first. Just because I can run a cash register don't mean squat. I'm studying you like a hawk, seeing how you do everything. Y'all got a nice place here. People walk in the door, and they feel good. That's special."

Being under scrutiny felt like torture, and I probably shouldn't mentor Eve on how to run a successful business, as I'd forgotten about inventory this month. "I can't take credit for that vibe. This shop's been in my family for three generations. My sister and I tried our wings in the real world, but this shop is very important to us. It's our home too. We're highly motivated to keep the shop profitable, but we're learning the ropes as we go."

"I hear what you're saying, but it ain't the whole ball of wax." She laughed and did a mini happy dance with her arms. "Ha! I used an idiom about wax in a candle shop. My lit teacher will crow at my cleverness."

"You're welcome to take notes on how we run our business, but keep in mind Sage and I have only been running the shop for a short while. You would get better business advice elsewhere."

"Don't think so. I feel this place inside me. It speaks to me. Besides, your family and mine go way back. Logic doesn't mean as much as emotions to me. My heart, body, and soul tell me to stay, so I will."

"Auntie O and MawMaw are friends. That what you mean?"

"I mean their parents, and likely their grandparents, were friends. In sociology we studied how like attracts like. You and I may not look alike on the outside, but inside, where it counts, we are very alike. I'm smart enough to recognize my likes and dislikes. Gerard is too. We are the MawMaws and Auntie Os of our generation. Good chance we'll be friends forever."

"That's a long time."

She grinned. "Yeah."

* * *

That evening, Sage and Brindle ate dinner at our place. The men grilled burgers on the balcony, while Sage and I made a salad and roasted asparagus in the kitchen.

I tore the lettuce into a big wooden bowl. "Busy Sunday at the shop."

"You happy with Gerard's cousin?" Sage said as she blotted the asparagus dry.

"Yes, is the short answer. The longer version is that it feels like she's always been there. She plugged right in, and we should give her as many hours as she wants. With Gerard on the weekdays and her on the weekends plus a few pickup shifts for her here and there, we'll have some days off from the shop."

"Good to know, Tabs. We need help, so I'm glad we found the right person. I want to get back in the shop, but I want to work fewer hours."

"You sticking with the nursery part time?"

She scowled at the roasting pan. "Nope. Mary Nicole came out to the waterfront and started raising sand about every little thing. I quit this afternoon. She can have the place. Word is Ms. Chatham will get out on bail tomorrow, but she will likely sell the nursery to pay for her attorney. I want to look at other nurseries, with an eye to one day opening a nursery of my own."

"Go for it. We'll make it work. Hopefully, Auntie O and Frankie will come home soon."

"I dunno. Frankie's family is hunting him now. If he returns, he'll be easy pickings for them."

I moved the clean radishes to the chopping board and went to work. "I doubt he'll walk away from Auntie O at this point, which means we may not get her back either. Eve can fill in the staffing gaps, and I can hire another part-timer if you get going full-time on plants again."

"Don't be giving my job away just yet. I need income, though Brindle and I have some news."

"Tell me."

"Can't. We agreed to share it together after dinner."

I disliked waiting, but dinner passed quickly. After everyone emptied their plates, I turned to Brindle. "Let's hear your news."

He pushed back from the table. "I reassessed my career goals. Whereas I initially wanted to climb the corporate ladder and become the *senior partner* at our law firm, that's no longer my goal. I like doing my own thing and pro bono work. In other words, I aspire to be more of a champion for the underdog."

"Congratulations!" Brindle had always been something of an odd duck in his multi-partner firm. "I think you'll be much happier."

Quig echoed my sentiment and followed with, "How soon can you make the change?"

"My partners are buying me out—their idea, not mine—so I'm on my way out the door anyway. Good riddance to them." He took a deep breath and glanced over at Sage. She nodded. "The big news is Sage invited me to move into her place. We're working out a plan to share living expenses. I'll sell my condo to pay for new office space. Some of my furniture will be fine in an office, so I can minimize startup expenses."

"Sounds great." I glanced at Sage and just to be sure I asked on the twin-link, *This is what you want?*

I do. Brindle and I had a long heart-to-heart talk last night and this morning. He really cares for me. He may not be my Quig per se, but he's the guy I want right now.

To make sure I understand, you two will be a couple? He's not staying in my room?

He's staying in my room. We'll rent a storage unit short-term for his furniture if needed. At some point we may upgrade our apartment furniture, though that isn't a burning need now.

I'm with you all the way, Sage. Brindle may be your Quig. You won't know unless you try.

Sage gave me a sly smile. "I'm happy about Brindle's choices, and I'm happier we have an extra staffer in our shop now. I'll help Brindle find office space and set up his office tech. I know computers and billing, so I'm his IT department."

"We'll be a great team," Brindle said.

And there'll be no sexy receptionists either, Sage said in my mind.

That's my sister. Wondered if all felt like sweetness and light now.

She chuckled on the link. *Not likely. But best to be myself with him. He needs to know what comes with Sage all the time, every day.*

I've got a feeling he won't be scared off by the real you.

You think he'll understand about our extras?

Time will tell. Quig handles it okay, what little he knows of our extra gears.

"I'd like to propose a toast," Brindle said, raising his glass. "Here's to good friends and new beginnings."

"Hear, hear."

Chapter
Thirty-Nine

O n Monday, Gerard barked out a warning. "Here comes trouble."
   I glanced up from my dusting to see an unwelcome face
peering through the shop window. Vito Morelli. Dressed in midnight black clothing, he looked like a poster child for vampires.
Gerard might as well have said "dead man walking," and I would've
had the same gut-wrenching dread. "Oh, no."

"Don't bolt on me," Gerard said, reaching for my arm and drawing
me behind the counter with him. "I want nothing to do with this guy."

That strong tether reminded me not to go invisible and hide,
though that's what every message receptor in my body shouted in
my head. "Smart man." Vito's paranormal talents of energy thief and
para-hypnotist combine into a lethal combination. Not someone any
sane person should engage.

I thought Vito had returned to Chicago. Had he been hiding
in Savannah for days? His continuing presence didn't bode well for
my family or friends. Though he remained outside, I felt the man's
malevolence through the glass and shuddered.

The door chimed ominously to signal his entry. Holy smoke.
This could be an out-and-out showdown of powers. I could notify

my twin to come downstairs to help, but Vito drained her last time. Very bad idea. I didn't want Sage in the same zip code as this man.

Vito sauntered up to the counter oozing malignant charm in a pale green cloud. I treated his arrival the same way I would a rattle-snake's. I didn't take my eyes off him, and I shielded Gerard and myself with white light energy. I'd pay for the intensive energy burn later, but I couldn't take the chance he'd harm us.

"Did ya miss me, *Bella*?" Vito asked.

"Mr. Morelli. To what do I owe the honor of your visit?"

"Sadly, I must leave your fair shores."

I risked a breath of green-tinged air. "You're returning to Chicago?"

"My travels are not your concern."

Clear as mud. "Well, then. Enjoy your trip."

He gazed at me through lowered lashes. "Always. The world is my oyster. Indeed, my travels have taken me far across the seas, but I adore Savannah. I will return."

It occurred to me he might be reading my thoughts. I bolstered my mental barriers too.

"You intrigue me, *Bella*."

We'd been through this before. "I have a boyfriend."

"I am a man. One day you will know all of me. That's a promise."

"Sage isn't here," Gerard blurted out. "Your cousin isn't here either. Leave town already, for crying out loud."

Vito's gaze never wavered from mine. He said, "Tell *Frankie* there are no hard feelings. Tell Sage she stole my heart. And tell yourself to anxiously await my return. Twins are the absolute best playmates."

He swept out of the shop, and I felt the immediate urge to shower off his green stench. Instead, I lit our sampler aromatherapy candles. "Good riddance. I hope that's the last we see of him."'

"Sounds like he has a twins fetish."

"He better fantasize elsewhere." Anxious to change the subject, I glanced at the stack of envelopes by the register. "Is that today's mail?"

"It is. Nothing much, only a few sales fliers and bills."

"Hand 'em over."

A popular a cappella group sang "The Little Drummer Boy" on our holiday music channel. "Glad Vito is leaving," Gerard said. "While you detox the shop, I need coffee from across the street. You in?"

"Yes."

"Back in a few."

I decided to call the number I'd discovered on the phone bill the other day. The one that might link to Auntie O. I punched up the number on my cell phone, but I didn't hit send. I couldn't. What if the cops were monitoring my phone line? Same for the shop telephone. They possibly had warrants for all our phones, despite the case being closed. I erased the number.

Never thought I'd be thinking this, but I needed a burner phone with a secret number. One of those that you paid for so many minutes of calling.

Just then, Blue Hair strolled into the shop with two friends. Not Blue Hair, Fawn Meldrim. I knew her name now, and I'd had her dad thrown out of here. She had to know about his alcoholism. Proof being that she'd come to the shop several times since the incident, so she didn't hold a grudge.

I wouldn't know if she'd help me unless I asked her. "Fawn?"

She stopped and looked my way. "Yes?"

"Can we talk?"

She clomped over to me.

"How's your dad?" I asked.

"He's in jail."

"Still?"

"He's trouble, Ms. Winslow."

"I'm sorry to hear that. My dad left so long ago I don't remember him, and Mom passed earlier this year. I miss her fiercely. But right now, I need to contact my aunt, and I'm scared to use my cell phone or the shop phone. The cops might've tapped them."

"You can use my phone," Fawn said.

"Thanks. I'll pay you ten dollars for the favor."

"Keep your money. I have an unlimited plan. Anyway, you kept the shop in business, despite everything that's happened. This is my safe place, and I can't put a price on that." Fawn placed a small phone with a tooled leather case on the counter. "Talk as long as you like. I'll be in the book nook with my friends."

"Thanks."

Once again, I punched up the string of numbers, this time on Fawn's phone. A man answered on the first ring saying, "Crocodile Dry Cleaning."

I laughed aloud at the old code Sage and I used as kids. "It's raining cats and gators."

"Tabby?" the man asked.

"Frankie?"

"Oh yeah. You calling on a clean line?"

"Absolutely. Borrowed a phone from a customer. Are y'all okay?"

"Better than okay. We hoped you'd call us once the coast cleared. Your aunt's been on edge all day. Here she is now. I'll put you on speaker phone."

"Tabby?" Auntie O said. "How are you, dear?"

"We're good, and it's great to hear your voice. I've missed you so much, and I've been so concerned about you two. Life on the lam can't be good for your health."

"Our health is fine, sweet girl. I miss you too. I'd love to see you and to be in that sunny stillroom mixing up candles and soaps with you."

"Are you coming home? The case is closed. Turns out the owner of the nursery and her niece conspired to kill Loren Lee. Frankie is no longer under suspicion of murder."

"We heard that, dear. Even so, I've been worried sick about you girls."

"We're okay. Sage and I hope y'all will come home now."

"Not yet," Auntie O said. "The story of Frankie's heritage went nationwide."

"Frankie's cousin, Vito Morelli, came by looking for him. Stirred up trouble every time."

The silence on the line crushed my hopes of a Winslow family reunion. I heard mumbling, then Frankie's voice came through loud and clear. "Stay away from anyone with the last name of Morelli. They're dangerous."

"Figured that out too. I know what he is, Frankie."

"Don't say it."

"I won't. Anyway, Vito left a message for you. Said there's no hard feelings. Does that have more significance than the words imply?"

More mumbling. "Stay away from anyone in Frankie's family," Auntie O said emphatically. "If they return, close the shop and leave town."

My throat closed. "I don't understand."

"Promise. If he brings others, the outcome will be different. Meanwhile, buy a burner phone and text this number with the code phrase. At some point we'll change phone numbers, but I want us to always have an open line of communication if there's an emergency. Carry the burner with you until this threat is past. You hear me?"

Her stern words infused me with dread. "Yes, ma'am. I hear you."

"Good. We'll keep our phone charged so you can call night or day. See if you can find a short-term renter for our place. Don't price gouge anyone, stay with the going rate in our neighborhood, less if it's someone you know and trust. Store our clothing and personal items, if you would."

"Of course. What about the T-shirt place?"

"Frankie will handle that separately, dear. We'll set up a new bank account for the apartment rental."

"I feel like you're about to hang up. There's so much I want to tell you. Quig gave me a locket for our three-month dating anniversary. Brindle and Sage broke up and then got together again. He's living with her now and starting his own law practice."

"That's for the best, dear. You girls have a clear path now, and if I'm not mistaken, have hired someone to help in the shop."

She had excellent sources, as usual. "Part-time. Eve is taking a few shifts."

"Eve. Of course. She's exactly who you need. Have to go. Minutes count on this disposable phone."

"Love you!"

"Love you more."

The call ended.

Sage and I were on our own, though we could reach Auntie O in an emergency. I quickly deleted the called number and turned my focus to the familiar scents and sights of the shop. It still didn't ease the heaviness in my heart. I'd found Auntie O, for all the good that did. Auntie O and Frankie weren't coming home.

Losing her again socked me in the gut. I wanted to see her, to hug her, to tangibly feel her love. She held our family together. Silent tears welled and overflowed.

An ugly sob slipped out. I turned my back to the shop. The need to cry overwhelmed me. I couldn't be strong for one more second. The strength I needed to hold back faded when someone's arms encircled me. Blue Hair, um, Fawn. Her friends hugged me too. The energy embraced me. I felt less alone and less withdrawn. I absorbed the boost of courage.

"Thank you," I managed to utter after a few delightful moments of group energy sharing. "I needed that."

"Sure you did," Fawn said. "We felt it."

My eyebrows shot up. "You did?"

"Yeah." She scrunched up her face as if in deep thought. "I had the sense you get when you're standing in the tidal zone, your toes curled into the sand. You know the waves can't knock you down, but instead they wreak havoc on the shifting sands beneath your feet. You're still standing strong, but they're a force of nature. They win every time by undermining you. I didn't want life to knock you over. I had to hug you."

"You got all that from a few tears?"

Another art student piped up. "For me it felt as if the happiness in the shop flickered like a candle in a breeze. We couldn't let that flame go out. We figured the call upset you."

I pressed Fawn's phone in her hand. "Thanks for the loan. I appreciate it more than I can say. My aunt is safe, but she won't return any time soon. That made me sad. Really sad. As if my mom died all over again."

"Grief is that way," Fawn's friend with the nose ring said. "In psych class we learned how sadness is a part of grief. So is acceptance.

On one level you understand your mom is truly gone, and your aunt can't come home right now. But your inner child yearns for the safety of a parent, even when you're doing great in life. And you are doing great. You've got a home, a business, and a steady guy."

Tears threatened again. "Don't forget my cat. Harley would do anything for me."

"Yeah," Fawn said. "He's okay, but know this. People in this community care about you and your sister. We want—no, we need you to keep doing what you're doing. It's important."

I blinked and tried to absorb her words. My heart nearly burst open. "Thanks. I appreciate that." Heat steamed up my collar. "I like having y'all here too."

Gerard strolled in with two coffees. "What'd I miss? Is Oralee okay?"

"She's fine. I'm fine. Heck, we're all fine."

Chapter Forty

The sea breeze whipped around my head, alternately cloaking my vision with hair and parting to reveal a panoramic view of the Tybee Island beach as we arrived at our destination. I drew ocean-fresh air deep into my lungs, savoring the raw energy where sky and water met earth. The elemental rush of the seashore centered me as nothing else did.

After Sage learned of my conversation with Auntie O, she whisked us off to the beach. This time I'd brought along a winter jacket and a knit cap, which I tugged on my head now to keep my flyaway hair tamed.

"I needed this," I said.

"Me too." Sage drew in a deep breath. "I keep meaning to ask you about the alley takedown. We've never encountered anyone as powerful as Chris. How'd you stop her?"

"Somehow I tapped into everyone's energy, even Quig's. Especially Quig's. I think he's a mirror talent of some sort, Sage."

She chewed her bottom lip. "I've never heard of that before."

"We've always known we can take and give energy. When I stood in the alley with Quig, our bodies touching, I did more than draw energy from him. His energy fused with mine, creating a mirrored shield that reflected Chris's dark currents, so she attacked herself. It's why she went down so fast. She expected no opposition, therefore she couldn't deal with an overload of her own dangerous energy."

"Wow. Weird in a fascinating way. Did you tell Quig?"

"How can I? He doesn't know what we are or what we can do. I want him to see my face when he looks at me, not some monster's. I want him to feel comfortable around me."

"He's lucky to have you, and he knows it. I didn't jump on the Quig train at first, but I'm proud of you for going after what you wanted. You chose him, and y'all are bonded so tight everyone can see it."

"Our friendship kept growing. He is wonderful in so many ways. It sounds hokey, but he completes me."

"Stop so I don't get jealous. You sure he isn't a latent energy talent?"

"Who knows? He told me that in his family the men always know their women on sight. He doesn't seem to be keeping anything from me, but maybe I have to become his family member to learn his deepest secrets."

"If you two get married, will you tell him our secrets?"

I shrugged. "How can I answer that without betraying someone?"

Sage watched gulls wheel overhead on the air currents. "He didn't ask you how we stopped Chris?"

"Nope. He lives in the moment, having accomplished his two major goals in life."

"What goals?"

"To become medical examiner and to be with me." I drew in another deep breath of bracing sea air and wished it were warm enough for me to float in the gentle waves. "Enough about my life. Are you and Brindle solid?"

Sage laughed in a knowing way. "Oh, yeah. Solid as I can be with someone. We're good together, and I've forgiven him for getting spelled."

I beamed at her progress. "You two have good synergy, so I'm glad you have a second chance as a couple."

We walked a few more paces before Sage said, "Moving right along, you comfortable with me helping run our shop now?"

I took my time answering. "When Auntie O left the first time, I knew we could do it. But after flailing around on our own, I rejoiced when she returned from Florida. I'm less optimistic this time, even though I know more about running the shop."

Sage collected a seashell, tucked it in her pocket, and walked along the shore. "Nobody knows the future, Tabs. Heck, I thought I wanted the assistant manager job at the nursery, but upon reflection I sought Loren Lee's approval. He pretended to be a good person, but I didn't see through his act until he died."

"You brought out the best in him. Loren Lee liked being around you. I never saw a dark side of him when I visited the nursery. Sure, his management style bordered on brusque, but managers like that are common. The good energy of plants steadied him somewhat, because he didn't blackmail people at work. He got up to no good at home on the evenings and weekends, when he lived in that sterile house."

"Are you rationalizing how we misread his character?" Sage asked.

"Is it working?"

"I won't make excuses for Loren Lee. I wanted a mentor. I blame that on not having a dad for most of my life. I won't make that mistake again." She glanced sideways at me. "On the other hand, I enjoy helping Brindle set up his office. Maybe that can be a part-time gig for me now, getting offices up and running. I want to work in our shop on Monday, Wednesday, and Saturday. I feel bad I that I put so much on your shoulders this month. I won't leave you hanging like that again."

That left me with Tuesday, Thursday, Friday, and Sunday. Fine with me. "We got through it is the best I can say."

"The shop is flourishing. You did good by hiring Eve, Sis."

"Glad I did something right. Even when I thought I excelled at taking care of business, I overlooked routine tasks. The shop is too much for one Winslow and Gerard. We need you there. Your skills complement mine."

"Once I realized how stressed a full-time nursery job made me, I knew my future lay elsewhere. Trying to win that promotion cost me my enjoyment with plants. I prefer being my own boss."

"I understand. Limited thinking blinded me to my shortcomings. I'm not a powerhouse. I'm as human as the next person, more so, because of our secret vulnerability. For goodness' sake, a dark arts practitioner and a combination psychic vampire/para-hypnotist attacked us. We must be on our guard for threats."

"Absolutely. I can't do it all either. Our focus remains on The Book and Candle Shop, no matter what else happens."

"Right. We had a wake-up call this week." I walked some more before I found the courage to say what else I needed to say. "Having Auntie O here gave me a built-in lifeline. Without her, life is scary. There's so much danger out there I never knew about."

Sage stopped. The surf pounded on the shore. Dolphins frolicked in the waves. I put my hands in my pockets and soaked elemental nature inside me. It felt glorious.

"Most people avoid danger, but we attract it," Sage said. "Bottom line is, each person must stand tall on her own two feet. That's the secret."

"That's true to a point. It isn't the same for twin energetics. We were always close. However, during this investigation when I felt apart from you, I faltered."

"I felt the same void when Quig moved into your heart. I made more selfish choices that kept us apart. I couldn't deal with not being in your heart."

I hugged her close as energy and love surrounded us, radiating out like a strong beacon. "You are always in my heart. Always, always, always."

"Darn straight." Sage hugged me back. "We've got this."

Acknowledgments

Though all errors in this book are mine, of course, some very nice and smart people helped me get it this far. Critique partner Polly Iyer slogged through the trenches of every chapter, as did my freelance editor Beth "Jaden" Terrell. They are truly women of great ideas and vast publishing insight. My agent Jill Marshal of the Marshal Lyons Agency took this series on and had first editorial crack after it left my hands. From there, Tara Gavin of Crooked Lane Publishing came on board in a big way. I also could not manage the travel aspect of marketing published books without the unwavering support of Craig Toussaint, a mainstay of my life.